THE CRUX

THE CRUX

Giampaolo Rugarli

Translated from the Italian by
N. S. THOMPSON

COLLINS HARVILL
8 Grafton Street, London W1
1990

COLLINS HARVILL
William Collins Sons & Co. Ltd
London · Glasgow · Sydney · Auckland
Toronto · Johannesburg

BRITISH LIBRARY CATALOGUING IN PUBLICATION DATA

Rugarli, Giampaolo
The crux.
I. Title
853′.914[F]

ISBN 0-00-271473-6

First published in Italy with the title *La Troga* by
Adelphi Edizioni, Milan, 1988
First published in Great Britain by Collins Harvill 1990

© Adelphi Edizioni S.P.A. Milan 1988
English translation © William Collins Sons & Co. Ltd 1990

Photoset in Linotron Bembo by
Rowland Phototypesetting Ltd,
Bury St Edmunds, Suffolk
Printed and bound in Great Britain by
Hartnolls Ltd, Bodmin, Cornwall

For Marisa

DRAMATIS PERSONAE

The Living

CARLO PANTIERI, police inspector
MIRELLA JENCA, ruined maiden
ANTEO BIRAGHI, magistrate
RANIERO CONTI, magistrate
DR GRUVI, physician
ELVIRA GATTI, mother in distress
GERARDO OPITZ, construction boss rolling in money
LUCILLA OPITZ, anxious daughter of Gerardo
CARDINAL MESCHIA, eccentric prelate
LAURO CROCE SABBIONETA, cabinet minister
ORAZIO LA CALENDA, cabinet minister
CIRO DE FIORE, presumed terrorist
UNCLE GIACCHINO, patriarch full of wisdom
BYRON, hall porter

The Dead

ASSUNTA, wife of Pantieri, equivocal housewife
SIGNORINA CANDIANI, schoolteacher, hard as nails
PETER ILYCH TCHAIKOVSKY, celebrated composer

Passers-by, onlookers, nosey-parkers, beggars, nurses,
stretcher-bearers, doctors, porters, policemen, Carabinieri,
warders, gamblers, casino proprietors, tourists,
out-patients, in-patients, politicians, nuns, priests,
rats, a pregnant goat, and an abundance of dead and injured.

The action may be supposed to take place in Rome, in Lavinio,
and in Calabria, some time before the Year Two Thousand.

Night, rain, snow, mist, terrorist attacks,
epidemics, inflation.

PROLOGUE

. . . in the flame-like bracts of a bougainvillea. It had been a long flowering and, although it was well into October, the wall opposite persisted in holding onto its tangle of flowers and fantasy. Inspector Carlo Pantieri sighed. He was fretting because he had seen the old lady, when it would have been so much easier to have refused. He looked across at the bougainvillea again, then at a chink of sky that was aflame with the sunset. Down in the street he sensed the usual frenzy of the crowd and for a few seconds the resentment he felt with regard to his last visitor abated. Those ramblings of hers, coherent but still demented, distracted him a little from the inevitable plunge into the people thronging the pavements. He hated humanity or was, perhaps, afraid of it. He was a solitary man, and an indolent one. His world revolved around his colleagues in the Police and around criminals, between whom he saw analogies because they dealt in illicit favours and small pay-offs. It also revolved around the judge Biraghi, his temporary and unwelcome flatmate, and around Peter Ilych Tchaikovsky. There were two extraordinary merits about Tchaikovsky with which he couldn't argue: one was that he had composed music, and the other was that he was dead.

"It's worse than a plot," said Signora Elvira Gatti, aged 86, of Tradate (Varese), folding her hands in her lap. She began to wring her fingers. "And it's even worse than a revolution, it's creeping into every family."

"Even mine?" Pantieri asked, with a bitter smile. He was thinking about his childless marriage and his wife who had died just a few months ago. He remembered her hat, decorated with flowers and little birds. She hadn't been a woman, she'd been a second-hand clothing emporium. All the world's idiocies and their relics had found shelf-space in the poor woman's mind: her overcoat with its foxskin collar, the Sundays she shipped herself off to Mass, the calls she made, the historical novels she read, the pulp magazines, the washing-powders and the plastic give-aways that went with them. Passing away in less than two days, she'd left him not so much a memory as a trail of Dixan washing-powder.

"Oh!" the old lady exclaimed, and her hand shot to her mouth. "I hardly dare, and I don't want to hurt your feelings, I know how these things are, and anything I say could be held against me in the future. But anyway, your wife, God rest her soul, was involved in the business and I think she was close to promotion. If it hadn't been for the tragedy of her death, she would have become a priestess of Monte Sacro."

"A priestess? And what do you know about Monte Sacro?"

"I know everything, Inspector," purred the old lady with a hint of self-satisfaction. "You live there, in Via Monte Pelmo, number 5, and there's no lift. You see, this is the time for new appointments. I'm certain they've already chosen new priestesses for Prati, for Testaccio and Aventino – now *there's* a high-class neighbourhood for you, they put up a lot of film stars. Your wife was very much involved."

Pantieri reflected. The old lady was imparting strange, incredible fantasies to him, but showed that she had some of her facts straight. Therefore someone, leaving aside the possibility of the decrepit old granny having done it herself, had been making inquiries about him. A fact that worried and annoyed him at the same time.

"Signora," said the Inspector severely, "you've had somebody spying on me."

"You don't understand," replied the old lady, a shade irritably. She placed a hand on his desk to emphasize what she was saying. "We're all being spied on, disaster looms about us all. And do you know why? Because at the root of it all there's the Crux."

"The Crux? Oh, you mean 'the crooks'."

"Absolutely not," enunciated the old lady with a vigorous

shake of the head. "Most of today's crooks are common drug-pushers, part and parcel of this ridiculous age. What's a little morphine or heroin, cascara or magnesium citrate? Humanity's always been on drugs. It's a way of alleviating their consciences for having put Christ on the cross. No, Inspector, you heard me correctly. I meant precisely the *Crux*."

"Well *I*," Pantieri observed, scrupling to put a Cartesian emphasis on the personal pronoun, "have never heard of it."

"In Latin *crucio* means 'I torture', from *crux*, a cross. It means suffering and death. Think about it, Inspector."

These were times of satiety and suspicion. They had begun in the 1960s, when a bomb exploded in a large city bank, killing and maiming. As an outrage, it had been mindless, but it had inspired ingenious explanations from others in articles, essays, monographs, lapidary inscriptions, lyrics and impassioned novels. Afterwards, more bombs had exploded and there had been more deaths. A series of cruel, subversive acts had been set in motion, and as the novelty wore off they came to look even rational. Now everyone kidnapped, maimed and murdered every day of the week, and people took this savagery in their stride, as part and parcel of the world in which they lived. Eyebrows were no longer raised, though it was still considered good manners to react with outrage. The institutions of democracy successfully claimed their positive right to prosper, even if they had to change their ways, so as not to leave the field open to terrorism, to the notion of "anything goes", and to other impulses which were strangling liberty. It was a reasonable claim. This was the background then, but had it really anything to do with that enigmatic word? The Crux . . . The Inspector thought he had come across the word once before, a new expression going the rounds or seen in a leaflet. A sound that had slipped away with the other sounds on the street, a hazy jumble of slang. The Crux . . . It was probably a new fashion house, or was it 'Crux', the latest dog biscuit? Perhaps it was a new dance or a new beat, like reggae? And from which catacombs of his mind did such useless junk surface anyway?

Pantieri lit a cigarette. His fortieth, was it? He smoked like a factory chimney and had a marked aversion for his bronchi, those ramifications which didn't know the virtue of simplicity. He looked out of the window at the chink of sky. It was dark now, the great Adagio of Tchaikovsky's Sixth lapped over the rooftops. He seemed to sail off into space, leaving detestable humanity to swarm below. He too had a house to go to, except that Biraghi would be waiting for him and the prospect did not fire him with enthusiasm. Unless it was the feeling that something had now been torn apart right in his very own home; his wife had been on the verge of becoming the local priestess.

"I don't understand," the Inspector mumbled, passing a hand through his hair. "What do you want me to do? Do you want to make a charge? A complaint? Or maybe a statement?"

"How could I do that?" the old lady replied. "It's all too much: piracy, unlawful restraint, armed robbery, hijacking, kidnapping, obscenity, rape, heresy, sacrilege, corruption . . . But these are only the symptoms. The real evil lies deeper; I fear they want to cause a mutation in the human race. And I'm also worried about my son. I love him. He's a first-rate physician, an academic, you know."

"A mutation in the human race?" Pantieri asked wryly. "Couldn't we just hope for its destruction?"

"You're just teasing me, Inspector," the old lady complained. "There are some things beyond my ken, they're matters for priests and accountancy tutors; but I remember a thread which ran along pre-established lines. The home, a husband and wife, children, cakes, the Christmas tree, Mass, grandchildren – but now all I have is a great fear . . . perhaps a fear of dying. Are you afraid of dying, Inspector?"

"Me? Oh, I'm immortal," Pantieri smiled, but instantly corrected himself. "I don't know, I try not to think about it."

"That's not true, you do think about it, a great deal. And you are afraid, very much afraid. So am I. That fear's always ruled a man's actions. But now it's different. We claim we can root it out. We want a world that can face the future with its eyes open. A great many people are saying it, but I'm not sure what they really want, myself."

14

"Signora, I've listened to what you've had to say with interest, but now if you will excuse me, I have no idea how I can be of assistance, and unfortunately I have no more time to devote to you."

The old lady opened her waterproof canvas handbag, fluttered a shrivelled handkerchief and modestly blew her nose; she seemed on the verge of tears, but checked herself, observing very softly: "Your time is precious, I know, but I'm in danger. And what's more, so is my son. The Crux know I'm on their trail, they know everything about me and about my son, they've threatened us and are going to kill us. Inspector, I'm asking for your protection."

"Protection?" asked Pantieri with a start, and yet there was something in the darker recesses of his unconscious that was troubling him. "My dear Signora, these tales you've been telling me are all fantasy. You're mistaken, or disturbed. A doctor will be able to give you something to settle you down. What about your son now, he's a medic, isn't he?"

"This is just what I feared," sighed the old lady. This time she couldn't hold back her tears. "You think I'm a poor madwoman. Oh well, I'd better go, and trouble you no longer. But beware, the Crux will strike very soon."

She rose with a sudden ease, almost grace. It was only in that moment that Pantieri noticed her and observed her with real attention, fixing her in his memory. She was small, thin, slightly stooped with age and dressed completely in black. The only spot of colour was a blue shawl wrapped round her slender shoulders. Before she went out, her hand lingered on the doorframe and, with no malice, but in a stern voice, she had spelled out her ominous words: "Inspector, the Crux will destroy you."

15

ACT I

ONE

Via Nomentana was chockablock with cars. Pantieri's Fiat 124 nosed forward jerkily, five metres then stop. With the darkness, the weather had changed. Sheets of rain were falling and produced a black gloss on the asphalt; purulent crowds of pedestrians were caught in the fleeting red of the traffic lights. Rome was not a city real and proper with a well-defined physiognomy; if anything it was an agglomeration of cities linked by their instinctive feeling for gangrene. Acres of monuments and history that, taken all in all, meant not a thing to Pantieri; he'd lived in Rome twenty years and had been twice to St Peter's and once to the Capitol. On the other hand, he was fond of Monte Sacro with its tangle of winding streets, its grey blocks of flats built with no lifts, the Virginia creeper which clothed the crumbling walls and the few pines which had escaped the bulldozers. The oddest assortment of things accumulated by the roadside and the refuse collectors never bothered to take them away. It was an untroubled ruin of inverted umbrellas, mattresses, wastepaper and old furniture. Grasses and sometimes anaemic little flowers grew among the rubbish.

Back home, Pantieri found his friend the judge, Anteo Biraghi. He was a high-ranking magistrate; with his bespectacled moon-face and his suspected hypogenitalism he had every qualification for judging in a calm, impartial manner, except for an indefinable gleam of madness in his eyes, which could also have been a look of crystallized terror. He was sitting in a corner of the kitchen, with his legs apart so as not to vex an overexpansive stomach. Every so often he poked two fingers down his trousers, either to attend to an itch or to instigate some mysterious and subjective state of well-being. He had been a witness at Pantieri's wedding and, when Pantieri became a widower, had installed himself lock, stock and barrel under the Inspector's roof, on the plea of affording comfort and company. He had promised to go as soon as the construction of his small villa in Lavinio was completed, which was now a question of days, if not of hours. Even if he wasn't an encumbering presence, he was still a human cancer. Strangely ill at ease, with his nose in the air and his fanatical, darting eyes, he was like a bloodhound sniffing for its prey.

"Good evening, Carlo," he said with measured effusiveness. "I was just thinking about that meeting that La Calenda, the MP, fixed up, six or seven months ago now, I think it would be . . . your wife, poor dear, was still alive."

"What are you on about now? It's an exaggeration to call that a meeting, I think. Didn't some four or five of them get together? All the bigwigs in the governing party. But it was more like a visit to La Calenda than anything else. He was in hospital at the time, recovering from a bout of hepatitis."

"Well, the newspapers made a lot of it . . . And there was something odd as well; Croce Sabbioneta wasn't invited."

"Nothing of the kind. Croce Sabbioneta was in Russia on an unofficial visit, or perhaps it was a diplomatic mission. He couldn't have been in Rome and Moscow at the same time, could he?"

What a bore the political scene was, thought Pantieri irritably. He could remember that gathering well enough. In fact, it had been his turn to lay on the necessary security: since terrorist groups had taken to using guns, the gentlemen of the establishment never set foot anywhere without bullet-proof limousines, police escorts, bodyguards and the rest. Not very heroic, but you could understand. Of course, according to the official version it was a matter of preserving those precious brains for the good of the country. Everything sprang from a spirit of service but . . . God, they were a pretty humble crew! Their speeches seemed to have been picked up in some second-class railway carriage – all right, so banal language could sometimes clothe great ideas. Not one of the political parties had a clear outline of its own, they were all dug in to defend their own heritage of power. Democracy had become a mere show. Ideologies had been abrogated, with no regrets. Perhaps the trouble was that, in Italy, it was often those at the bottom of the class, those who never made the grade, who went into politics. True, there were one or two exceptions. Lauro Croce Sabbioneta was probably one. But what an impoverished mind! What a lack of inspiration!

"Something must have happened at that meeting," Biraghi was musing. "Something very important."

"I don't think so," Pantieri murmured. "I was there . . . of course, I didn't hear what was said, except for one or two jokes as they were saying goodbye. Dr Gruvi was there with me, too."

"The Reader in Clinical Medicine?" asked the magistrate ironically. "You mean that he'd taken the trouble to pay his respects in person? A strange man, that academic. He invents puzzles for the magazines in his spare time. Signs them with the pseudonym 'Protomartyr'."

"Well, La Calenda was his patient," Pantieri replied. "When you're looking after the Minister of the Interior, you can't behave as if you were treating a laundress."

"That's the trouble. But you were telling me you'd picked up one or two jokes as they were leaving."

"Jokes? That lot couldn't be witty if it tried."

"Sabbioneta's a cultivated man, even if he wasn't there that time. You say he was in Russia? A coincidence no doubt, but a strange one."

Born into a poor family near Forlì, the last of twelve children, he had been baptized Lauro because his parents had presentiments of the glorious laurels that would one day crown his brow, and Croce, perhaps recognizing that this supernumerary was a cross to be borne in a family that was already far too large. By the time he was twenty there was already talk of the young Sabbioneta; an article of his on the poetry of Vincenzo Padula attracted praise from Luigi Russo. A talented amateur actor and fascinating public speaker, the child prodigy became a Professor of Italian Literary History two days before the outbreak of the war. He was wounded and decorated in Libya. He was saved by a miracle, but fortunately the scholar was exceptionally robust; besides, in his student days, he had been a boxing champion. Then, the Resistance and, with the end of the war, years of intense work: his University chair, his articles for *Corriere della Sera* and his correspondence with Father Agostino Gemelli. Some infirmities, inevitably. The ex-athlete suffered perhaps from rheumatism; he evidently felt the cold because he was seldom seen without his overcoat, which was always the same blue cashmere. He had entered politics rather late in life, more or less when Dossetti decided to take a bow, and he knew immediately that his would be a leading role. The leading role, in fact. With his hand on the helm of government, he had imposed himself on whatever difficult situation, above all as a thinker: his stubborn fundamental opinion that politics was not the art of the possible but the ethics of the matter in question had won everyone's esteem. Whatever happened, it was usual to wait for Sabbioneta's judgement before expressing an opinion. The man's only weakness, if it could really be called such, was his passion for stamps. His collection was justly famous; after all, he was the owner of the blue Eleonora of Zimbabwe without perforations, and the acquisition of such a rarity said it all.

"You're making a storm in a teacup," Pantieri smiled, "and I don't understand why. You know better than I that before Christmas Sabbioneta will be charged with forming the new government . . . one of national solidarity. Not a very exciting prospect, perhaps, but a different distribution of the spoils will bring some order, even if there's no end to the scandals. Even the police are now looking to the villains for their cut . . ."

"I don't think anything will change either," Biraghi muttered, lowering his head and poking two fingers back down his trousers. "A disappointing conclusion: so much for reinvigoration – that'll never come now."

Talk. Meaningless talk. It never changed the world. Better to miniaturize it, thought Pantieri, lock it away behind the walls of a house. He looked around him and smiled wanly: the colourless things in the apartment, the cretonne-covered armchairs, the chandelier, the decorated plates hanging on the wall left him feeling sad and resigned. Only a panoply of arms in the hall sometimes managed to spark his imagination; it was an ornamental display of weapons in the worst possible taste, and certainly clashed with such an unheroic setting, but it succeeded in evoking marvellous scenes from the books of his childhood. Most of all, he was excited by an antique, rusty poignard and pretended to sink its pointed steel into the fat belly of that boring fart Biraghi, twisting his guts out from a wound which swam with blood, rigatoni, and the pandects of jurisprudence.

"Would you mind," said Pantieri, cutting him short, "if I listen to Tchaikovsky?"

It was the surest way of being left in peace; and from this point of view the ideal composition was the *1812 Overture*, but that was too much of an open provocation. He settled for the Piano Concerto, whose *attaque* might succeed in bringing even Biraghi to forget politics and terrorism, at least for a while. His wife used to become tetchy when he turned on the record-player to put an end to her wearisome conversation. She'd died six months ago, and now it seemed as if he'd never even known her. A volvulus, something nasty to do with the intestine; she'd passed away in less than forty-eight hours, under the surgeon's knife. That surgeon had read his mind and done him a favour. But these were wicked thoughts with which he profitlessly tormented himself from time to time. He wasn't really guilty of Assunta's tragic end, nor was he even guilty of never having loved her. For a moment he pictured her again as she used to be, drying her hands a little spasmodically on her apron, her untidy blonde hair dried out from all the perms in the neigh-bourhood hair salons, her cheeks glowing, her hands attesting her long predilection for detergents. An insignificant woman, or perhaps a woman he had never understood. Every human being held a secret and his wife was certainly no exception to the rule, but he'd never attempted to penetrate the enigma; too much trouble to burden yourself with anyone else's soul but your own.

"It'll put off the solution to our problems," Biraghi went

on, his voice over-reaching the tempestuous sound from the piano; "all of the problems afflicting us: 'Partyocracy', property speculation, corruption, the services in disarray, unemployment, alcoholism, the Crux . . ."

"I beg your pardon?" Pantieri gave a start, in spite of himself, and hastily switched off the record-player. "I didn't quite hear what you said."

"Crooks. The scourge of criminality."

The old dear he had met down at Division, rabbiting on about priestesses and mutations, had left a weight on Pantieri's mind, a dim foreboding. He was afraid his very own home might be concealing a mystery, while being aware that there were no rational grounds for his fears. Biraghi knew nothing of the old lady's ramblings, and, in speaking of "the Crux", had simply committed a slip of the tongue. And yet that enigmatic word had a wicked and enticing sound to it.

"Almost the whole of the Press is on the same wavelength as the society we now live in," the magistrate was saying, speaking as if to himself. "The newspapers go overboard about futile things, like rent tribunals and changes in pension structure. They waste rivers of ink on tomfoolery like that! To say nothing of the television! They never discuss ideas. Take Edward von Hartmann's . . . Here the laws are a cosmetic to slap on the face of a woman who needs tarting up."

"It's a tough job, yours," Pantieri commented sarcastically. "You judges have to supervise the make-up job, it seems to me! I'm not talking about you, I was thinking of that Prosecutor of the Republic, Raniero Conti . . . He's a person on the up, that, and sees the law – and its implementation – as a way of getting there. A shifty, cynical so-and-so. Anyway, leaving gossip aside, I've no wish to talk politics."

"Alright," Biraghi assented. "Besides, I'm going out soon. I've got an explosive appointment, but I don't suppose it'll interest you. I won't tire you any longer tonight with my commentaries. However . . . I don't want to open an old wound, because I do understand . . . but since poor Assunta's death, you're getting to be a real crosspatch. You were pretty misanthropic before, but now . . . Well, just remember I'm a friend and that I do try and stick by you."

"How could I forget?"

"I'll be moving into my little villa in Lavinio in a few days' time," said Biraghi. "Not far from the Convent of the Blessed Oblate Sisters of S. Daniela Crisci; I'm placing myself in the odour of sanctity. I could go straightaway, I think everything's in order, apart perhaps from the floors to be cleaned. Perhaps you'd prefer to be on your own?"

"I'm not sure."

"Listen to the man!" sighed Biraghi. "By the way, I've taken a small liberty. I've put a box away in your cellar. Let me repeat, it's only a question of a few days: it'll follow me to Lavinio very shortly. And it's not to be touched. I know perfectly well you wouldn't go and open it . . . but I wanted to warn you, all the more so as the contents are a bit *sui generis*."

"*Sui generis?*"

"Absolutely. Eight pairs of *Mastomys natalensis*, and the females are pregnant. They're beauties! Arrived for me specially this morning from Nigeria. A friend brought them who lives out there. Right under the nose of the Customs. I make shift with a bit of black-market dealing, myself!"

"Well I'll be damned!" blustered Pantieri. "And I don't follow . . . I've never heard of these creatures, supposing that's what they are. I don't want any trouble with the other residents in the block. And furthermore, I don't understand what the devil you want with your pregnant females . . ."

"The *Mastomys natalensis* are rats."

"Rats?"

"Rats, mice, rodents. They're valuable little breeding animals, better than the chinchilla. They never fall ill, they're robust and they're prolific breeders. They're just the thing to speculate in. Loads of money to be made: *Mastomys* furs are valuable."

"I don't like the idea of these rats in the cellar, I don't want any trouble. And they'll make a mess, not to mention the smell . . ."

The magistrate stood up and stretched. He was pleased with

25

his animal farm, and looking forward to lucrative business in the future. He wandered aimlessly round the apartment, his attention turning from this to that, and lingered in front of the hall mirror. With accomplished fingers, he straightened his tie, which he still knotted too long and too tight. He consulted his watch two or three times as if he were worried about being late for something, then, before going out, peered into the umbrella stand and suddenly rummaged down in it as far as he could go. He pulled a dirty sleeve out and began dusting himself off with rapid, irritable gestures.

"I lost my keys," he explained to Pantieri, who was looking at him in perplexity. He went out giving a farewell smile that was an equal blend of cordiality and contempt.

Pantieri switched the radio on, catching fragments of a news bulletin: the Rt Hon. Orazio La Calenda was fighting strenuously for a new law on civil rights and institutional reform . . . This new law was an excuse to block any real change and suppress guarantees afforded by the law; but then one had to admit they weren't cast-iron anyway. The debate about the new law, like any other debate, was only quibbling; it lent a respectable air to what the conflicts were really about – jobs for the boys and perks. Jobs like the chairmanship of a bank, perks like a fat tender. The Minister of the Interior was from Calabria and vaunted his aristocratic blood; nearer seventy than sixty, a wizened bachelor who was sparing with his words and even more so with his praise. According to some, he had links with the Mafia, while others said he was close to the American Secret Service. There was a rumour that he had a son, an illegitimate one who had never been recognized, and that this heir, conceived so many years ago, had turned out a bad lot; a criminal element, as bad as could be. But perhaps this was the evil gossip of his enemies, trying to visit the sins of a possibly non-existent son on the head of his poor father. La Calenda got on people's nerves, he represented a construction bosses' and big landowners' interest that was hated by the predominant industrial complex.

The bulletin continued with insignificant items: a hundred kilos of the purest heroin seized in Ventimiglia; bandits had released the pharmaceutical industrialist Galdeni for a ransom of five thousand million lire; there was still galloping inflation and the price of potatoes had suffered another leap; in the Upper Volta it was feared there was an outbreak of the plague . . . The plague? . . . Did that still exist? Now, wasn't it rats that transmitted the fatal disease? Pantieri lit a cigarette and decided to go and check the cellar. Not that he was worried about the possibility of plague; good God, on the eve of the twenty-first century there was no chance of such a possibility, at least in Europe, but it wasn't worth while annoying his neighbours in the block. Biraghi should have realized he'd acted off-handedly. It was thoughtless. Rash. The box of rats had to go as soon as possible.

It was dark and there was a musty smell, as nobody visited the basement very much. There wasn't a single family in the block who frequented it as a rule. It was a series of damp, narrow rooms where the furniture they knew they'd never use again had been buried once and for all, which avoided the nagging doubt that comes from having thrown something out for good. More than a cellar, it was a graveyard of old junk. Pantieri wasn't long in catching a muffled squeaking, an intermittent hiss that kept starting up . . . Squee, squee . . . lamented the little mice imprisoned in the box. They ran about in the small space available, banging into the sides, so that on top of their cries there was the sound of their scratching paws, and muzzles striking the wood. Pantieri lit a candle-stub and peered through the grill that covered the top of the box. They were small mice of singular appearance: they looked like Lilliputian lions, their heads fringed by a thick mane and with long clammy tails ending in a tuft of hair. There looked like a streak of cruelty in the creatures' eyes, but this was merely a fanciful impression. With the dark, their captivity and hunger perhaps, they had no reason to look anything other than untrustworthy.

Pantieri went back up the stairs and, on the point of going in through the main entrance, he stopped for a moment to have

27

a look at the sky. It had stopped raining and a wind had risen, blowing the clouds apart here and there; strips of cobalt and *encre de chine* had broken through, while the moon sent out whispers of grey. From the thickets of Sacrofano, Castelnuovo, Morlupo, Campagnano – thickets transformed by speculators into villas at two million lire the cubic metre – the wolves descended. In the cemetery of Prima Porta, like the Italic splendours in Santa Croce, the shades of Romulus and Remus, the Popes, the ancient trollops of the Suburra, and the more recent ones in Via Vigna Clara and Via Tor di Quinto, gathered to meet; the tireless Marchese Casati took photographs. To the north the sky seemed to settle down; the recent lacerations, vivid as knife-slashes, knitted together and suffused into a clear night.

It was then that the fleet appeared: at first they looked like aeroplanes, seven, eight, perhaps even more, but they had no wings, they were too large and moved along at a ponderous pace that defied the laws of physics. Pantieri thought they might be helicopters, but the sausage-shaped outlines and immense size led him to discard that hypothesis. Then he thought of an interplanetary invasion, with space ships unloading hordes of extraterrestrial conquistadors; at this supposition, he felt more relief than alarm because in his heart of hearts he looked forward to the joy of having a master who would teach him what to do, what not to do, where to go and where not to go; in short, how to live. But as the fleet moved on, even the extraterrestrial conjecture proved false; those cigar-shapes, so black in the sky's cerulean, evoked scenes from the Belle Epoque, not the future of space travel. They were airships.

The fleet dropped down a little, described a wide arc, proceeded in the direction of Via Aurelia, then let the night swallow it up. Publicity, Pantieri thought; simply publicity.

But as soon as he was back within his own four walls, the presentiment of disaster that had taken hold of him after his conversation with the old dear suddenly surfaced again; only now it was more intrusive. He slipped into the bedroom and contemplated the wardrobe, which remained crammed with his wife's things. Pantieri had locked it six months previously and never re-opened it; but now he thought he saw some scratches around the lock, marks left by a penknife or something larger, as if someone had unsuccessfully tried to force it. Absurd. Who could have been interested in going through his wife's underwear? Biraghi was a magistrate in the Court of Appeal, it wasn't even thinkable . . . What a base suspicion!

Still, it was better to take a look over it and make sure. He searched among his bunch of keys and with difficulty, as some rust had formed in the old lock's workings, he succeeded in opening it. Remorselessly he began to rummage through the drawers which had belonged to his wife. He took care not to throw things about the place, but put everything back as he had found it; this consideration being a way to avoid showing disrespect for poor Assunta's memory. There was a tart smell of cosmetics, armpit and mothballs. He passed in review pathetic things of questionable coquetry: woollen vests, archaic knickers, others microscopic, suspenders, packets of sanitary towels, nighties long and short, a pair of flannel pyjamas.

By now he was persuaded he wouldn't find anything unusual, and began to feel ashamed at having violated the privacy to which even a deceased spouse is entitled. Aimlessly, he went on through the domestic haberdasher's, and the wear and tear in some of the garments, the reek of wax emanating from the pullovers (this was a hallucination caused by his bad conscience) and the bunches of dried lavender peeping out from the linen activated a forgotten piety in him. That was the moment when he came across the cardboard box buried under a pile of stockings and handkerchiefs. It was an ordinary box into which he looked without wanting to, convinced he would only come across insignificant trinkets. But he was wrong.

The telephone brought him back to his senses. Its penetrating ring seemed to add solemnity to his discovery, underlining that moment in his life in a crucial way. They were calling him from Division: there had been an explosion at the Discount and Savings Bank in Via Due Macelli. Twenty dead, possibly more; a hundred injured. They thought it was a terrorist attack.

TWO

To picture some things, you have to have seen a war and a city after an air-raid. The reporters spoke of huge craters, gaping abysses, clouds of smoke, the acrid smell of cordite and all the nonsense reporters write on these occasions; but it's also true that words aren't photographs; they can't capture things like a mirror; the blood written down on paper isn't the blood soaking pavements and débris. The reporter can't delude himself into thinking he transcribes reality; if he's lucky he can evoke a misty resonance or stir up ambiguous sounds in the mind. Groans, cries and sobs. Death, real death, is steeped in formalin, incense, church, priests, earth and no one knows how to report it.

A rough voice called him over, "Pantieri, over here, quick!"

It was Dr Raniero Conti, Prosecutor of the Republic; a stocky, vulgar man, very full of himself, a martinet.

"Here I am, sir," responded Pantieri calmly. "Forensic will be here shortly to look things over."

"The bastards!" snarled the magistrate. "This is terrorism, alright! Okay, so they wanted to plant a bomb, they wanted to blow up a bank, but could they wait till tomorrow? Not bloody likely! Had to be tonight, didn't it? Tonight, when I'd tickets for the Sistina, stalls, front and centre, second row. Can you beat it, Pantieri?"

He was fuming; he enunciated each word, afraid no one could grasp his personal tragedy.

"Enough is enough," he complained, while consulting his pocket watch with its sacrilegious transcription, 'Mon âme avec le diable'. "I've no peace anymore. Yesterday afternoon they snatched the wife's handbag. Silly cow. A million lire gone,

Pantieri, a cool million. Then that twerp of a son gets netted in a round-up of punks. Dirty lot, mixed up with the Crux, that's it, crooks . . . It's one buggering thing after another."

"Everyone has his troubles, sir," muttered Pantieri wanly; "we get our deserts."

That slip of the tongue between "the Crux" and "crooks" hadn't escaped him (but was it really a slip of the tongue?) and he clearly remembered that Biraghi had committed the same error only a few hours earlier. In the back of his mind a danger signal was vexing him, but it gave him no clue as to where he should watch out.

A crowd had gathered. It was proving difficult to contain it as it pushed and shoved; they all wanted to enjoy the show. The jostling interfered with the work of the emergency services until the public and the forces of law and order came to a tacit agreement: the curious didn't step over a certain line and in return the police didn't obstruct the sight of the injured being taken away to the ambulances.

Pantieri had no time for the Prosecutor; he couldn't stand his blunt, graceless manner. He suspected that, rather than looking for the truth, Conti occasionally preferred to fabricate it. Other suspicions were less definable (but were none the less odious for that), and simply fuelled his antipathy. That inscription on his watch, which he displayed on every possible occasion, was infantile, but irritating all the same. A magistrate had to be neither satanic nor angelic; his job was to accept the facts in their humble objectivity.

The police made way for a black Mercedes, which came to a stop beside Pantieri. The Minister of the Interior, Orazio La Calenda, emerged with the Rt Hon. Lauro Croce Sabbioneta.

La Calenda was drawn and moody; he took Conti to one side and confabulated with a worried look. Sabbioneta was sprightly and went to join the crowd, the simple people who loved him for being an honest man. They liked him living in a convent on the Aventine, lodging with the friars, even though he had a modest apartment in Via Serpentara; they liked the Franciscan simplicity of his diet: a glass of milk, an onion, a cheese vol-au-vent, a mandarin orange crêpe. They found it touching that there had been but one love in his life and when his fiancée died in the bombing, he had dedicated the bitter future to the adoration of her cherished memory. (These snippets, divulged by a weekly magazine, were promptly and irritably denied, but it was still common knowledge that the illustrious politician was almost an ascetic.)

"Are there many lives in danger among the injured?" Sabbioneta asked Pantieri as he took off his blue cashmere overcoat and his jacket, and rolled up his shirtsleeves.

"Some could bleed to death."

"Then I offer my blood," Sabbioneta proclaimed, thrusting out his bare arms.

"My blood too is at your disposal!" bawled the Minister of the Interior from a distance, and he came over waving his arms. He stood beside Sabbioneta and in stentorian tones bellowed: "Justice will be done!"

"What justice?" asked Pantieri under his breath, knowing from long experience that there is nothing more crooked than what we are used to calling "the law". Fortunately no one registered his comment; there was now a crush of doctors and photographers around the two politicians, one group busy with their blood-letting, the other clicking away for the morning editions.

Conti wriggled out of donating blood and sought cover with Pantieri. La Calenda sidled up to him and said something in an undertone, but those standing closest picked up a scrap of the dialogue: ". . . like the Sorcerer's Apprentice".

The Minister of the Interior made a gesture to indicate that it was time to leave and Sabbioneta retreated towards the black Mercedes, shaking hands all the while and patting the unwashed heads of the little children thrust at him as if he were the Pope. The ministerial car set off, preceded by the sirens of its motorcycle escort.

"The bastards!" whispered Conti to Pantieri, waving his arm in the direction of the now distant black limousine. "Think they can bullshit the whole world, they do. They can bullshit these numbskulls here . . . this filthy mob, that's all they can bullshit."

32

"If I'm not being indiscreet," said Pantieri softly, "what was the Minister of the Interior saying? What's all this about the Sorcerer's Apprentice?"

"A load of balls," said the Prosecutor of the Republic, fuming, and for an instant the colour left his face. "A smooth way . . . a cultured, a refined and educated way . . . of saying 'we don't know what the fuck's going on.' Hell's bells! Pantieri, will you look who's coming now!"

It was Cardinal Meschia who was coming now, followed by his usual retinue of the faithful, of layabouts and radicals. For some the Cardinal was a saint, for others a troublemaker; it was suspected that the Holy See could be numbered among the "others". On he came, towering above the crowd which genuflected and prostrated itself before him. He was wearing his usual red overalls full of holes, patches and grease stains. With his unkempt white hair and his kindly blue eyes, his hieratic figure invited the crowd to prayer, and led them to think that a bomb explosion was after all only a minor upset. The Omnipotent was armed with bombs of quite a different kind.

Having imparted his blessing, he came up to Pantieri for information: how many dead, how many injured, how many arrested. The illustrious prelate's pity was directed especially towards the latter, and he experienced a sense of disappointment on learning that for the moment no one had been hauled off to jail. Consoling prisoners was one of his favourite occupations.

"Do you think Baget Bozzo will write an article on this?" he asked Pantieri, frowning with an uneasy air. "Merciful heavens, it was lucky the bank was closed and the destruction limited to employees and passers-by . . . What if it had been in the morning? . . . Well, I shudder to think. Is it the work of organized crime or is there a political twist to it?"

"I'm afraid there might be a political twist."

"It's the beginning of the apocalypse! The month of January in the year of judgement!"

What filled the Cardinal's life was his expectation of the apocalypse, his aversion to Baget Bozzo, and his concern over world famine. The apocalypse was an opinion, and on opinions

33

it is better not to debate. Baget Bozzo was a trustworthy political commentator, but he unleashed mysterious allergies in the eminent prelate, who had only to see the hated signature to start mauling the rag which had dared to give him space and, overcome by a destructive rage, he would then rip its pages apart, fling the shreds onto the floor and tread them into the ground like dirt. As regards world famine, he had been taken to hospital many times, suffering from the effects of his hunger strikes in protest against it. Some of his other ventures had raised eyebrows. At the head of a crowd of outcasts from a shanty town, he had once overseen the sacking of the restaurant "Il Passetto" and, worse, had attempted to set fire to Villa Ada, wishing to transform its green oasis into a dairy farm.

"You were in charge of security at Dr Gruvi's clinic six months ago, weren't you?" asked the Cardinal. "I refer to the meeting of the leaders of the majority party, when the Rt Hon. Sabbioneta was not invited."

"The Rt Hon. Sabbioneta was in Russia," Pantieri explained. "Why do you ask, Your Eminence?"

"Baget Bozzo's talked a lot about that meeting. Now why did it take place when Sabbioneta was in Russia?"

"I really have no idea, but as far as I have been led to understand, it was a matter without any political significance."

"Do you mean that Baget Bozzo has just been jumping to conclusions?"

"I haven't read the articles myself."

"Well, no matter," said the venerable old man with a sigh. "Let us think about those poor people devastated by the explosion. You don't think, Inspector, that these are the warning signs of the apocalypse, do you? And mild warnings, at that, because the account to be paid with death will run into the order of millions and hundreds of millions, if death still has any meaning."

"One can hope it might be the apocalypse," was Pantieri's comment and he noticed a small ulcer on the back of the Cardinal's hand. Considering the fame and profession of his interlocutor, he wondered if it might be the stigmata, but he rejected this appealing notion with brutal realism. Then he added: "If it were the apocalypse, that would explain everything."

"We humans always think we can find an explanation . . . And yet we've managed to explain almost nothing . . . Isn't it about time we thought of a world which based its logic on the absence of logic? The eternal verities are very few and all elementary: take food, for example. I'm interested in things to do with food; I'd like everyone to have enough to eat. The rise in the price of potatoes is alarming: potatoes and beans are the meat of the poor. Now if you will excuse me, I must go and bless the corpses."

Pantieri took refuge in a bar and had a coffee. He lit a cigarette. His eyes were bloodshot and he was tired; he looked about him but couldn't pick out any definite images; all he perceived was greenish mist interspersed with the glare of neon lights. Thus, when she appeared in front of him and he recognized her, small and frail as she was, and black as night except for the patch of blue made by the shawl around her shoulders, he thought his tormented brain was playing a nasty trick.

"You see, Inspector," said the old lady softly, "you wouldn't believe me, but all this was bound to happen. And it's only the beginning. By the way, only a quarter of an hour ago they nominated a priestess for Monte Sacro. The ceremony was blasphemous and shameful, a disgusting business."

"I'd dearly love to put you in handcuffs!" exclaimed Pantieri. "You're going to tell me everything you know, and you're not leaving here until you do."

"What more do you want me to say?" went on the old lady, in a murmur. She was sad, resigned. "I'm only a poor old woman, and this is a colossal affair brewing . . ."

"I'm listening," promised Pantieri. "You'll tell me everything, otherwise . . ."

He did not succeed in finishing. Someone had touched his arm. Conti was giving him a sardonic, suspicious look.

"Thought I'd have a coffee myself," the judge enunciated. "This joint'll be coining it in tonight! What a shambles!

35

Nothing doing at the Sistina, it's closing, be open at a 'date to be confirmed'."

The moment's interruption was enough. The old lady disappeared, with her blue shawl and her secrets. Pantieri looked about him, dejected: he peered out among the swarm of cars, ambulances and gapers. She'd vanished into thin air.

The barman had recognized Conti and piped up: "What the crux going on?"

"What the crux!?" yelled Pantieri, slamming his fist on the counter. Two or three glasses fell off and smashed into pieces.

"But *Dottore*," whined the barman resentfully, "I was only asking what's going on."

"Pantieri, you're tired, you're in real bad shape. Best go and get some sleep, eh?" ordered the Prosecutor, with feigned consideration.

THREE

He didn't follow Conti's advice. He buried himself in an emaciated pine grove at the end of Via Nomentana, where children played during the day and lovers discarded their contraceptives during the evening. Night breathed on his face, caressing him like the Adagio in Tchaikovsky's Sixth. The raindrops were music to him. There was a sweetness in the past, or perhaps it was sweetness because it was the past; nothing far-fetched in the reflection – it was as reassuring as the party in power.

There had been an employee at Division, one Mirella Jenca, 24 years old, from Papasidero (Cosenza), and he'd felt a faint pang of love for her. A love that was troubled and anxious. He was ashamed to admit it. If he'd taken a fancy to her it had mainly been because of the rotundities which adorned her fundament. It was somewhat disgusting. Was passion (or the attempt at it) only justified because a woman had a beautiful a . . . ? The suspension dots were printed by his own imagination. Well, after all, why not? One loved as one could and as one knew how. But there'd soon been gossip. A police officer, and a married man as well, flirting with a typist in his office, well, nobody would have created a scene, times had changed, the permissive society had wormed its way into police stations as well, but nevertheless, Heaven knows, aesthetically, officially, and responsibly, the usual wisdom was you don't poach in your own preserves. And yet, even though he was aware of jeopardizing his promotion to Chief of Police in Cremona or Frosinone, he hadn't had the courage to do without Tchaikovsky; and if he'd really liked women, he wouldn't have accepted such an inglorious outcome. Instead, it had been Mirella Jenca,

24 years old, from Papasidero, who had handed in her notice and disappeared. It had been fruitless searching for her, not that he'd really tried.

And now (three years had since elapsed) it was Mirella's image that came floating into his mind. It had happened before, but prior to that unusual day he'd felt obliged to cancel it out, forcing himself not to think of her and so not to suffer. Perhaps the trouble was something else; something inside him was twisted and perverted, he didn't know how to get close to a woman with the sincerity every human being needed. Without being aware of it, he'd treated the women in his life (few and far between) as inscrutable objects, though objects, too, of a guilty, animal yearning. Rather than try and make himself understand, he'd preferred to see his more insubstantial fantasies reflected in these rather unsuspecting and surprised creatures. His face sensed a familiar caress and he abandoned himself to a mush of tender feelings.

Spirit of sweetness, he thought, and as he surrendered to his memories, he was embarrassed to find himself in thrall to a sort of mental masturbation, except the vulgarity of the action was absent – there was only the magic of invented kisses. All the same, he forbade himself from thinking about those profane curves, even though they embraced . . . With Mirella he had had an opportunity and, as always, he had been defeated. At the end of an old Carné film, only at the end, alas, Arletty explains to Barrault that there's nothing more simple than love; but since his childhood, at home, in church and at school, he'd been taught that love was a very complex thing: the spirit and the gonads had to be in tune and on their interaction depended eternal melodies. Among the many labyrinths of the world, love was love, and that's all there was to it. Out loud, he asked the night: "What does it mean 'to be in love'?"

He lit a cigarette and looked at the packet: still two left. Anyway the tobacconists would be open before long. It was cold and damp; he pulled up his collar and was aware of being frozen stiff. Never mind. Squalor and neglect – how delightful! Up to that point the radio had fed him a diet of pop songs and dinky tunes, just the thing for amorous regrets, then the *cupio dissolvi*; but the light of dawn brought back the horrid sounds of the time-signal and the usual know-all voice began to recite the world's affairs. Inflation could never be deplored enough; according to a well-known theory, it was the most iniquitous of all taxes.

The sky was half blue, half ashen; soon it would start raining again. Night's labyrinths faded out, to be replaced by the furtive scenario of buses, the racket as cafés ran up their metal shutters, and humanity on the march towards wages, salaries, stipends and backhanders.

He turned the car round and went back to Division. Apart from the tragedy in Via Due Macelli, it had been a quiet night. No bloodshed, no robbery, no theft. Only a prostitute hauled in for soliciting. Generally no one bothered, but this one had gone too far. She'd had quite a binge and was still under the weather.

"Wheel her in," said Pantieri to the duty guard. "And send someone to get me some cigarettes. Let's have a coffee, too, and make it strong."

A sheet of rain was falling across the windows, blurring the outlines of the trees and roofs. The bougainvillea blossomed in magenta mistiness, thick wads of cloud faded away above it. Pantieri ran a hand through his hair: every time he expected a visitor he thought it suitable to be seen concentrating on a pile of papers, but it was only a ploy, because he never read a word, he was too anxious over the impending confrontation. Before raising his head, he knew it was her, he recognized her footsteps, her smell, and he felt drained.

"Mirella Jenca, Inspector," intoned the duty guard. "Age 27, from Papasidero (Cosenza). Married. Arrested while soliciting five Dominican friars."

She was thinner and her face was pale; her make-up had run and whiskers of mascara and eye-shadow were streaked beneath her eyes. She was smiling her special smile, soft and ironic; meanwhile, she straightened her split skirt, which gave him a glimpse of a leg blue with the cold. Her backside was even more bewitching . . . indeed it was . . . yes, why didn't he genuflect as one would before a miraculous apparition and

39

beg her permission to cover the miraculous, beatific, polished sculpture of her a . . . with kisses? Suspension dots came to his aid. Thank goodness she sat down straightaway.

"I want something to put on," said Mirella. "I've been freezing all night. Your men wouldn't give me a blanket. A little kindness wouldn't hurt."

"I'm sorry," Pantieri replied, and, taking off his jacket, he handed it to her with an uncertain smile.

"Now you'll be cold yourself," she parried, but was only being polite, for she quickly covered her shoulders and breathed a sigh of relief. "I'm always worried about that little lesion on my lungs, you remember, the one I told you about. When I was a little girl, they sent me to the country and it all cleared up. In actual fact I don't think I was ever tubercular."

"No, of course you're not tubercular, never have been. So, tell me about yourself. Life's full of coincidences, I was thinking about you only last night."

"What d'you want me to say? I go on the game a bit, I can't deny that."

"You should stay sober, and you shouldn't solicit people, otherwise you run into the Merlin Act and then there's unpleasantness. Well, I'm not pressing charges. As far as I'm concerned the matter's closed, and off you go."

"You're letting me go? But listen, I want to tell you how I wound up like this. I'm not happy you've got to hear about it. What we two got up to was all above-board, more or less."

Pantieri looked out of the window. Trickles of water were running down the panes; through them he saw a grey village crowning the summit of a mountain. A winding road took you up there through oaks and olives, and on the valley floor flowed the mysterious river Lao which, once upon a time, had submerged a city and later a hoard of treasure. The village was populated more by sheep than human kind, and was called Papasidero; he had discovered it some time ago on a love-quest, and had been intrigued by that Greek-sounding name which seemed to want to bring the stars closer to the earth.

They had been guests of Mirella's ancient relative, Uncle Giacchino, an illiterate peasant who nevertheless knew all the secrets of the world. He knew when it was time for grafting, and when it was time for bottling wine. Then Pantieri remembered a ruin gripping on to the summit, a castle abandoned for more than a hundred years, which the popular imagination linked with terror and superstition; people spoke of spirits there. Uncle Giacchino told stories about the unrelenting ghost of the last feudal baron, who had been deserted by his beautiful wife and had spent a lifetime searching and waiting for her; then, after his death, his waiting had never ceased, as he wandered restlessly among the now crumbling battlements.

The phantom used to appear unexpectedly, but mostly during the winter, when logs crackled in the fireplace, the reels ticked off wool into skeins, and werewolves played with snow under the blue light of a full moon. Pantieri had always wanted to go back there, with its cold and its sheep-tracks fresh with snow. A limpid world, composed solely of light and colour. Or perhaps the end of the world, like a last act, when fiction and reality melt into one. That distant night beside Mirella he had kissed those fascinating curves and then listened to the rustle of the leaves in the wind; he thought he had secured a truth or at least caught a glimpse of it.

"It's my husband who puts me on the streets," Mirella murmured. She lit a cigarette, then hesitantly offered the packet of Marlboro to Pantieri. They inhaled a few lungfuls in silence.

"You're married then?"

"A year ago. My husband's from Calabria, one of the 'honoured society'. He gives me a lot of freedom . . . Travels a lot . . . Business I don't understand . . . He's a big shot in his home town. Needs a lot of money. He loves clothes, shows, trips and cars. And his weapons. Everyone thinks he's rich and that's what makes his life sparkle. He loves to put on a front. The fact is he's just a second-rate guy, but can't resign himself to such a depressing thought."

"So he puts you on the streets because he has a problem with his prestige?"

"Well, up to a point. He does get by, sometimes he earns quite a lot. You know how it is . . . with all this inflation, it helps with two wage packets coming in. Of course, appearances count an awful lot for a Calabrian. We only have one yardstick, one philosophy to live by: 'Losing face'. We can put up with squalor so long as people pretend not to know. And to excuse ourselves for all the dirt that falls on our heads, we always manage to find a bit more falling on other people."

She slipped off without giving him time to ask anything else, leaving his head spinning with conjectures and regrets. Finally the duty guard arrived with his coffee and the cigarettes. He was excited and, stumbling over his words a little, he said: "Sensational news, Inspector! They've arrested the culprit of the bomb attack in Via Due Macelli. Dr Conti will be here in a moment."

"I can't stand that man and his arrogance," Pantieri sighed. "Anything else?"

"They've fished an old lady out of the Tiber. Police surgeon swears she was strangled, then dumped in the river. Small, thin, dressed in black. A blue shawl was floating beside her."

FOUR

Perhaps the key to the solution lies at home, Pantieri thought, ruffling his hair with his habitual gesture. It was time to think about that cardboard box, or rather about what it contained. He'd seen enough dirty photographs, it was part of his job and nothing would have surprised him. And yet he was disturbed by that sudden revelation that his wife, a fairly stupid and sexually aseptic woman, had kept those forbidden images like holy pictures.

It was incredible. So many years he'd lived with the woman and conceived an unflattering view of her: there'd been no passion in their intimacy, it had the dull cadences of a school poetry reading. But he had misconstrued her. What had Assunta's secret been? Perhaps someone had asked her to keep the compromising box for a while and she hadn't given it a moment's thought, or perhaps she'd kept the pack of relics for her own shameful and secret delight?

Trollop, thought Pantieri, and was ashamed of himself, because his wife's memory now kindled a spark of desire in him – once contaminated, the memory became naughty, disturbing. Sensual enjoyment in degrading circumstances was the inheritance of a Catholic upbringing; the thought of guilt was a prelude to pleasure, which gave one all the more of a lift, the worse the sin attending it.

But in all probability this was beside the point, because among all those squalid photographs he had found one anomaly, a faded snapshot taken by a cheap camera. It was a family picture: a man with his arm around the shoulders of a young boy, holding him close. There was an evident similarity between the two, they must have been father and son. More-

43

over he thought he recognized the man, or at least had once seen him, but it was difficult to call him to mind, as the photograph was faded and very old. His policeman's nose told him that of all those embarrassing scenes, it was precisely this one of a father and son, caught in a pose of maudlin devotion, that was perhaps the most embarrassing of all. He had left the box with its obscene contents in the wardrobe, but had put away in the safety of his wallet the snap-shot immortalizing the sanctity of paternal love.

While he was driving the old 124 along Via Nomentana in the rain, a mortal tiredness overtook him: he hadn't slept for two days. He searched for a music programme on the radio and was inundated by the "Pas de deux" from Tchaikovsky's *Nutcracker Suite*. Tchaikovsky was certainly an intrusive guest.

A raindrop landed on the windscreen which the wiper couldn't reach. It resembled a woman's face, presumably the face of his schoolteacher, Signorina Candiani . . . She'd sent him outside the classroom, accusing him of constructing a blow-pipe and darts (out of his maths book!) for taking potshots at his classmates. Him of all people! He'd explained, he'd asserted his innocence, and while he was all in a fluster at his desk a dart armed with a pin had flown across the classroom and buried itself in his cheek. Despite the pain, he'd been satisfied: he was now sure his innocence would be vindicated. On the contrary, his schoolteacher explained, the victim is always the culprit and had sent him out. After that, Pantieri had transformed punishment into a state of election.

As soon as he was home, he went back to rummaging through the stockings and handkerchiefs in the wardrobe, without any qualms; the only sensation he had was that some-one else might have been there before him, turning Assunta's relics upside down. The cardboard box was open and the pornographic photographs scattered about. He hunted like a maniac through every corner of the house, in the vain hope of turning up further evidence, but all he came across were the emblems of his bourgeois respectability and that was all. He found a scrap of paper, grey with dust and age, thrown away in the umbrella stand, a venerable list of things to buy or

44

already bought: oregano, basil, sugar, coffee, two crux and saucers . . . no, that wasn't it, it was crockery, cups and suchlike crucks like that old crock who'd been strangled and dropped in the Tiber.

The door opened and in came Biraghi. He was just back after having breakfast at the bar on the corner. Every morning he went down to have a *cappuccino* with a sprinkling of chocolate on top, and four brioches. He said it was for settling the glycemia in the blood, a sacrifice he underwent for the good of his health. His lips were still dusted with brioche crumbs and sugar. Under one arm he was holding *Il Messaggero*, which was black with headlines and exclamation marks.

"Fascinating this mystery of the Discount and Savings Bank," commented Biraghi, unfolding the paper. "There was no doubt it was a device with a timing mechanism, one of those which uses acid . . . A difficult debut for the new chairman, Gerardo Opitz . . . our construction boss will be sorry he didn't stay in the business."

"The terrorists don't give a damn about Opitz," replied Pantieri. "It's not their business to do Nemesis out of a job. They sow confusion, that's all."

His eye fell on a bottle of Glen Grant left on a sidetable. He unscrewed the plastic cap, but was swamped by corrosive fumes and his eyes immediately began to water. It wasn't whisky.

"What's this filthy stuff?"

"Trieline, it removes stains. I needed it because I got my trousers dirty yesterday with the plaster and rubble. It's an extraordinary product, trieline: in actual fact I ended up putting a hole through my trousers, but they were torn anyway. Even so, be careful, it's a bit poisonous."

"Well, damn your eyes. What's the sense of keeping it in a liquor bottle?"

"You're right, I'm sorry. Anyway, life's so transient . . . 'Hic aliquo mundus tempore nullus erit.' As I was saying, you've got to admit the Opitz business goes beyond the bounds of decency. You don't put a notorious property speculator at the head of the country's largest credit institution. He's just a racketeer; he can't tell a bank vault from a morgue! And what are his qualifications? Why, he's a friend of La Calenda, as well as of that murky pool Sabbioneta."

"Well, some of the stances Sabbioneta takes can be annoying, but he seems to be above-board."

"I don't think so. On another matter . . . I took the liberty of going into Assunta's wardrobe, as it was open; I was looking for a towel. It would never have crossed my mind, otherwise I wouldn't have dreamed . . . I'm *so* sorry."

"If you're alluding to the photographs, they're mine," Pantieri lied, blushing. "Some material evidence, confiscated last week. I shoved it away in the wardrobe there while I was waiting to draw up the report."

"Of course, of course, no need to explain . . . I just didn't want to look like a nosey parker."

"No question of it," said Pantieri, cutting him short. "But there is something else: I'd be grateful if you could remove those rats."

"Don't worry," Biraghi smiled, "they'll be clearing out today. I'll be off too, I suppose. I think they'll have finished cleaning the floors at the villa by this afternoon, then I can move out to Lavinio. Ah, the seaside! I can't live any distance from the sea, I can only breathe properly when the air smells of seaweed."

"I went down to see those rats of yours," Pantieri persisted, ignoring his lyrical excursion into iodized air. "Revolting. I can't think what's got into your head."

"You didn't touch them, did you?" asked the magistrate with ill-concealed alarm. "You don't touch little creatures that revolt you . . . And then, even if . . . The *Mastomys* belong to the rodent family and exhibit its noble characteristics. They multiply very quickly. There's been one birth already: eight little rats, each one no bigger than a bean. They can't even walk at the moment, but they'll soon be able to reproduce. You'll see, they'll multiply very quickly."

★

"You done that enema yet?" asked Conti.

"No sir," replied the guard. "He's not eaten, hasn't touched a thing for twenty-four hours."

Pantieri had no liking for Conti's methods. Okay, a slap might fly during an interrogation, but not torture, that was another matter. Beaten on the soles of the feet or with needles of all sizes driven under the fingernails, anybody would confess to any sort of crime. The enema was administered so that the person being interrogated wouldn't soil himself under torture, a thing which really got on the Prosecutor's nerves. But according to the guard, this time they could dispense with the formality.

"What evidence is there?" Pantieri asked.

"Pantieri," said Conti, lighting up. "All the evidence in the world! Point one: near the bank, an hour or two after the explosion, municipal cop sees this bloke dressed up in a blue suit, looking suspicious, who asks for directions and speaks with a marked Southern accent. The accused's got a suspicious look, a blue suit and he's a Southerner. Point two: he's got no visible means of support, and we're looking into that, but I bet you anything you like he's a pimp or perhaps something worse. Point three: he joined the majority party in 1962, then cancelled his sub, three years later. Dubious, to say the least. Point four: in 1969 he signs up with the Jehovah's Witnesses. And I don't care for that either. Fifth and decisive point: we found a fuse at his place and a carbide bomb."

"I beg your pardon, sir, but is that what you propose to build your case on? Point one: looking suspicious doesn't mean a thing, respectable people do it all the time: they're either shy or embarrassed. A devil-may-care attitude's the prerogative of delinquents. And I think everyone's got a blue suit, I know I have and so have you. And in any case, a terrorist doesn't go chatting to a policeman on the beat after he's set a bomb off. Point two: a pimp's one thing, an arsonist's quite another. If you could properly equate the two, we'd be in trouble. Rome would have been razed to the ground by now. Point three: joining a political party is not an indissoluble marrriage. Anyone's entitled to resign. Point four: the Jehovah's Witnesses

47

have never hurt a fly. It's true that every now and again they go and hide away somewhere waiting for the end of the world to come, but then it doesn't and everything reverts to normal. However, who knows, sooner or later they might get it right. Fifth and final point: a high-explosive device is one thing, but a carbide bomb's quite another. Even little boys make them, for playing with, more than anything else. Take a look: does your case still stand up?"

"Pantieri," Conti snapped, "lay off the defence counsel bit and fetch me a couple of screws. No, hang on – fetch me in the accused. I want to see him, I want to take a good look at him."

The accused was one of those people who instinctively arouse dislike, maybe even revulsion. He was dark, hairy, with a moustache, tall and well-built, but with short arms, and gaudily dressed. The jacket had huge lapels, the blue shirt was wide open, almost to the navel, and an improbable collection of chains and necklaces dangled on his hairy chest. He rang a bell, though Pantieri couldn't for the life of him remember how.

"De Fiore, Pasquale, known as Ciro," recited the screw. "Age 38. From S. Nicola Arcella (Cosenza), his place of residence. Identity still to be checked, cables sent to all Divisions. States he's currently living in Rome, has been a sales rep for household electrical goods, now employed working as a film extra."

"Ciro," sighed Conti. "You may as well confess, we've got you nailed."

"But I'm innocent," De Fiore replied. He spoke with a pronounced Calabrian accent and his voice seemed to emerge more from his nose than his mouth. Every so often he stroked his moustache, worried that a hair might have taken a wrong turning. He betrayed no emotion; far from it, he looked irritated and at odd moments his dark eyes flashed with menace as if implying that come the right time and place he'd straighten out the guy who'd shopped him. From the unnatural gleam of his excessively even teeth it was clear that the organ of mastication had been replaced by dentures, and discarding the supposition that caries might have taken such a toll on a man short

48

of forty, the inference was that the accused had lost his teeth in the course of some rather animated discussion. He whistled as he spoke: "The name's De Fiore, we're held in great respect in Cosenza; my aunt's the great-niece of a first cousin of the Della Cibbia – they're barons. So what do you want with me?"

"Ciro," sighed Conti again, "let's get things straight. I don't give a toss about the De Fiores, nor about the Barons Della Cibbia. You bring me a cast-iron alibi, one I can check."

"I got nothing to do with that attack. When that bomb went off, I was home, washing my hair, wasn't I?"

"We've only your word for that," put in Pantieri. "Anyone to confirm it?"

"Just myself. No one else. The wife'd gone out."

"So where was she, this wife of yours?" Conti asked in an angelic voice.

A glare of rage flashed in the eyes of the accused, who for a moment seemed poised to pounce on the judge. But he pulled himself together, and, enunciating clearly, he exclaimed: "So you want to know where the wife was, eh? Well, she'd nipped down the shops for a lettuce for her spoiled husband who's a fussy beggar and can't eat unless he has a couple of leaves of salad on the side. I worship her, the wife, like the Virgin on the altar."

"Don't be an ass, Ciro," said Conti severely. "You ought to go on the stage! . . . Right, listen to what we've got on the wife."

The guard paused. His face shone with a bitter satisfaction, then he announced spitefully: "Jenca, Mirella. Married name De Fiore. Age 27. From Papasidero (Cosenza). Arrested yesterday evening, later released on the orders of Inspector Pantieri. Profession, tart."

A long silence descended. Everyone looked at Pantieri as if he were now the accused.

"Why d'you let her go?" snarled Conti.

"I didn't know she was the wife of this lot," explained Pantieri. "Didn't even know the gent existed."

"Pantieri, why not go and fuck yourself?" sighed Conti, then reverted to De Fiore and said in honeyed tones: "Is that right, then? You worship your wife? Like the Virgin on the altar? Taking her cunt round in procession . . ."

"Mr Prosecutor," mumbled the accused in a strangely meek, wheedling tone of voice. "I swear by my mother's memory, may she turn in her grave this very moment if I'm not telling the truth, I didn't know my wife was in with the Crux."

"The Crux?" repeated Conti. For the first time in the interrogation, he spoke with a wisp of understanding, almost of complicity.

"I mean double-crossing me, on the game," explained De Fiore. "You put me in such a state I don't know what I'm saying."

Pantieri gave a start. Perhaps coincidences just kept piling up and nothing more; however, that singular slip of the tongue was always the same and kept cropping up with such frequency (and at such crucial moments, too) that he was gripped by the suspicion that one part of humanity was exchanging the fatal word as a sign of recognition, making itself known and recognized as belonging to a different world. He lit a cigarette and wondered why he should have been so lucky (or unlucky?) as to be on the outside of it when it would have been more convenient and restful to subject his will to this fantastic Crux and pension off the tormenting stimulus called free will.

The guard, who had returned after a brief absence, announced excitedly: "The accused's relatives have all arrived, sir! Mayhem, out there. Eighteen of them: uncles, cousins, in-laws of cousins and nephews of in-laws, four godfathers and the best man."

"Arrest them, all of them!" exploded Conti. "No, kick them out! What do they want? Pack of savages!"

"They say they've come to spring the accused, sir, and swear they won't go away until he's off the hook."

Suddenly an old woman dressed in black burst in, followed in vain by two policemen. Before the bystanders had time to react, she flung herself round De Fiore's neck and began crooning: "Oh, what a handsome boy you've grown! What a build, what a complexion! The weight you've put on! And all these wonderful chains: they could put you up on a shelf with the

Madonna del Carmine! Auntie wants to dress you up in solid gold, my little boy! Take one and two, take one and two, and the evil eye won't get at you!"

"Holy smoke! Arrest the old faggot!" howled Conti.

The guards made a move, but the old woman dropped on all fours in the middle of the room and, focusing her witch's eyes hypnotically on the floor, she went on with her litany: "Auntie's expecting you home, and she's going to make you fried bread, sausages, boiled eggs, ring biscuits and roast kid. You'll eat so much your belly'll be like a barrel!"

They heard a scuffle outside and it seemed as if more people were about to burst in, but this time the forces of order prevailed: some cries burst out in an indecipherable language, then a voice bawled: "Lay off! I'll kick your arse for you, you son of a bitch!"

Finally, there was silence. The old woman remained on all fours and the guards looked on as if turned to stone; they couldn't bring themselves to make a move. The Prosecutor wiped his forehead with a handkerchief. De Fiore spoke regally: "Auntie, I'm stuck for words, you've touched my heart, you have, and I don't know what to say. But I thank you, Uncle, my cousins, relatives and godparents. Thank you, all of you. A family's still a thing to warm the heart, better than a board of directors at Fiat. But now you'll have to go, Auntie. I've got to be alone to meet my destiny. Justice will shine like crystal, because my hands are innocent of that blood, and they're not short of the necessary protection."

The old woman began to pout, but, encouraged by some neat footwork to her posterior, she was forced to move; she proceeded on all fours, stopping now and then in a last attempt to resist, until she had to yield to the kicks. When she reached the door she fired her parting shot, addressing the most tenacious of her persecutors with foam at her mouth, and hissed: "Up yours, and that long line of bastards you come from!"

She disappeared. Savage cries hailed from outside the exit and it could be inferred that the luckless eighteen were mounting a fresh attack, but suddenly a deathly hush descended. Conti and De Fiore went back to looking daggers at each other, but with a secret connivance. It was the Prosecutor who broke the silence: "Find the accused's wife and bring her to me here, now!" he ordered, fixing Pantieri with a meaningful look, then he went back to addressing De Fiore. "You left the majority party in 1965 and I want to know why. I bet you let yourself get snaffled up by some organization, some secret society . . . Am I right?"

"I swear on my Auntie's life," De Fiore exclaimed, "may she die with her boots on, I have never, never had anything to do with the Communists."

"Communists? What have they got to do with it?" Pantieri interjected. "And cut out all this swearing, otherwise you'll put your whole family at risk."

"And the Jehovah's Witnesses?" chimed in a guard. "You don't accept injections, right? You object to holy statues, pictures, medals, right? You're against symbols, you have to destroy them. And seeing as a bank's a symbol of capitalism, you put a bomb in it. Come on, you prick, confess now and the Prosecutor'll jail you with extenuating circumstances."

"I didn't put no bomb nowhere."

"What about the carbide at home?"

"Oh, stuff it! You're talking crap! Crap and more crap. I once went fishing, I knew it was forbidden, but everyone does it . . . So I wanted to make a big noise and light up the village festival, I've got to go to S. Nicola next week. Look, we're having fireworks there."

"Listen, sir," concluded the screw, addressing the Prosecutor. "We're just wasting time. He's only buggering us about. You leave him to me. We've got some good needles, we'll give him a little manicure and learn him how to behave in decent society."

Dr Conti appeared to hesitate, then slowly nodded his head: "Only size two, no more. Won't be necessary to hurt him too much. After all, he's a sensible lad. He'll come round. I want to see him afterwards myself, alone."

He was about to go out with his operatic strut, when Pantieri touched his arm: "I'd like you to ask the accused what the Crux is."

"The Crux?" repeated Conti ambiguously; either he didn't understand, or was pretending he didn't.

"No good looking at me," said De Fiore with a shifty smile, but he now wore a look of brazen deceit. "It's a word I've never come across."

FIVE

The eighteen Calabrians had left police headquarters, but had not gone away; they had settled on the pavement a few strides away and were bivouacked with their cargo of suitcases held together with string, and their loaves of bread, sausages and penknives. They were forever eating; being on a journey, they needed more sustenance than usual. To the reporters they insisted they would only leave the day De Fiore was released. Any number of ways were tried to shift them: fire hydrants, towing trucks and foam extinguishers, but without success; they moved a few paces forward or back and stopped where they were. The attempts had to be abandoned. For a little while they came to be accepted into the city's integral tissue and became a presence not unlike that of the Colosseum or the Temple of Vesta: historic, concrete, taken for granted. When they disappeared no one even noticed.

At lunch time, Pantieri drove the 124 without choosing a destination. From the radio came disturbing news: the Middle East situation was alarming, potato prices might have to be pegged. Was it possible that the phantom Crux was responsible for all this as well? Even for the unstoppable rise in the price of potatoes? He was immersed in these thoughts when he saw her a few metres ahead, walking along the pavement. She had changed out of the slit skirt, her uniform for plying her trade on the Lungotevere, and was wearing a plain suit. She looked anonymous in the middle of an anonymous crowd.

He hailed her with a beep of the horn and she immediately got in; so quickly that, as soon as the car moved off, she appeared to breathe a sigh of relief, as if she'd been unexpectedly rescued from some danger.

"Well, long time no see!" Mirella said. She was a little out of breath.

"Quite," said Pantieri, with a bitter smile. "What's more, I'd have seen you again anyway. Judge's orders. I'm supposed to arrest you."

"Not again!" she looked ready to cry. "Why don't you arrest the people who murder little children or set bombs off?"

"Bombs is precisely what it's all about. Your husband's been pulled in for questioning, as you know very well. You've been home and changed."

"My husband's got nothing to do with it. At least I suppose he hasn't. As for me, I know nothing about it."

She was pale. She fished around in her bag for a cigarette, but her hands were trembling so much that she thought better of it. The car went through Monte Sacro and on towards Talenti. Here the Rome of the Caesars and the Popes was more than ever an abstract idea, a fable served up for ignorant tourists. A miasma of grey apartments melted into the sky, which faded to deep blue in the distance; yellow leaves whirled down from the sparse trees and the usual deposits of rubbish were piled by the roadside. Further on, sheep were grazing in fields that were already marked out for new developments; it was all that survived of the age when the countryside knew nothing of bulldozers.

Pantieri stopped at an *osteria*, the usual old rustic place, tarted up and decorated with strings of garlic, peppers, corn cobs and dusty bottles. A minstrel, accompanying himself on the guitar, was singing the heart-rending story of the Roman boatman.

"There's an enigmatic word," Pantieri began. "I hear it cropping up now and again. I don't know what it means, except that it means a conundrum. And it's not any organization we know. It seems to be used as a password . . ."

"I don't follow."

"When the girls in the Via Veneto spread the word round that 'it's raining', what do they mean?"

"That the Vice Squad's coming with the Black Maria."

"Exactly. Now what's 'the Crux'? What can you tell me about it?"

"Dr Gruvi mentioned it, I seem to remember. Gruvi's a top medic. He cured me of hepatitis, but I've got to be careful, it could be followed by cirrhosis. He talked to loads of people on the telephone about it, and I was very curious . . . I was worried, I hadn't grasped what he was on about, I thought he was talking about 'cracks'. Gruvi's a big-time quack, but he's also a dirty old man. So I got the impression he'd something against me, and I sulked. I asked him for an explanation, saying that if you wanted to insult a person you should have the guts to tell them to their face, and call a spade a spade, without mincing words, because I got the drift anyway. Well, he laughed his head off and I was left looking plain daft. He explained that he meant the Crux, a scientific fact, something like a pandemia, if I've got the word right. After that, I didn't take any notice."

"I'm going to pay this Dr Gruvi a visit," sighed Pantieri. "But first I'll have to place you under arrest."

"Oh, please don't do that. I've got nothing to do with any bombs, you know that better than I do."

"We'll talk about it. Meet me at Doney's after seven, there's always a crowd there and no one'll notice you. But do take care."

He left Mirella at Monte Sacro and carried on to Via Monte Pelmo. For anyone coming from Viale Adriatico (having passed the cinema Antares with such pleasures as it has to offer), Via Monte Pelmo is a narrow street, climbing towards the left; it has a little shop that sells squishy persimmons, existential as relics, and a garage that smells pleasantly of lubricants and platinized points. The trees are episodic, the hedges a fragile screen between the immodesty of the public highway and the modesty of the private kitchens with their fragrance of cabbages. A few oleanders are eternally waiting to flower.

On this scene the slovenly profile of Byron the porter stood out dramatically, like that of a signalman waving his red lantern along the tracks in an attempt to stop the train on its way to the bridge that is unexpectedly down. He had a sophisticated, romantic name, but was actually a brute grown fuddled with wine. He could barely speak, communicating telegraphically, with very long pauses which enabled him to gather his resources for a further venture into speech. He was laconic to a degree: "Dr Biraghi's gone. Says he'll phone. Note from messenger."

The note risked entire sentences that Byron would never have been able to construct, but to make up for this, it was of Sibylline obscurity:

THE TREASURE HUNT IS ON. JUST BEYOND LA STORTA, ON THE LEFT, THERE ARE DAYS AND NIGHTS OF LOVE, WITH A SWIMMING POOL AND A TENNIS COURT. IF YOU CAN AND YOU KNOW, INVESTIGATE.

A FRIEND

Crazy, thought Pantieri and, thrusting the piece of paper into his jacket pocket, he wondered whether he was near to going crazy himself. The earth's axis appeared to be shifting.

"Well? What are you waiting for?" he asked the porter, who was looking at him curiously. For a moment he was even afraid that the brutish Byron might be hiding something.

"Rats," the porter objected, poking an exploratory finger up his nostril. "Administrator's phoned the sanitary inspector."

"Hasn't Dr Biraghi removed them?" enquired Pantieri, peeved, and he dived down into the cellar without waiting for a reply.

The rats' squeaking had become intolerable, the more so now that it was compounded with menacing little howls, angry shrieks and desperate yells; the light of a candle exposed a scene of brutal horror. Seized by a sudden frenzy, the rats were tearing each other apart: the newborn had already been devoured and two adult specimens lay dead with their heads half gnawed. A trickle of sticky blood was beginning to drip onto the floor.

Byron joined Pantieri. "Rabid beasts," he commented. "Very bad beasts. Administrator very browned off."

"It's a disgrace," said Pantieri in an undertone. He rushed up to his apartment to phone Biraghi, but couldn't get hold of him. No matter, he'd catch him later, he'd make quite sure of that.

Now he had Dr Gruvi to consider. He returned to his car and drove back down Via Nomentana in the opposite direction; at the underpass he turned towards Castro Pretorio . . . My God . . . Domenichelli, Gondrand, Franzosini, Angelo Dani, the lot: every one of their huge removal vans had congregated in Viale dell'Università, creating a traffic jam which, thanks to the local police, was now totally inextricable.

From the vans to the wards of the Faculty of Medicine there was a swarm of porters laden with obsolete impedimenta; they were moving hospital beds, patients in their nightshirts, chamberpots, enemas, bedpans and urine bottles and creating an unspeakable confusion. It was like a circle in the *Inferno*, a clamour of cries and oaths; doctors in white coats were flapping all over the place, amid a flurry of pleas, proposals and imprecations.

"The paracentesis!" yelped a young intern, trotting hither and thither as he repeated the meaningless invocation to one and all.

"What's going on?" Pantieri asked a policeman.

"I don't really know," the disconsolate officer replied. "It looks like Dr Gruvi's moving out."

"Moving out?"

"Yes, they've made him a consultant at Carsoli. Now how d'you like that!"

"But Gruvi's a leading light!"

"I know, but he was one of Prof. Officinale's mob, and now Officinale's been retired. Each Professor has got his own crowd, and as soon as he gets tenure he boots out his predecessor's lot and puts in his own."

"Listen, I need to talk to Gruvi."

"In all this mayhem? You'd better try again at Carsoli. Give it two or three weeks."

At that moment a savage cry rose above the uproar and silenced everybody, if only for a second; doctors, porters, nurses (lay and religious) and the sick suspended their frantic activities and looked towards the source of the howl. Gruvi was apostrophizing two porters who were so bowled over by the blast, they dropped a geriatric case with a huge swelling between his legs.

"Handle him like that and you'll rupture him!" Gruvi fulminated. "Here's a case of bilateral orchitis – did I say rare? It's unique! – and you manhandle him like a blooming cupboard!"

"We're not equipped for these removals," said a porter in self-defence. "He would have been better off trussed up in a sling."

"Imbecile," Gruvi replied. "Find a nursing sister, they've got gumption; and see you get some help."

Pantieri elbowed his way through the crowd and waved an arm to secure Gruvi's attention; he showed his ID card and introduced himself.

"And what do you want?" thundered Gruvi. "Do you realize what they've been getting up to? Just think, they'd diagnosed a tumour! A tumour – I ask you! The testicles would have been hard as wood and nodulous. It was nothing more than a common or garden orchitis. But a splendid example, a textbook case. Well, what do you want?"

"I have to speak to you about a police investigation."

"Hmph! There's a bar roundabout here, let's go and have a coffee."

There was a touch of disorder about the doctor's appearance; he was wearing a yellow gown that was ample and billowing, an antiseptic kite which kept him floating between earthly miseries and a heavenly summons. Every so often the leading light tripped over his gown and at that moment perhaps a patient rendered up his soul to God; at first Gruvi looked penitent, almost apologetic, then with a furious gesture he crammed his black Homburg on his head, and clenched his teeth in a grimace of vexation. His hand trembled as he lifted his coffee cup and a little liquid spilled onto his gown; he swore under his breath and smiled. Then, all of a sudden, he went into an ecstasy, contemplating a damp patch on the ceiling and for several minutes was lost in a daydream about lilies-of-the-valley, feminine hair-dos, orchitis – who knows? Finally, he returned to earth and asked coldly: "And how can I be of help?"

"Doctor, have you ever heard of the Crux?"

59

"It's too long a story. I'm an academic, a man of science. I'd rather not talk about it, at least not right here and now. And then, I don't feel at all well. If this supposition didn't smack of pulp fiction, I'd say I had the symptoms of poisoning. But it's not possible. I haven't eaten anything that could have upset me, and at Ernesto's last night in Via Cassia, the mushrooms were above suspicion . . . Acute hepatitis, perhaps. That would be a bore."

"I'm sorry you're not feeling well, but people have been murdered. The guilty must punish – I mean the law must punish the guilty."

"I know. I'm in danger myself . . . grave danger, I suppose."

"All the more reason for helping me get at the truth."

"Very well, but I feel it's my duty to warn you that the last and only person in whom I confided has been killed."

"Killed?"

"Killed. An old lady came to see you yesterday afternoon, asking for your help and protection, but you wouldn't listen. At dawn this morning, that old lady was fished out of the Tiber. Strangled. You know all about it."

"I spoke to some old dear, but she was very confused, seemed the worse for drink, not reliable at all. Besides, I would never have thought . . ."

"No need for excuses. That 'old dear' was my mother."

"Your mother! But her particulars, the surname . . ."

"I was the son by her first marriage; she remarried. She was getting on and what she said didn't always hold water, but she could still see straight, believe you me. Arterio-sclerosis makes for fantastic lucidity. If she hadn't come to speak to you, Inspector, she'd still be alive now . . . What a tragic farce! Got herself murdered because someone was frightened of what she could tell the police, and you didn't even want to listen to her!"

"I'm sorry."

"Never mind. You want to know about the Crux . . . I'll only tell you what I feel absolutely sure about. Deductions I've not yet been able to prove I'll keep to myself. I don't want to equivocate, I simply can see no virtue in jumping to conclusions. After all, I could be wrong. It all began about five years ago. We were a sect, a secret society, something akin to a masonic lodge, whatever you like . . . I don't really know why we called ourselves 'The Crux': it wasn't my choice, and it wasn't my place to criticize. Oh, I certainly gave my opinion, but it was scarcely an important question . . . There were many of us: all famous, rich, powerful people. We were organized into isolated cells, so I can't give you any names beyond those in my own: there was Lucilla Opitz, daughter of the construction boss, Gerardo – he's the new chairman of the Discount and Savings Bank . . . the man at the very top was Raymond of Touraine."

"Raymond of Touraine?"

"An assumed name, behind which was hiding a public figure who didn't want to be identified, even though I wasn't slow in finding out who it was."

"Why Raymond of Touraine? And why a sect?"

"Do you know Les Baux in Provence?"

"No, I don't know Provence. I went to Paris once, many years ago, a package tour organized by Division. Saw the Louvre, Place de la Concorde, some tart who did a striptease, ate some liver pâté: that's all the France I know."

"Too bad, too bad. Les Baux are full of history, legends, and above all, dreams. Take no notice of the guide-books that tell you to go there when it's sunny or at sunset. Nonsense. Les Baux should be seen in the rain and wind. They're all crooked and clawed, their ruins are caked with blood. They were the refuge of cut-throat brigands under the leadership of a sinister character called Raymond of Touraine, who ravaged Provence for thirty years. His cruelty was legendary. He disappeared in 1400 in the waters of the Rhône, near Tarascon, drowned, presumably."

"An evocative alias," Pantieri commented, with a hint of irony. "Programmatic, if I can put it like that. But why this sect?"

"A desire for abasement," the doctor confessed, simply, "or indeed a death-wish. Forgive me, but I must return to Les Baux. You won't be able to understand, you haven't been there and so can't, and then it's impossible anyway to put a visual description into words. But imagine a picture slashed with white, black and grey brushstrokes, the only possible colours, any others would be fictitious. Red, maybe. That's the colour of blood, and darkness, it's another form of black. Les Baux are tinted with death. To tell you the truth, death and all that attends it fascinated us: famine, poverty, disease. Think back to the times of Les Baux: there were outbreaks of plague, cholera, smallpox, you could die of starvation, a fellow could be knifed at the drop of a hat, prisoners were put down like dogs after being tortured. We were tired of this antiseptic world with its universal guarantees of daily bread, insurance cover, pension rights, leisure, contraceptives and abortions on demand. That has to do away with backstreet abortionists. Don't you find that disgusting? We were horrified by all this impassive sexuality, free from its eternal accessories: passion, jealousy and above all, sin. No way! Ours was a sect that meant to restore some dignity to sin. In these depraved times, it's become the only victim."

"I see, but what did you actually do?"

"Nothing much. An occasional orgy, the odd black mass, a grave desecrated now and then . . . The usual stuff. The real trouble started when I realized that even the Crux was becoming politicized. What I mean is that at a certain point our misdeeds, our peccadilloes, were themselves being turned into instruments. Each wrongdoing corresponded to a certain logic, a certain plan. It no longer derived from a maybe simple-minded pleasure in committing evil. We were no longer a pack of scoundrels, but conspirators in the service of a party, or rather of a tendency within a party. It was no longer sins we were concocting, but the most vulgar political crimes. This was repulsive."

"I see," observed Pantieri sardonically. "But up to now, Doctor, you haven't offered me a single concrete particular, nothing that can serve a police inquiry . . . In my wretched job, it's the facts that count and the proof of those facts."

"There was one fact about six months ago," Gruvi sighed. "The Minister of the Interior was admitted to my clinic for a check-up on the after-effects of hepatitis."

"Orazio La Calenda?" asked the inspector rhetorically. "Are you referring to the famous visit of the party leaders? There was more fuss made about that visit than necessary, in my opinion. As luck would have it, I was there too, in charge of security, and I honestly didn't notice anything abnormal."

"Of course!" Gruvi exclaimed, coming back down to earth. "Now I remember I met you at the time. Anyway, I'm sorry to give you the lie, but something out of the ordinary did happen. Don't take offence, it was a detail bound to elude the ear of someone not in the know. I'm not bad at anagrams, I suppose you know I contribute to *Sphinx* magazine under the name of 'Protomartyr'. I've got an eye for certain tricks. So, as the meeting broke up and people were saying goodbye, one of the participants distinctly said: 'We'll wait until it's time to set up a plaque for our friend Cleon V.I. Cercato.' An improbable name, nasty. When the Minister of the Interior heard this he was upset and annoyed; he'd understood the meaning and probably agreed, but he was afraid of a gaffe, an indiscretion. At least that was my impression. Don't you remember, Inspector?"

"I don't remember what he said about our friend Cercato, but there was a brief moment of embarrassment, even though I'm damned if I can see any particular meaning. It was the usual bit of banter among friends; for a few moments there was a drop in the rowdiness and gush. It often happens when you're chatting along just to keep the conversation going, rather than to satisfy an intimate need."

"No, it wasn't like that. The allusion to our friend Cleon V.I. Cercato was a coded message, a signal to confirm an agreement reached. Obviously, I can't swear this interpretation's correct, I could be wrong. It's incredible the number of spectral shapes hidden inside the folds of words! Anyway, a few days later another instance occurred."

"Another instance?"

"Yes. La Calenda came to the clinic for the usual analysis, and by chance, the purest chance, I caught a snatch of him speaking on the phone. He was saying: 'We'll set up the plaque to Cleon V.I. Cercato very soon.' He knew I'd overheard, and

I knew that he knew. He looked in a panic. I talked to my mother about it. I used to tell her everything. Well, almost. I had unlimited faith in her judgement, the more so because, as I told you, she could see things as a result of her arterio-sclerosis that normal people couldn't. I'll be even more frank; I confided to my mother what, in my opinion, the message meant: an epigraph relating to an execution. And then my mother was killed."

"It's disconcerting," Pantieri admitted, ruffling his hair as he brooded. "But perhaps we could get at the truth quite soon, if you'd confide in me as well . . ."

"The key to the message?" the doctor interrupted excitedly. "I most certainly will, but not right now. Tonight I'm having a talk with . . . let's call him Raymond of Touraine."

"The boss of the organization?"

"If you want to put it that way. He'll be able to guess . . . pinpoint . . . indicate . . . I'd be very much out of order if I spoke to anyone else before him. Oh, damn it! I do hope I won't have to take to my bed this evening of all evenings! The fact is, I'm feeling worse and worse . . . as if I'd eaten something that was off, but I can't understand when. Bah! I hope I haven't caught acute hepatitis. It starts like this, you feel an upset, nausea, dizziness . . . I'll spare you the symptoms that follow, because they'll give you the shivers. But I'm not going to be ill. I've got to see Raymond of Touraine at all costs."

"Wouldn't you just give me the translation of the message?"

"No," replied the academic. "I've already wasted too much time and this removal's costing me an arm and a leg. Thirty thermometers gone missing, one patient deceased, and one unmentionable incident between a porter and four nuns. We're being helped by the Oblate Sisters of S. Daniela Crisci. They're ladies who take a little handling. No, that's enough chatter for now. The fact is, Inspector, there's something nasty afoot: I'm feeling more dead than alive."

SIX

The sky, swollen like a black bladder, rumbled and crackled; then it began to pour. Water began to inundate the roads and piazzas, flooding the basement floors got up as desirable garden flats; the drains filled up, gurgled, and brought a storm of sludge streaming into the barracks-like blocks of flats in the farthest outskirts. A greyish mustard colour spread evenly among the ruins, the loansharks and the shanties; the city poured back into the innocent countryside and was like the dense, surging flow of a sewer.

Pantieri, at the wheel of his Fiat 124, anxiously watched this tide as it rose before him, dragging along carcasses of cats and dogs, wastematter and rotting leaves. Everywhere else rain washes and cleans, and symbolically wipes out sin, but not in Rome; here a storm is an unguent of vices, an aspersion of filth, it is a shower of every household's bodily discharges restored to them by the gods of the tempests.

Back at Division, Pantieri ran into Biraghi. The judge had joined the investigation in the role of observer and, had he wished, would have given Conti a hand.

"I've had trouble with your rats," the Inspector complained. "I went down to have a glance at them this morning and they were tearing each other apart like wild animals."

"It's all a matter of physiology," smiled Biraghi, poking a couple of fingers into his fly. "Question of space . . . when animals, and human beings as well, feel confined in too small a space, they go to the bad. And you should know that lies at the root of urban violence, at least according to modern sociology. The high population density of the megalopolis induces claustrophobia, and the claustrophobia induces the savagery."

"If you say so, but the basement of a block of flats isn't the place for breeding rats. Let's hope there's not been a flood down there . . . it could be your damned rats have all escaped."

"That would be a pity. I'll send someone round as soon as I can. You're right, it would be better to make more suitable arrangements for them."

Biraghi and Conti greeted each other with scant enthusiasm. They were divided by mentality, habits and political persuasion: Biraghi had anarchistic tendencies; he was a freethinker, slightly mad, and tenaciously at odds with the entire world, while Conti was a time-server, an unscrupulous bungler and belonged to the regime. The two had even once been rivals in love, but a Judgement of Solomon had put an end to the quarrel, because the lady they were fighting over chose to dump them both and marry a manufacturer of sanitary appliances. The two interpreters of the criminal code had been mortified to notice how wafer-thin and insubstantial was the activity on which they were engaged.

"I can't understand it," Biraghi murmured, ironically. "I presume that severe methods have been applied to the accused, and yet he hasn't confessed."

Conti looked at him askance. "Your Honour," he observed, "the truth is I can't make it out either. The man's a slob, a swindler, a shady character, but we've no confession from him and confession's the queen of proofs."

"Mr Prosecutor," interrupted Pantieri, "I have another idea. Maybe De Fiore's implicated, maybe he isn't, but in any case he's a minor figure. For me, the bomb attack on the Discount and Savings Bank's the result of a conspiracy, possibly an international one . . ."

"The Libyans," Conti observed. "Worse than our bloody Southerners! Just Bedouins, aren't they? Living in a desert . . ."

"Impossible," said Biraghi, ironically. "I mean, I don't believe in an international plot. Dr Conti here's in the regular pay of the CIA and he'd know if there were one."

"What's that? Don't try and be funny," grumbled the Prosecutor of the Republic. "Look, there's the Czechs, they're hotheads . . . Remember '68? And the Palestinians? The Syrians? The Jews?"

"We can't go off the evidence," Biraghi sighed. "I feel that we have to search closer to hand, very much closer, but for now I'm obliged to serve up clear, apodictic evidence. Until we have a confession given to us by the guilty party or whoever . . ."

"Or by whoever!" Conti emphasized. "Take De Fiore's wife, that little tramp. You had her discharged, Pantieri, instead of holding her for playing the tart in a public place. Well, what's become of her?"

"Disappeared," the Inspector lied, ruffling his hand through his hair with his usual gesture.

"Pantieri," said Conti solemnly, "I've made investigations. That bit of tail was a temp at Division, she's been your mistress. We know, it's all there. Don't start getting ideas about covering up for her, or we won't be friends any more. I'll ruin you, take my word for it. Now, you'll have to excuse me; I'm expected for supper by the Minister of the Interior. His Excellency La Calenda wants me to brief him on the case. See you in a couple of hours: we'll have another go at the Calabrian."

He left them with a brief nod and went strutting out, while Biraghi couldn't restrain a pitying look. The magistrate walked over to the window and examined the sky with a preoccupied air.

"It'll rain for two or three days," he said. "October in Rome! . . . I don't think you'll find out who was behind the attack, it's too big a thing. Besides, in cases like this, it's always the last person you suspect. Yes, it must be someone above suspicion and pretty important . . . I'd start looking among the politicians, bankers, entrepreneurs, magistrates."

"It could be Dr Conti."

"I don't think so, he's got no sense of humour. A felon's got to have a sense of humour – if his crime's brutal, at any rate. If you're into mangled corpses you've really got to love the grotesque, otherwise what's the sense of it?"

67

"It's almost seven," Pantieri exclaimed. "I'm sorry, I've got some urgent business myself and I must run."

"In the rain?"

"In the rain."

He ran all the way to Doney's. Mirella had waited for him and fortunately had not been soaked. But now what? Pantieri didn't stop to think. He didn't even consider the possibility of being spied on or tailed, still less did he worry about compromising himself with the porter for witness. He took Mirella back to his apartment in Via Monte Pelmo.

Whenever there was an outsider in the house, the furniture and things left him feeling vaguely uncomfortable. This time he looked at the cretonne-covered sofa, the display cabinet with its gleaming sets of glasses, and beyond a closed door the quilted bed, which had almost smacked of Hollywood all those years ago but now would be a hard job to sell even in the Porta Portese flea-market – he looked at them and judged them with loathing. He imagined that the most recondite meanderings of his soul would be rummaged through and the obvious, the second-rate, would be brought to light.

"Aren't you happy to have me here?" asked Mirella, nestling into a corner of the sofa.

"Very happy. But they're out looking for you, and I don't know how long I can hide you. Would you like to listen to a record? Some Tchaikovsky, perhaps?"

The *Pathétique* was back on the turntable. First there were essential notes which defined the melody; they were muted, drawn from a distance; then the orchestra added its full voice, sepulchral and powerful, a surge of love and the unattainable. The artful melody seeped into his soul, impelling him towards disconnected emotions, poised on the edge of madness (whispers that could not be caught, moans to which there was no response). He smiled at himself. There was no sense getting drunk on music, the less so as it was only he who was drinking.

"A letter arrived for you this morning," said Mirella, all of a sudden. "I'm dying to know who's written to you."

"Who told you about that?"

"Nobody, but it's sticking out of your jacket pocket and

68

you're forever on the point of losing it. Not a difficult deduction."

"It's a strange message, announcing a treasure hunt. Once you've passed La Storta, there'll be days and nights of love with a tennis court and a swimming pool. That could be the Bela Motel . . . Lovers tend to make for those chalets."

"But what do you think's hiding at the Bela Motel? I've got the feeling it's a macabre way of pulling your leg."

"Could be, but I think I'll go and take a look . . . Perhaps after midnight, when the traffic's quietened down and the chalets have closed their doors. It's the best time for investigating the world's secrets."

"And Dr Gruvi?"

"We had a very long chat. He explained what the Crux is, or rather, what it was. Our doctor friend knows something, without question: he spoke to his mother about it, and she's been murdered. Poor old thing. Strangled and dumped in the Tiber. And she'd come to me for help! Gruvi thinks it's a political intrigue or something of the kind . . . He's promised to give me the solution to an enigma, but first he's got to see Raymond of Touraine."

"Raymond of Touraine?" asked Mirella slowly. Her face showed neither mirth nor surprise, but a vague doubt.

"Yes," the Inspector explained. "It's the pseudonym of the boss, the head of the organization. It all seems a bit too fantastic to me; that is, I can glimpse some fragments of truth, but I'm not able to formulate the complete picture."

"The complete picture? Maybe you're just assuming there is one," said Mirella, talking almost to herself. "It's all so jumbled up, so haphazard . . . I've come to know a great many people in my job, important people, sometimes very important. There's no understanding powerful people; there's one who used to come to me because he wanted to be humiliated, nothing else. He was in total despair. He came to mind hearing you talk about Raymond of Touraine, not that it's got anything to do with it."

"I must go," Pantieri said. Certain memories made him suffer and made him curious; and curiosity added another kind of suffering, oozing shame. "I'll see you later, perhaps very late. You must absolutely not go out of the house. Besides, it's coming down in buckets – never stops."

"You're leaving me alone?" mumbled Mirella, and her voice was full of spectres.

Pantieri sighed and found that his mouth was dry. He touched her on the knee, which made little sense as he realized he'd embarked on an explanation of what causes storm clouds. A proper lesson on cumulus and nimbus formations, but it was Mirella who had asked for this clarification. Nevertheless, was there no connection between the knees of a beautiful girl and the storm winds? Mirella's skirt was drawn up much more than modesty allowed; at school under the eye of his teacher, Signorina Candiani, such a state of affairs would have been regarded as sheer effrontery. Now the pupil for his improvised course in meteorology was showing her panties, very scanty ones. Those most confounded garments had a name, a fashionable obscenity . . . weren't they called G-strings? What an obscene, what a superb a . . . thought Pantieri, clinging, however, to his suspension dots. If he could have flaunted such a salutary posterior to passers-by, he thought, he would have been both proud and indignant (proud because he had appropriated it, and indignant because modesty was worth respecting). His hands pulled at the skirt, probing about, trying to come ashore, despairing at the breadth of the beach-head. Four or five times, he dumbly repeated: "The North wind or *tramontana* . . ."

Then he stopped, because they'd passed on to the next lesson.

Immediately afterwards, he fell asleep; he knew he had no time to lose, but the mediation of sleep, however brief, was indispensable in order to put reality back where it belonged. Wipe clean what had happened, cancel it out if possible, relegate it to the realm of dreams. The *tramontana* was a wind that brought storms and that was that; but what was this whim of picturing school again, where licentious exercises took the place of logical analysis? Half an hour later, he woke. My God, it was late! He dashed off to Division, a world where every vice was known, as pure as a little boy at his first communion.

SEVEN

De Fiore was already being grilled, or at least it looked like it. His hands hung down by his sides, his wild black eyes were threatening, evoking an insurance policy called 'vendetta'.

The accusers' part was growing progressively flimsier; it had started off as a Shakespearian tragedy, and now tailed off into a bit of Chekhov. Conti was no longer his old ruthless self, while Biraghi was ironic, detached and careful not to say too much. As for the accused, he was parrying with a lavender-scented pastoral world, quite incorrupt.

"My very dear inquisitors," De Fiore declaimed, smoothing out his moustache with an arrogant gesture. "You've got to understand the world I come from, then you'll see how my innocence'll shine forth, and I'll be clear of this mess. I was brought up respectable, you know, work and the home, that was it. When did I ever come across a copper before now?"

"That's enough," muttered Biraghi. "We ought to call in a film director, he'd make us a brilliant movie."

"Yeah, and then I'd shove it up your arse!" De Fiore hissed.

"De Fiore," said Conti softly. "You said you were a respectable man. Well, I'm a man of the Crux, that's to say, let's come to the crux of the matter: you're speaking to a judge."

That damned slip of the tongue cropping up again, that password of theirs! Pantieri was now convinced that the key to the mystery lay there, hidden behind that alluring and obscene word; all it needed was to dispel the mists around it, acquaint himself with the Crux, identify with it, and perhaps learn to love it. A very heavy silence fell, broken suddenly by a consort of flutes, harness-bells, and tambourines out in the street.

"Gypsies passing," Conti explained, as he stood by the window. "Sensuous, lascivious music, that. Makes me think of transparent veils, rotating bellies and bums all a-jingle. We've all got a bit of Scheherazade in our blood."

As the melody faded in the distance, Pantieri abandoned himself to its flood and called to mind Yvonne De Carlo's navel from a film of many years ago. Scheherazade had never existed, women as sweet and beautiful as those Hindu bayadères were a dream. Sex and love were nothing but a trap set by the imagination. How glad he would have been were he kneeling right then in front of Mirella! To be obliterated, wiped off the face of the earth. But he didn't know if he was thinking of her, or of a character he'd invented; as for the real Mirella, her hands were marked with life's lessons. Perhaps Scheherazade's hands had also been chapped and suffered chilblains, warts; maybe her nails were lacquered with red varnish. The colour of death, according to Gruvi's philosophy.

"Lovely singer, Mino Reitano," De Fiore put in. "And Rossini's Cenerentola's very nice. Heard it three years ago at Cosenza."

"So who gives a damn?" said Pantieri. "Let's get down to brass tacks. What did you want that explosive for?"

"You already asked me that," De Fiore sighed. "It was for making firecrackers for the village festival, I swear it, knock on any door of anyone in my family. I know nothing about this disgraceful business my wife's putting around."

"De Fiore, we've made investigations at the Vehicle Licensing Authority. You're down as the owner of a very pricey motor car. Out with it then: where did the cash come from?"

"I come from a rich family, don't I? Very rich. Best flock in the whole of Cosenza, thousand head of goats, maybe five."

"Your uncle was a poor herdsman, got ten years for manslaughter. And he's not even your uncle, because you're actually a foundling. Nobody knows who your parents were."

"Okay! Look, I had a win on the State Lottery, and at cards with my friends, a big win."

"The likes of you?" cried Pantieri, smiling grimly. He was infuriated because that human dreg had married Mirella, had

72

dared to seize hold of a treasure on which he shouldn't even have raised his eyes. The Calabrian was probably innocent of the bomb outrage in Via Due Macelli, but he was guilty of having ventured along paths where he had no business.

"Okay, okay," said De Fiore, giving in. "You know my wife's on the game, but I never took a penny. Alright? Now, that's enough. You can't crucify a man of honour. Blood and mucus in my nose, I don't want any bruises. I'm only flesh and blood, like anyone else. I'm not one of the Crux, I mean, one of your crooks."

It was then that Pantieri went for him, gripping him by the throat. He squeezed with hate, he hated him because he had ruined Mirella, had turned her into a prostitute and exploited her, because he was a liar, and he latched on to mysterious and powerful connections. De Fiore's jugular veins swelled and looked like bursting under the pressure of his hands. A jet of blood spurted from his nose.

"The Crux – you don't know about it? Is that what you're saying?" Pantieri gasped in his face. "You keep talking about it, but you don't know anything about it . . ."

"Pantieri," put in Conti, "let it go."

"You're making a mistake," rasped De Fiore. "I haven't got a clue what the Crux is!"

"Pantieri," Conti insisted, "drop it."

A guard had to rush in to rescue De Fiore because Pantieri, beside himself with that slimy throat and the stink of the body, would have carried on squeezing.

"Mr Prosecutor," De Fiore gasped, "he's off his head, I don't know anything about this Crux."

"We're wasting our time," murmured Biraghi, who had watched the scene, impassive as a statue. "I have a different opinion."

He went out without waiting for a response, all the while fiddling with the buttons of his fly, tracing the route he found familiar and reassuring, while he waited for the one that would give a lead in the investigation.

"Pantieri, you're an oaf," Conti muttered, shaking his head. "I wouldn't have thought it of you. Why the fuck you start rambling on about this Crux? So De Fiore trips over his big tongue, and now we got to send him to the cells again."

Ciro De Fiore set off, escorted by the guard and, passing in front of Pantieri, he spat on the floor.

"Rough folk," Conti observed, "but they have their own kind of dignity."

"Mr Prosecutor," said Pantieri, "I was convinced that Ciro De Fiore had nothing to do with the bomb in Via Due Macelli, but now I'm not so sure. The evidence we've got doesn't tally. The question is the Crux. I mean . . . I'm hearing it too often. I've even heard it from you, sir."

"What are you getting at, Pantieri?"

"Nothing. The fact is that twenty-four hours ago, or little more, I received a complaint from a poor old dear. She was trying to tell me about the Crux. This morning she was found dead. Someone thought she'd better be silenced. Then I met the old lady's son, Dr Gruvi, and I'm finally beginning to understand. Very soon I'll know a lot more . . ."

"And what secrets did he confide in you?" Conti asked sarcastically, but there was a touch of anxiety in his voice.

"Just gossip, nothing precise. I'll have to investigate . . . find confirmations, explanations. Most of all, I must know a name."

"You've done well telling me this. At supper, His Excellency the Minister of the Interior, La Calenda, conferred wide powers on me. We saw eye to eye on the essentials, and I'd even venture to say we're now in perfect harmony. Now as for you, Pantieri, get out and investigate, you have my full authority. And keep me posted. Especially that, you got to keep me in the picture."

There had been a cutting edge to Conti's voice; what he had come out with was not an order, not a plea, but a threat.

There was a knock at the door, which had remained ajar. There was no time to say "Come in" or "Wait" before Cardinal Meschia, for it was he, stepped brashly in. His red overalls looked more greasy and tattered than usual, most certainly because of a huge dark stain (wine? rust? paint?) which had blossomed on his chest. Conti kneeled and crossed himself piously.

74

"Do rise from that uncomfortable position," said the Cardinal jovially. "With all the damp around, you risk picking up a nasty chill."

The Prosecutor of the Republic rose from the floor and asked: "And to what do we owe this great honour?"

"I was just passing by . . ." the Cardinal replied, hesitantly. "Actually, to tell you the truth, I've received a strange phone call from Dr Gruvi. You will know him, I'm sure, Mr Prosecutor . . . Reader in Clinical Medicine at the University of Rome and now transferring to the hospital at Carsoli, one of those acts of humility our country asks of the best of its sons. Gruvi is an academic, and a leading light. In his spare time he enjoys puzzles and cryptograms, pastimes like that; he contributes to a magazine under the name of Protomartyr. Not a pen-name of which I approve, but I've seen worse . . ."

"Yes, I know, I know," said Conti with ill-concealed anxiety, "but the phone call? Why should he bother you in particular?"

"I've no idea," the Cardinal replied. "I couldn't understand a word of what he was saying, or almost nothing. He sounded like a very sick man, thoroughly feverish, in a delirium."

"When I met him, in the early afternoon," Pantieri put in, "he seemed a bit off colour. He was worried he might have caught acute hepatitis . . ."

"Then he *was* talking nonsense," the Cardinal concluded, deep in thought. "The fact is he kept going on about someone being in trouble and he had to be warned. But he didn't tell me the person's name."

"Fiddlesticks," commented Dr Conti, as a footnote, his face brightening.

"Up to a point," specified Meschia. "Gruvi was beside himself all afternoon trying to find this person in danger, but it was a fruitless effort. Perhaps he thought it would be easy for me to find him. Unfortunately, just at the crucial moment the call was interrupted. I tried ringing his home, but they told me he wasn't there. Therefore he must have been phoning from a public booth or a pied-à-terre. I don't know what to think, I'm a little worried."

75

"I'll have investigations underway immediately," Pantieri declared and stepped outside to give the orders. He was in a stew; once again he had touched on the truth and, like a fool, had not been capable of grasping it.

"Your Eminence was referring to his friendships," Conti muttered. "It's there we should be fishing, is that right?"

"More or less," the Cardinal agreed, "but I really couldn't think who it might be. I have so many friends, from all walks of life, the humble and the powerful. The Holy Father, if I might dare call him a friend . . . but who on earth would wish to do him any harm?"

An anxious silence descended. Pantieri conjectured that those present were asking themselves what would happen to Christianity thus brutally bereft of its leader. Nothing, because the great merit of the Pontificate was its continuity; a Pope dies, there's another one produced, as popular wisdom had it; but my God, what a horrifying trauma for the world! . . . The Vicar of Christ, victim of an assassination . . . It was monstrous.

"Not a word to the press," the Cardinal ordered. "They're capable of fabricating goodness knows what. Not that I'm referring to Baget Bozzo, who I have to say isn't a hired pen . . . But if someone could bridle that tongue of his . . ."

"We don't breathe a word to the press," said Conti, "unless it's something that's particularly confidential, secret or delicate. But this doesn't seem to me to be the case. Gruvi was drunk and talked on the phone as any drunk would. We'll have some news of our famous academic tomorrow, I'm sure."

"The only question is," said Pantieri ironically, "what kind of news?"

"Pantieri," the Prosecutor rasped, "that's enough!"

The Cardinal raised a hand as though intending to impart a quick blessing. The ulcer which Pantieri had noticed before was a bright red and had grown, and was beginning to secrete pus. Conti froze, contemplating the sore in fascination; his gaze expressed rapture, envy and a devouring curiosity. He could not contain himself and, putting a hand over his mouth, he whispered: "Even you, Your Eminence?"

"What?" asked the Cardinal, taking offence; that tone of complicity and mystery was lacking in respect. "Forgive me, Mr Prosecutor, but on many occasions I fail to understand the judiciary. Their brains seem to be full of sawdust. Just think about the price of potatoes! Three thousand lire a kilo! I wonder how ordinary people will manage to eat . . . Perhaps it foreshadows a horrifying famine? Italy could suffer the same fate as India . . . a terrifying prospect, isn't it?"

"Terrifying," breathed Conti, mortified. "It's enough to make you wet yourself, if you'll pardon the expression."

Cardinal Meschia completed his tetchy blessing and left.

"Pantieri," snarled the Prosecutor, "don't go getting ideas in your head. That there's holy madness for you: it's holy alright, but it's still mad."

"Am I to suspend the investigations into Gruvi?"

"Not on your life. You never know what you may come acrux," said Conti with deliberate sarcasm and strutted out.

It was two hours to midnight and the bizarre appointment which someone had arranged at the Bela Motel. Pantieri got into his 124 and drove towards Ponte Milvio. He didn't turn on the radio. He already knew that all he would hear would be of more killings, more strikes in protest against them, more funerals, more passion of one kind and another. He also knew that the lira had slipped, notably against the mark. The price of cigarettes and petrol would be up. And the basic rate of income tax would be up too. He knew it all.

He stopped at the turning into Via degli Orti della Farnesina and killed time by contemplating the sky. It was no longer raining and the clouds looked like breaking up. A strange cobalt moon glowed in a patch of clear sky, then all of a sudden the airships reappeared. He counted them: twenty-four. No, it wasn't advertising. Who would be so crazy as to incur the enormous cost of filling the sky with cumbersome dirigibles, precisely when he could be sure that, what with the bad weather and the late hour, no one, or almost no one, would be looking up to see what lay above? It was another mystery to add to the rest. Or was someone interested in spying on Rome? With its slow, quiet flight, an airship was an excellent observation post;

77

you could surprise everyone in their lies, their betrayals, their shabby deeds . . .

The spirit of the world was compromise. It was hypocritical to point an accusing finger against those in power. Government and Society each reflected the other, and that worked well enough. Yes, there was terrorism . . . What was that, though, but a boil, a benign boil, offering an outlet for noxious humours that might cause damage if not set free? Disgruntled societies had revolutions, which was another matter. He looked up again and saw that the airships had disappeared; the moon, too, had become hidden behind a lowering cloud. A night for murder, a night dense with foreboding.

He was assailed by a sense of discomfort, and with the unease of living in such a chaotic age, came a pang of hunger. Perhaps he had fallen under the influence of Cardinal Meschia or perhaps he was searching for an eternal truth. He spotted a rundown trattoria, and went in.

"What would you care to order, sir?" asked the proprietor affably. "We've got some excellent young trout from Piediluco, arrived this morning. We could make you a lovely *trota alla mugnaia* our crux' speciality."

Pantieri made off like a thief. Now he was beginning to suffer from hallucinations. After the familiar slip of the tongue (was it how others spoke or simply what he thought he heard?) that proprietor had struck him as an insidious conspirator, whereas he was nothing more than some poor devil who doubtless couldn't even bring himself to doctor his customers' wine. He got back in the car, casting suspicious glances in all directions. The radio announced that unknown terrorists had assassinated the Prefect in Milan, and that the price of potatoes had risen again. Five thousand lire the kilo, so they said. Naturally . . . it was obvious . . . Everything was going to rack and ruin and everyone was looking the other way. People were living in a dream, waiting to be jarred awake by a horrified shriek. He headed towards Via Cassia.

On foot, he started towards the Bela Motel, hoping in his heart of hearts that the trip would prove to be to no purpose. He slipped on a stone and landed in a puddle, getting to his feet splashed with mud and cursing at his own stupidity. He was surrounded by nothing but silence, broken every so often by the rumble of traffic. A huge cloud was sailing towards the diaphanous white of the moon; it spread out and the tops of the pines vanished, sucked back into nothingness. It began to rain again.

At the top of a slope, no further than a hundred yards away, a flash split the darkness, and then many others in rapid succession. But they weren't lightning flashes, they looked like fireworks or flashbulbs, white bursts of magnesium that lit up the sky's inky blackness. The curtain rose on a strip of earth, and on that strip, a stage of mud and soaking grass, Scheherazade appeared. Or at least it looked like Scheherazade. She was naked, and swayed her hips as she walked, the way they teach you in the television studios and among the Blessed Oblate Sisters of S. Daniela Crisci. More women emerged with her from the shadows, no less shameless in their obscenity but equally beautiful in their explosion of bestiality. They were dragging someone by the hair, and that someone was dead.

They were wanting to show him a sample of the sacrificial rites in which the Crux delighted: sex and blood instead of *vermicelli aglio e olio*. Scheherazade was howling like a wild animal and so were the other women. It lasted only a few seconds; darkness gathered again and silence returned to guard the lovers in the Bela Motel as they measured out their mutual passion.

Pantieri dashed forward, but at the foot of the slope he fell once more. He knew he had slipped on a human body, a body as cold and hard as marble. He was straddling the corpse like a lover, his lips brushing the ice-cold lips of a dead man. The damp of the rain soaking his clothes gave way, about the level of his heart, to a more noticeable and disagreeable feeling of moisture, almost as if an oily liquid had begun to spread across his shirt. He rose to his knees and with fumbling hands struck a match: Dr Gruvi lay with his arms stretched out, his face white and set in an expression of ironical resignation, his dinner jacket darker than the night and, skewered by a poignard, his breast was red with blood.

The headlights of an Alfa Giulia lit the scene. A familiar, sardonic voice asked with feigned good humour: "Pantieri, what you doing? Fooling around with corpses?"

He didn't need to raise his head, he knew it was Conti.

ACT II

ONE

There were two disconcerting circumstances about Gruvi's murder: the brutality of the crime, perpetrated with a cruel and unusual weapon, and the discovery of a note transfixed below the poignard's hilt. It had been written in block capitals in Indian ink and its message comprised only a few inexplicable and mocking words: "That a plaque might be set up to Cleon V.I. Cercato."

They had rushed back to Division without even waiting for the forensic squad to finish their examinations. It was evident that the murderer, whoever it was, was not in the vicinity, and that moreover the truth was hidden by deceptive appearances, and clues specifically designed to distract attention. The scrutiny Pantieri had insisted on carrying out at the top of the slope had yielded no result; the bacchanalian women he had seen, or thought he had seen, the sinister shades, obscene in their nakedness, like unchained demons out to conquer hell, had vanished. Not a trace had been found to lend credibility to that luminescent prelude to the crime. All they had collected was mud; they got splashed all over with it, and Pantieri's fruitless rummaging through the soaking grass and boggy ground had given rise to vexed, sarcastic glances.

"Pantieri," Conti began, "you got to give it to me straight."

"I was carrying out investigations."

"Right, but the fact is, we tailed you right from your first move. And, worse luck, two hundred metres short of the Bela Motel, we had to get stuck bang up somebody's arse and we were hanging around for ten minutes – which leaves ten minutes to explain. You better tell me what you got up to, and come clean with it."

It was almost an accusation. And how long had they been tailing him? Perhaps they already knew he'd hidden De Fiore's wife in his apartment. But there was worse. The poignard driven into Gruvi's chest had come from the display in his entrance hall. He'd recognized it straightaway by the arabesques on the hilt and its two notches, which made the rusty old blade unmistakable. When had it disappeared? He didn't remember noticing anything out of place, but then he took for granted the things he normally had around him. That poignard could have disappeared some time ago.

"Dr Conti," Pantieri said, with little conviction, "I'm a public servant, not a murderer."

"*Excusatio non petita . . .*" the Prosecutor joked. Then he thrust the back of his hand under Pantieri's eyes. "Take a good look."

Just below the wrist a pustule had grown, the size of a bean. The skin was scaly and violet, puckered and shrivelled over the slight swelling.

"Like it?"

"What?"

"My pustule."

"No, it's revolting."

"You're an idiot – you haven't a clue! It's a beauty. You're just churned up because you don't have a gong like this!"

Pantieri looked Conti in the eye to assure himself that he was only joking. But Conti wasn't joking and he wasn't out of his mind; he was brimming over with complacent joy, as if that boil had accorded his human condition its necessary justification.

"A real beauty," repeated the Prosecutor, vehemently.

"I don't have any pustules," Pantieri mumbled, meekly. "I'm sorry, there's no excuse."

"Never know, even you might grow one. If you'd only listen to me . . . But I doubt it. You couldn't ever raise a big 'un like mine – maybe just a wee one. A little boil, or a small scab. But you're not up to it."

"In your place, I'd call a doctor."

"Holy smoke! I knew I was wasting my time! Pantieri, you've not understood a damn thing! You think I'm ill? Poppycock! This pustule of mine's harmless, see? It's a badge, a mark. It's not got to get better, it's got to stay like it is! If I'm lucky, maybe I'll get another. I'm well in, I've arrived, I'm one of the boys, I belong. I'm not a criminal who disappears into the bush to do academics in."

"Is that an accusation?" asked Pantieri. With a start, he remembered the ulcer on the back of Cardinal Meschia's hand. Was the Crux imprinting its own stigmata?

"Not, at any rate, for the moment," said Conti softly. "But you've got a hell of a lot of explaining to do. For example, who owns the murder weapon?"

"I do," Pantieri replied, making an effort to speak calmly, even though his heart was in his throat. "It's the best piece in a display at home. Someone stole that poignard from me."

"Oh, someone stole it? And where's your proof?"

Now they'd got him. Maybe he could have done without that dangerous admission; he wasn't sure that Conti knew of the dagger's provenance. They were always bluffing during interrogations, it was normal practice to pretend you knew everything, when in fact you didn't. But if he'd lied and the magistrate had challenged him, well, yes, he would have been in a worse mess.

"No," whispered Pantieri, swallowing hard. "I can't prove a thing. But I'm a public servant and I give you my word of honour . . ."

"Your word of honour! And why should I believe that? I don't believe in honour, Pantieri: I don't give a monkey's about it. Honour's like a twat, it's okay when it's fucked. You think I'm so gormless I'd take anyone at his word? I learnt about that as a boy: I swore by Almighty God, Jesus Christ, the Holy Ghost, Our Lady, on my mother's grave . . . And it was all false! Incredible my mother never had a stroke! Lived to be ninety, she did, died of old age. I perjured myself on her and lengthened her days!"

"That's a matter of opinion. I've never perjured myself and I care about my honour."

"You bastard, where d'you keep your honour, then? You've gone and hidden a witness, don't think I don't know. That

Mirella Jenca, De Fiore's wife, you've got her stashed away in your flat, haven't you? And for all I know you're having it off with her right in the very same bed you did it with your poor wife, where the poor woman gave up her soul, too . . . It's okay to cuckold the dead, isn't it? She was a good woman, your wife, and now you come and spit on her hallowed memory. So where's all this honour of yours?"

"I swear to God . . ."

"Ah, you filthy perjurer! We've photographed you, filmed you, bugged your phone, and you swear to God it isn't true? I hope you rot in hell!"

Something inside Pantieri began to crumble. In a flash, the scenes of his life passed before him like some faded, tedious film: little white lies and deceptions he'd woven (to his own cost, moreover), the resigned acceptance of a job he didn't care for, an unfortunate marriage, and squalid escapades with worthless women; weren't these all falsehoods and worse than the one he'd just perpetrated? They created the picture of a mediocre man deluded into thinking he could find a moral dimension, which was probably impossible. Conti was right: perjury, call it a venial or a mortal sin, as you like, was the subterranean basis of existence.

"It's true," Pantieri murmured, "I have hidden her in my flat. But she's got nothing to contribute to the investigation, I'm sure of that."

"And who do you think you are, making my judgements for me?"

"I made a mistake, but I'm asking you not to involve the woman."

"Pantieri, you can get stuffed. But don't worry. I'm not going to touch the lady, at least, not for the moment. Nor you either. I'm going to give you some rope, I want to see where you end up. But just watch your step."

"You won't go thinking that I'm implicated?"

"You've still not understood. Now listen, and listen good. What I need is an instigator, a perpetrator and an accomplice. Now pay good attention to what I'm saying. I'll spell it out for you in simple language. I didn't say *the* instigator, *the* perpetrator and *the* accomplice. Used the indefinite article, didn't I? I'm a magistrate, I know the law. The law's a pussy-footing, hypocritical reflection of society's thirst for revenge. For one reason or another, passions come crowding in, sparks of hate fly, and you've got to exercise a calming influence. But someone gets his balls in a twist and goes over the top. That's where the courts come in, to make vengeance respectable. It's not a question of fixing on the right target, but of clamping down on dangerous movements. I've got an ideal solution for this case . . . A fascist millionaire as instigator, an ultra-lefty as perpetrator and a public servant as accomplice. This way I'd see to satisfying the whole gamut of society's pet hates in one fell swoop. And you'd be just the ticket as accessory to the crime, the traitor conspiring within the administration of justice, a fifth columnist. There you are, a prize defendant!"

"But that's preposterous," Pantieri protested. "It's our duty to find the culprit, not to invent him!"

"Pantieri, you really don't understand a frigging thing, do you? In this world everything's invented. Everything's at the mercy of the imagination, of the chaotic, the arbitrary. Politicians invent your politics, designers invent your clothes, engineers your machines, writers your novels, and banks your high interest rates . . . and we dream up culprits. To be frank, though, where Gruvi's suicide is concerned, it's difficult to think of you as a culprit, much simpler to think of you as *the* culprit. You'd had a meeting with the victim, you were nabbed at the scene of the crime five minutes after it happened, the murder weapon belongs to you, and you've buggered us about in a real pig's arse of lies and half-baked notions . . . extraterrestrial lights and these blow-jobbers prancing around . . . what jury would believe you innocent?"

"But I *am* innocent!"

"Look, old son," smiled Conti, spreading out his arms, "You've got you forty-eight hours to prove you're in the clear. Forty-eight hours to bring me a culprit. Mark my words: *a* culprit. See how I bend over backwards to help you?"

He went out squaring his shoulders and puffing out his chest like a turkey-cock. Pantieri sighed. He shot a glance at the desk

. . . an old habit, it was always possible that someone had left a report or note lying about. There was a sheet of carbon copy. My God, Ciro De Fiore wasn't a nobody after all, the Prosecutor's office in Genoa had issued a warrant for his arrest: he was wanted for the murders of a magistrate and a journalist, an attack on a school and several robberies . . . So he *was* a terrorist. Oh, no, there was a case that held water, alright. Whether he was responsible for the bomb attack on the Discount and Savings Bank remained to be proved, but a terrorist he was. He'd used forged papers in Genoa, but the identification was certain, despite the recent acquisition of a moustache. The carbon copy said nothing more. However, those few items were enough to tangle the web even further.

Strange. De Fiore had nothing in common with the usual run of terrorists; as soon as they were arrested, those people always declared they were political prisoners, refused a solicitor, swore they would drill the judges full of lead, and very nearly displayed a narcissistic state of bliss, as if they'd finally achieved the glittering prize which they'd coveted since their earliest childhood: they were finally in prison! (If nothing else, they had achieved one result: postponed any possible revolution by at least a century. Those who were seriously worried about it could set their minds at rest.) But this De Fiore . . . He simply didn't fit the picture of a terrorist; he was arrogant and whining, forever anxious to show off his bourgeois respectability, his connections, his delight in celebrating all the rites of a world that suited him just as it was.

Dawn was breaking as Pantieri arrived home. The porter greeted him with a strained smile.

"Cellar flooded. Rats all escaped."

"Are you sure?"

"Absolutely."

There was a smell of cigarette smoke and spirits in the flat; the ashtrays were overflowing with butt-ends and a bottle of brandy had been knocked over. Mirella sat waiting for him, cross-legged, in the middle of what had been their bizarre nuptial couch. She was certainly very beautiful: barefoot, her hair loose over her shoulders, impudent breasts, golden skin and soft, modulated lap, she looked untamed and alluring. Her hips merged into forbidden rotundity; it was hard to define an area or zone that wasn't contaminated by sin. She was hard and soft at the same time. Had he loved her? Or was he only beginning to now?

"There are some sandwiches if you're hungry," she said with a smile.

"Where did you get them?"

"I went out last night, but not for very long. I was bored to death, I felt like a prisoner, and I wanted to eat. I've got a right to eat, haven't I? It's a disgrace: ten thousand lire a sandwich! If it starts like this I'd like to know where it's going to end?"

"You promised me you'd stay put. The Prosecutor's office has been watching me, they know you're here. And I'm in trouble . . . Gruvi's been killed, stabbed through the chest with a poignard lifted here, from my place. The Prosecutor caught me beside the corpse . . . and now they suspect me; I'm the accused."

"I love you."

"Me and how many others?" Pantieri asked maliciously, then at once regretted the words. A stupid, spiteful remark. Or another throwback to his old schoolteacher, Signorina Candiani. She would ask him a question and he would cobble together some kind of answer, deluding himself every time into thinking he had scraped a pass. She encouraged these hopes, punctuating every silence and every stammer with a wink or a word, and only at the end, when he was sure he'd passed, would she pronounce sentence: Zero, boy! He'd learned to hate her and the rest of humanity with her; you couldn't trust anyone, and to be on the safe side, better to get your own shot in first. A stupid game: as with Signorina Candiani, he always came off worse.

"I love you and that's that," Mirella replied. She made a furtive movement with the back of her hand, perhaps she'd dried her eyes, but she wasn't the crying type, she knew what life was about.

"Okay," said Pantieri, "have you seen the display in the hall? All those weapons? The poignard that killed Gruvi was stolen from there."

"When I came in there was no poignard. And what's a poignard, anyway?"

"How can you say you've not seen one when you don't know what it is? It's a pointed blade, looks something like a spit. Never mind. Remember Papasidero? I've got wonderful memories of it. I don't know why, but I'm sure I'll go back. I'd like to go back when there's snow."

"Why don't you go straightaway? It's very beautiful without the snow, too. It's full of olives and oaks. When all's said and done, who's stopping you?"

"My God, life's got certain narrative rules that have to be respected. You can't anticipate the epilogue! I wish to goodness I could read what's going on inside your mind."

"I didn't steal the poignard," Mirella muttered after a long introspection. "I can understand you not trusting me, and I'm sorry. As for the rest, do as you like. But going off to hunt the killer, or killers, is a dirty game and I wouldn't be all that much use to you. Perhaps it's time to embrace truths that are less cramping than those you extract from solving criminal cases. Vanish, while you can."

"You may just be right," said Pantieri with a smile, "but right now I'm dead beat. I want some sleep."

He dreamed about a swamp, nearly six hundred years ago, with quivering reeds and jonquils and a seagull hovering on high. Then suddenly he heard the maddened shriek of chaffinches in flight, while concentric waves undulated through the green waters towards the muddy banks. There was a roar in the background, implacable as destiny and as alluring as death. It was both a threat and an invitation. It was the Rhône, swirling the body of Raymond of Touraine . . . Then the Rhône poured into his room, the current sweeping him away as well, or rather carrying away the last clear images that are found on the borders of sleep. Why was the building work on the site next door so noisy? The rumble of bulldozers intervened and someone on the floor above had gone to the toilet. The sound of silence had

been left at Papasidero. A gust of wind, and from the heaps of
leaves piled at the foot of the oaks a single one detached itself
and, like a curling paper, twisted in agony, brushed the street
pavement for a few metres, rose and then fluttered down. An
exhalation, the breath of silence.

It was three in the afternoon. Mirella was fast asleep beside
him. He paused to contemplate her and to reflect; who knows,
perhaps she had stolen the poignard and was in on it . . . But
why? Oh my God, at first glance the answer wasn't that bizarre,
it didn't take too much imagination . . . What with the price
of sandwiches! Or perhaps she'd been threatened, blackmailed?
The law could be more underhand than the underworld. He
looked unhappily at the girl, then, after a torment of temptations and reconsiderations, his eyes started to caress the area
below her spine. No, he was wrong to have doubts about her;
it was others he should mistrust. It was in that moment,
through the association of ideas, that he remembered the
rats.

He dived down to the cellar. Byron was snoring in his lodge,
hunched up in a rocking chair, while he revived his feet by
soaking them in a large bowl. No one could have woken him;
so much the better. The water, which had leaked in from a
sub-basement, was about two foot deep; it blocked the way
down the passage, unless one didn't mind wading knee-deep.
Pantieri took off his shoes and socks, rolled up his trousers and
courageously stepped into the morass. For light he struck
matches, one after the other, burning his fingers so as not to
plunge into darkness after too brief a time. He reached the
doorway to the area which belonged to him and peered with a
vague sense of anguish through the gaps in the planking. On
the mud which washed from wall to wall, as if stirred by
underground currents, the box which had contained the *Mastomys* was now adrift. One side of the box was stoved in, the
rats had disappeared.

He attempted to throw light on the muddy surface (but the
light from the matches was fleeting and deceptive), to try and
see if he could spot any survivors of the shipwreck, hoping
nevertheless that a whirlpool might have sucked the little

monsters away somewhere, maybe returning them to the sewers. He saw nothing. Nothing but an old cardboard suitcase which had burst its contents of moth-eaten woollens, useless letters and spent lightbulbs over the mud. He withdrew. His fingertips were beginning to burn, so he decided to make his way back in the dark, trusting his memory. After three steps, he froze. Something was nuzzling his leg. He lit a match: a dead *Mastomys* was trying to take refuge near him, circling his knee with its long, slimy tail. Framed by the sodden fringe, its leonine muzzle was open in a grin: trapped between its sharp, curved teeth it held a small, rusty nail.

He went back up the stairs in his bare feet, carrying his shoes, and stopped for a moment to peek in at the porter's lodge, in two minds whether to wake Byron up and put him in the picture. The brute was snoring – worse, he was gargling; a thin strand of saliva quivered between his open lips. His feet were gnarled; the yellow nails had deposits of thick, black grime which they had conserved for years on end, proof against the blandishments of bath salts and even of Palmolive soap. A dense, frothy liquid was floating in the footbath: between the two big toes, like a drowned man dragged onto the sand between two rocks, lay a dead rat which was casting a questioning, open-eyed look at the ceiling: this was pleasantly decorated with a roll of fly-paper and an Art Nouveau lampshade, complete with beads and tassels.

Pantieri stormed up to his flat and scrubbed himself several times, then flung himself at the telephone. He had to tell Biraghi immediately, at all costs. He tried his office, the restaurant where he had lunch, then an old aunt of his, where he finally succeeded in speaking to him.

"Those disgusting rats of yours have escaped!" he complained, without troubling to moderate his language. "There are corpses floating about the basement corridor . . . it's a frightful scene. There was even a rat in the porter's footbath. Would you like to tell me what you intend to do about it?"

"What do you want me to do?" Biraghi replied after a long silence. "It's gone and happened now. But we can discuss the matter. If you knew about Edward von Hartmann . . ."

"Forget about von Hartmann. Wouldn't it be better to call in a firm of pest control?"

"It wouldn't be any use: it's too late now."

TWO

The villa belonging to construction boss Gerardo Opitz was tucked away off Via Appia Antica. The rain was still coming down in buckets; Cecilia Metella's tomb, the rust-coloured pines, the rich men's villas and the greasy wrappers by the roadside were all being submitted to an equal wash.

Pantieri had telephoned asking for an appointment: he'd remembered Gruvi mentioning the cell the doctor belonged to ("in mine there was Lucilla Opitz, daughter of the construction boss, Gerardo Opitz . . .") and he had concluded that at Opitz's he might be able to gather further tesserae to render the mosaic more intelligible.

Opitz was fat and smooth, exuding worldiness and elegance, perhaps because his villa was full of top people: he was giving a party to celebrate his nomination to the chairmanship of the Discount and Savings Bank. The bomb attack had raised doubts about the appropriateness of the celebration, but in the end the prevailing opinion was that the best answer to terrorism was to take it in one's stride. Besides, the best of everything had already been ordered from Euclide's, not excluding *farfalle al salmone* and *penne alla vodka*. You couldn't just ditch that kind of delicacy.

Opitz introduced Pantieri to some of the guests, allowed him a glimpse of the noble figure of the Rt Hon. Lauro Sabbioneta and the more comradely one of Cardinal Meschia (the prelate was smoking a cigar), and then begged him for a moment's patience, giving him to understand they would be able to retire to his study later and talk freely.

It was a party coloured blue, reminiscent of Picasso's Blue Period. Subdued lighting tinged the scene light blue, and the guests, moreover, had dressed in conformity with the host's penchant for cool tones. Then, under the effect of a whisky he had drunk, they became dismembered to resolve themselves into a merry-go-round of mascaraed eyes, vermilion fingernails, wigs, back-combings, bracelets, necklaces, rings and porcelain-capped teeth. Everything was spinning: a vision of life caught in an endless paroxysm. There was an explosion of music. Hidden away in a corner, a small combo was playing and someone confided life's agonies to a microphone.

The guests were now dancing: they stood face to face, shaking their hips and fannies, whisking up their innards, waving their hands in the air with vague allusive gestures (or was it reproof?) and snapping their fingers. The synthesizer, with its unexpected improvisations, let out its shrill whistle as electronics and the jungle colluded. The Moog's noise was a ship's siren, the roar of jet planes, the hiss of tyres, a P38's report, but it was also the cry of horror emitted by the first caveman to grasp the certainty of death, the first to realize what death meant. Later, other less savage and more imaginative men had come to make conjectures about the soul, and so began the age of the harpsichord, the fortepiano and the pianoforte. But that first cry of horror, apparently forgotten, had never lost its urgency and, after thousands of years, the synthesizer had rediscovered it.

"Successful party, don't you think?" said Opitz, beaming.

"It certainly is. This music doesn't say much to me, though. My generation discovered rhythm, but I still prefer melody."

"You don't have to tell me. I'm very old-fashioned myself. However, in my work, I simply have to keep up certain relationships and friendships. And besides, one can't just reject the age we live in. Why don't we go into my study?"

They withdrew into a huge room, completely blue, of course, but for two easy chairs in white leather. They sat down, looking at each other in silence for a moment. The Moog's wail reached them more faintly, but persisted nonetheless in its suggestion of enticing thoughts of death.

"I believe you know Dr Gruvi," Pantieri began.

"Don't . . . don't! He should have been with us tonight . . .

It's terrible, distressing, quite heart-breaking. I read about it in the paper . . . and yet no one had it in for him."

"And yet he was killed."

"Most disturbing news. Deplorable how from one moment to the next one can . . . well, that's to say, depart this life. We all hang from a thread, a very slender thread. We're like leaves. Inspector, do please consider this as a gesture of friendship and allow me to make you a little gift of ten million."

"I don't follow."

"Please, I should like to give you ten million lire. My goodness, you take the trouble to come and visit me in the middle of the night . . . in this torrential rain. I hope you didn't come on foot? Believe me, it's the least I can do, a mere trifle. Please accept ten million."

"Signor Opitz, I haven't come for the party. I'm carrying out enquiries. Your proposal could sound a little ambiguous, if you follow me?"

"Nonsense. Why on earth should I wish to corrupt you? I only want to do you a small kindness, make you a little present as a token of friendship. Try not to misunderstand me. Now listen carefully, because this is philosophy. It's my conviction that everything has to be paid for. Have you never heard of the laws of profit? No one is willing to give anything unless he gains from it. This doesn't apply exclusively to business, it's a universal rule. It's engraved in the soul. Take my wife (I don't mean now, she's over seventy, and we've got over certain problems); if I wanted to make love to her, I paid her. In our early days, I gave her jewellery or whatever else took her fancy, but latterly I just paid her in cash. Simpler, quicker, more intimate. Better than a brothel. I want to be clear, however. My wife would have made love to me anyway, even for free, but you see, if I paid, she felt indebted to me, felt under an obligation. There was a perfect reciprocity, she became an authentic tart. Money is good, it generates warmth; it's spiritual, it's the only possible tie. That's why I want to give you the ten million, Inspector. I don't want our acquaintance to be fleeting, I want a little corner in your soul."

"Signor Opitz, let's forget about money. You can tell me

something else instead. Have you ever heard anyone mention a Raymond of Touraine?"

"Gruvi mentioned something. A ridiculous story. Wouldn't he have died some five hundred years ago, an evil spirit perhaps? Heavens, how could I ever pay off a spirit? The fact is, it's not a question I've ever thought about – maybe with two lorry loads of candles . . ."

"Do try and help me. We don't need two lorry loads of candles. I'm looking for a living person. I'd like an explanation, or at least a clue to follow."

"Perhaps my daughter knows something. Lucilla was a great friend of Dr Gruvi. Yes, I think it was quite a close relationship. I'll send for her."

Lucilla Opitz was beautiful. A minute scar disfigured her mouth slightly, but her features were perfect: her sharply profiled face had a tragic, profligate look; it was difficult to observe her with indifference. She was tall, and her body provoked desire, but not in the usual way. She suggested indefinable, or rather inadmissible, temptations; she aroused sordid thoughts, but whoever gave the slightest purchase to such thoughts would read only contempt in those green eyes of hers. She was a distant woman, too distant. There was a touch of ambiguity in her disdain, as if she knew that she deserved the same contempt she accorded to others and positively revelled in it. She dragged one leg: infantile paralysis.

"You want to know about Raymond of Touraine and the Crux?" she sighed, as soon as her father had left the room. "I can't tell you more than you already know . . . When it began we were a sect. We worshipped evil. It was quite a fashionable thing to do, you know, a way of letting off steam, an elegant way to stop people getting into worse trouble. It's the people who are bent on doing good – they can be the dangerous ones, wouldn't you agree, Inspector?"

"An original idea, but it doesn't help me throw any light on Dr Gruvi's murder."

"I'll spell it out: I don't know any more about the Crux and Raymond of Touraine, and there's nothing more I can tell you. Raymond of Touraine is the leader's pseudonym, but I've

97

no idea who he is. As for the organization, it has indeed been politicized and I myself pulled out some time ago. But I think there's another problem that needs investigation. Gruvi wasn't killed by a knife in the chest."

"He wasn't?"

"I mean that a corpse was dragged to the Bela Motel and a corpse had its heart stabbed. It seems to me straightforward enough. Besides, it'll be easy for you to check if I'm right – there'll be an autopsy I suppose."

"I think the post mortem's already been done, but I don't know the results. Anyway, the pathologist always writes at Dr Conti's dictation. But would you tell me how you've reached this conclusion . . . Though, come to think of it, I was struck by how cold the corpse was, like marble, and its rigidity . . . *rigor mortis* had set in. Furthermore, Gruvi was still alive at six that evening, because that was the exact time he telephoned Cardinal Meschia. At all events, the murder wasn't committed a few minutes before I arrived, but several hours before."

"Twenty-four hours before," Lucilla specified. "And not with the poignard, because the fact is Gruvi was poisoned."

"Poisoned? . . . Yes, he told me he was feeling ill and said the same to Cardinal Meschia. According to the Cardinal he was absolutely delirious. But why do you suppose Gruvi was poisoned?"

"It's not a supposition, it's a fact," replied Lucilla, simply. "I was present when he swallowed the poison."

A prolonged silence fell. It was still pouring and for a little while the blue study was filled with the Moog's lamentations outside the door and the hiss of the downpour outside the window. A loose gutter was spouting a cataract onto a hedge of hydrangeas; gusts of wind were shredding the night sky between the trees. It had been raining almost non-stop for two days. If the weather didn't improve immediately, the Tiber would burst its banks and the Nuova Magliana would be under water. Ah well, that was a working-class district; what could you expect? A yellow streak scored the heavens; it could have been distant lightning, or Very lights. Not very likely. It didn't disappear and it wasn't bright. It seemed more like a cloud of sand advancing towards the city; it wouldn't be the first time that sand from the African desert had been driven north to coat Imperial marble and tufa slums with mustard dust.

"I'm sure you're aware of the seriousness of what you're saying," observed Pantieri, ruffling his hair. He lit a cigarette and took two long drags, as he awaited an explanation.

"Of course I'm aware of what I'm saying, even if my revelation's nothing extraordinary. It was Gruvi himself who told me he'd been poisoned; he phoned me yesterday evening, about a quarter to six."

"A quarter of an hour before he telephoned the Cardinal."

"I don't know anything about that, and it doesn't concern me. He told me to bring him some cortisone at once . . . Gruvi was no mean doctor, he knew what treatment he needed. But I realized that it was a forlorn attempt, there was nothing really that could be done. I ran to the chemist's, then dashed round to his place, unfortunately it was on the other side of town . . . a quiet apartment in Via Caldonazzo; only Gruvi, myself and one or two others knew about it. I arrived about an hour later, there was a lot of traffic and I was having a spot of trouble with the clutch. Well, Gruvi wasn't there any more. Evaporated into thin air, or so it seemed. A chair had been knocked over and a trunk in which we kept some costumes was missing. The costumes were strewn all over the floor. It was rotten luck."

"Why didn't you report it?"

"I only thought of getting out, I was terrified. And I knew that by that time there was nothing to be done to help Gruvi; in fact, in today's paper . . . it's very sad news. However, seeing that you, Inspector, have come to find me . . . you of all people . . ."

"Why 'me of all people'?"

"Nothing," Lucilla mumbled, after a brief pause. "A strange coincidence, that's all. But I don't think it's you we should be talking about. Anyway, last night it was fairly easy to piece things together . . . I knew when and how Gruvi had been poisoned; as I said, I was there. It happened in Ernesto's restaurant on Via Cassia, exactly two days ago. Let's see, it was ten o'clock, more or less, and there was hardly a soul there, the place was dead, talk of a funeral! Then in came one of those publicity guys who plug this and that product and give out free samples: cigarettes for the most part, but also sweets, confectionery and cosmetics. He was carrying two boxes, a red one and a green one; he showed the green one to everyone else and the red one only to Gruvi. I was struck by that, even though I took little account of it at the time. He offered him a little slab of fancy chocolate, a revolting thing I thought, a mixture of aniseed, cocoa and honey. But Gruvi was a glutton. I remember, though, after he'd gulped it down in one bite, he made a rather tart comment."

"What did he say?"

"That it tasted of crap. But then he ordered a whisky and didn't mention it again. It was only when he phoned me yesterday evening that he said he was sure the poison had been administered in the chocolate . . . a really sneaky one that only begins to work twelve hours after it's been taken, which means it's too late to rush for a remedy."

"Could you describe the man who offered the chocolate?"

"I'm afraid not. You know how it is . . . It was dark, we'd been drinking, and we were preoccupied . . . There's a sort of person you just don't notice, they're more faceless than a slot machine. Besides, the guy didn't even say a word, maybe he whispered something under his breath, something I couldn't pick up . . . I remember a tall, well-built man, with a very thick black moustache, but I could be wrong."

"Did Gruvi tell you the name of the poison?"

"He mentioned two or three names, and spoke of amanitine, I seem to remember. They were all toxins with a delayed action, and all equally lethal."

"Why such a far-fetched poison?" Pantieri asked, almost to himself. "So as not to allow him time to take an antidote – Gruvi was a doctor, after all. With arsenic, you know about it at once, you can try doing something about it. And also to leave enough time to set up the scene with the poignard and incriminate me! But why?"

"Oh dear," sighed Lucilla. "You should speak only well of the dead. *Parce sepulto*, isn't that what people always say?"

"I don't follow," observed Pantieri hesitantly, passing a hand through his hair.

"You became a widower recently," Lucilla explained, "and I suppose you were fond of your wife. Well, I knew her."

"You knew my wife? Of course, she was a pretty nondescript woman, pretty colourless and our marriage was not a happy one. We didn't have any children and that kept us from worse unhappiness. We bored each other with all due propriety. Still . . . you know how it is . . . your wife's very like your country, and who feels ready to disown that?"

"Are husbands also like one's country? You see, Inspector, if you put it in those terms, your wife had no patriotic scruples. What I mean is, she was unfaithful."

"Unfaithful?" asked Pantieri, quietly, but without emotion and still less with any astonishment. He was a public servant, and, as such, had to reckon on his wife's adultery, much as he counted on his salary. It was a question of bourgeois sophistication. He couldn't even complain about never having suspected, because he'd never taken the trouble to ask himself if there were any grounds for suspicion.

"She was Dr Conti's mistress," Lucilla said, all in one breath. "It was an open secret. Only her husband was in the dark, of course."

"So why tell me now? What's the point? You said yourself: *parce sepulto*."

"Conti and your wife were hiding something, something more secret than their affair, which wasn't a secret at all, anyway. I'm not telling you this to stir up any posthumous jealousy, and not even to blame your wife; I want to help you find an explanation for the trap they set up for you at the Bela Motel."

"Do you mean that Conti could have a specific reason for wanting to get me into trouble?"

"I suppose so. A reason for putting you out of circulation, and especially for damaging your credibility. Conti suspects that you're in possession of, or could come into possession of, a secret which he was on the trail of with his mistress, I'm sorry, your late wife. You follow me? And mind, it must be a tremendous secret, one to make or break rich and powerful men, men who are feared, men who make history."

"I don't know any secrets."

"Possibly not. But it's more probable that you do know some but haven't recognized their value. As if you carried some capsule about in your wallet and didn't know it was poison."

"The photograph!" Pantieri exclaimed all of a sudden, and immediately bit his tongue. But by then it was too late, the dangerous confidence had escaped his lips. At all events, it was only a conjecture. There was no assurance that the faded snapshot he'd come across among a pack of pornographic pictures in Assunta's wardrobe was the banana-skin that was going to send history sliding off in a different direction. A man and a boy in a pose of affectionate familiarity, two faces that looked like those of a father and son. Better not to reveal anything more, and try somehow or other to remedy the gaffe.

"What photograph?" Lucilla wheedled.

"Nothing. I was thinking about an old photograph of Conti and my wife . . . The way they looked at each other, their smile . . . an indefinable air of complicity . . . stupid of me not to have suspected, wasn't it?"

"As you said yourself," murmured Lucilla, disappointed, "you can't have doubts when you don't want to have any. Why don't we go back to the guests and I'll introduce you to the Rt Hon. Croce Sabbioneta and Cardinal Meschia, unless you already know them? They're two extraordinary men, the kind who set the course of history."

In the lounge next door the Moog had fallen silent and the guests were swarming in two separate clusters around the Cardinal and the statesman; the man of the Church had attracted around him a gathering of young women, all milky cleavages and lips open more in suction than a smile, while the man of the State was surrounded by a garland of generals in uniform, ambassadors with dress swords, and bank directors in double-breasted suits and horn-rim glasses. (Sabbioneta had also taken the unusual step of leaving off his overcoat, which was, however, deposited in the cloakroom as though in a safe.) All people who were above the world's everyday problems, but who still contributed not a little to inducing them, thought Pantieri irritably. Take inflation . . . No, no, this misfortune at least could not be laid at the door of the governing class; the hydra-headed monster was goaded on every day by the rank-and-file: a Coca-Cola here, a T-bone steak there, and perhaps a bottle of wine, no wonder the lira was slipping against the mark.

"I'm inclined to see that the political interest prevails over the economic one," Lauro Croce Sabbioneta was saying, as if he had been reading Pantieri's thoughts. "There's no doubt we must put our own house in order, but do forgive me, I absolutely do not believe in the new legislation on civil rights and institutional reform that the Rt Hon. Orazio La Calenda, Minister of the Interior, has so much to heart. It's not new regulations we need, but a greater consensus. What's needed in politics is two things: a fresh start and a new deal. It's not easy. Grave injustices can be committed. But on the eve of the Year 2000, society very largely manifests itself in a concern for the proper allocation of resources. It may seem incredible, but even the exercise of corruption postulates moral rigour. The corruption of one or a few is unacceptable, but when corruption becomes universal, the very notion of corruption goes by the board. This is the only possible programme of government, one that can attract a large consensus . . . If we'd had the foresight to take the latest idealogues and put them onto the boards of directors as we did with the protesters in '68, we should now have less of a crisis on our hands. Let's not forget: you have terrorism when there's a shortage of jobs for the boys. And the best way of coming to grips with it now and to absorb it once more into the system is to promise immunity and reduced sentences: in other words, to corrupt it."

THREE

Opitz became aware of Pantieri's presence and went towards him; he took him by the arm and piloted him towards a window. It was still raining, but with less fury. The sky was split into two hemispherical vaults, one indigo, the other mustard-coloured; the line between them was a-quiver with lightning flashes. The broken gutter had stopped spouting and twittering. The noises in the background were more hushed and persuasive.

"What an incredible sky . . ." Opitz muttered. "It reminds me of a similar spectacle back in 1917, when the Spanish 'flu broke out. I was only a child at the time, but there are some experiences you can never forget. Do you understand? Spanish 'flu, the War, Fascism . . . Who knows, history could even repeat itself. I suppose you must find these ramblings of mine tedious . . . I understand, you're investigating a murder and all this political chat must seem to you beside the point."

"Not at all. I get the impression that politics and crime are intimately linked, each needs the other."

"Undoubtedly. As a rule, such political debate as remains is bogus. In reality, the debate is entirely about personalities. There are tremendous hatreds, such as we can't begin to imagine, mortal hatreds . . . and terrorism's sometimes been the secular arm here. It's a fact that the institutions have been taken over by the imperatives of organized crime, and whoever doesn't play along is thrust aside, if not worse. But it's best to shrug it off. As for me, tomorrow I'm giving a speech to celebrate World Savings Day, at the Protomoteca on the Capitol. I'll be illustrating my new duties as Chairman of the Discount and Savings Bank. I'll give rhetoric its due, but as far as savings are concerned, I'm going to pose a question that's bothering me. I'd be glad if you'd come and hear me."

"Of course I shall. But I didn't know you were an economist."

"That's a misplaced irony," complained Opitz, wringing his hands. "Do you know what I had to pay for the Chairmanship of the Discount and Savings Bank? Twenty thousand million down! No one else was prepared to pay a sum of that order. So wouldn't you say I have a sound grasp of the laws of economics?"

"Up to a point."

"The world's like that. I believe I've already explained my convictions to you and I'm extremely sorry you won't accept my modest gift. But I won't insist. I hope at least my daughter Lucilla was able to offer you some useful pointers."

"It was an interesting conversation. Gruvi appears to have been poisoned, but apart from that, it seems that there's a compromising document in circulation . . . one that could make trouble for a highly-placed person."

"I'm not surprised. The only real risk we run is that of being exposed. Denunciation doesn't try and change the system because it's part of the system, but it can substitute one group for another, or one leader for another. That's the political struggle for you."

"There's a lot of cynicism about . . . The speeches made by Sabbioneta . . . We all know he's a gentleman and an honest man . . . nevertheless, I was struck by such a pitiless description."

"It was crude and not very reassuring, but close to reality. Rulers and ruled are on very much the same wavelength. There was a point where the idyll threatened to crack apart, but then, thank God, along came terrorism, which took care to strengthen the old affections. It's terrorism that's saved democracy, that's saved our democracy; and since the game paid off, it's on the cards, I think, that groupings in the corridors of power may have created terrorist bands of one kind and another. Indeed, I think it's more than likely. The impending threat revitalized a flagging love for the established order and at the same time the personal vendetta, in the event the political struggle, was able to express itself with the necessary brutality. Of course, when you play with fire, you know what happens: a few wild mavericks start acting on their own account, outside any logic or control. Random phenomena absolutely unsuitable for subversion; if anything they rekindle the atmosphere of fear, danger and anxiety. A few people got it in the neck: magistrates, journalists, police. All very sad, but it served to reinforce the conviction that there must be no change, because change would breed a society that was wholly without pity. A certain kind of pity, anyway. What's more, we shudder at the thought of justice because we know we're all guilty. What we need are amnesties, not revolutions."

"What was the secret that Gruvi was keeping?" Pantieri asked, point-blank.

"I honestly don't know," Opitz replied, "and I can't even hazard a guess. If he was murdered, if he paid for whatever it was with his life, it can't have been a question of no account . . . In the next few days, I suppose, we'll know what's been brewing. Something will happen."

"But what?"

"I repeat, I don't know a thing," said Opitz coldly. "I've always preferred the rattle of money to the rattle of sub-machine guns. You get the same result, and perhaps more quickly. Who knows . . . Cardinal Meschia never fails to puzzle me . . . a saintly man, of course . . . a man of charity, a revolutionary armed with a crucifix . . . Don't misunderstand me, I'm not trying to insinuate anything. Perhaps it's because there's a certain kind of fervour I simply don't understand . . . But in a world where everyone intrigues, it wouldn't surprise me if a cardinal were involved in some kind of plot."

And yet to see him with his unruly white locks, engulfed in the miasma his cigar was spreading, like a smokescreen of macerating uncertainties hovering over two possible lives, with his red overalls all in patches, the Cardinal looked less like a conspirator than like a stylite dropped by chance into the middle of a society gathering. Besides, Meschia had already caused a scandal by refusing the canapés with caviar, salmon and pâté de fois gras; he had asked for and obtained a large onion that he was now biting into with relish under the fascinated gaze of the women forming a circle around him.

"We must return to simple foods," the Cardinal propounded, and in the heat of his discourse, he spat minute fragments of onion into the cleavages of the nearest ladies. "The delicacies I've seen in this house are an insult to poverty. We must never forget that even today, even at this very moment, there are people dying of starvation. Actually dying of starvation."

"People also die of thrombosis, people die of pemphigus," Lucilla objected. "One way or another, we've still got to die."

"Disease is one of the facts of life in this world," said the Cardinal severely, looking with knitted brows at the back of his hand. The ulcer that Pantieri thought he had noticed had grown a little. Above all, the living flesh was more visible, and every so often it discharged microscopic droplets of blood. The Cardinal polished off the onion in two bites and added: "It's in the nature of things that they can cease to function, or become corrupt . . . it's part of God's law. But we all have an equal right to satisfy our hunger and we cannot allow our fellow human beings to have nothing to eat."

"I was looking at the ulcer on the back of your hand, Your Eminence," murmured Lucilla significantly.

"I don't know what you mean to imply," complained the Cardinal, "but mine is quite a rare disease. The doctor's spoken of a burns syndrome, Lyell's syndrome, and he seemed rather concerned . . . As for me, I don't care a jot. God's Providence knows what is right. Mine is but a small indisposition compared with the misfortunes of so many people."

"Your Eminence," Pantieri broke in, "I wonder if you would allow me a word?"

"You again," the illustrious prelate smiled. "Our police are remarkably intrusive."

He took his leave of the ladies, tracing vestigial benedictions with two fingers through the smoke-filled air, and pushing the Inspector forward, he drew up by the side of the synthesizer that, right at that moment, expert hands had set going again. The noise of the rain was over and there was only the Moog's

wild, melodious lament. It elicited a perverse desire for languorous abandon, an analytic index of every lost opportunity . . .
His schoolteacher, Signorina Candiani, certainly didn't suspect that Mariolina Nava's proximity could excite him; in the misty chill of that heath centred round the teacher's desk children of ten didn't get excited in that way. Thick forests of hypotenuses shaken by the polar blast of sapphics and iambics. His hand was on Mariolina's knee: he wanted to touch her, and she too wanted him to touch her, because there was no mischief in her smile. Something new to experience, something beautiful. But he had never dared, paralysed as he was by the teacher's baneful presence. He'd never considered that, after that occasion, he'd have no further opportunity to touch the cherry of a little girl of ten. Who knows if the Cardinal . . . He immediately rejected the shameful suspicion: idiocy suggested by the Moog. What the hell. Living meant always doing the contrary to what one wanted to do, especially for priests.

"And what do we live for?" the Cardinal suddenly blurted out, perhaps himself influenced by the oozing melody. He came to himself at once and bit his hand to show his willingness to undergo self-punishment for that not very orthodox exclamation. With a sad smile, he explained, "Of course, that's just a manner of speaking: the Lord knows the whys and wherefores, and it's not for us to enquire. But melancholia sometimes gets the upper hand. And then this is an unhealthy place . . . subdued lighting, the smell of spirits and tobacco, and human bodies . . . *Vanitas vanitatum*. We should work and nothing else. Life is only that, work. Chekhov was right."

"Your Eminence, you surely know about Dr Gruvi . . ."

"Dreadful," the Cardinal assented, cleaning a tooth with a fingernail. "He was on the phone to me only yesterday and, yes, I did have a presentiment of something untoward, but not a catastrophe like this!"

"I'm afraid that the catastrophe's still not over. You remember that Dr Gruvi wanted to warn someone, someone under the threat of death?"

"The Holy Father?"

"No, not the Holy Father. But a very important person,

without a doubt. Gruvi's been silenced so that the crime that's planned won't be hindered. Someone's in grave danger and you've got to help me find him."

"Find him? If only I could, if only I knew, with all my heart, I'd be only too willing . . . but as I explained to you, the late Dr Gruvi's phone call was interrupted."

"Try and make an effort to remember. Some trivial word, perhaps, some inflexion in the voice could be enough to offer us a clue. After all, it's a question of saving someone's life."

"To tell you the truth, I spend all my energy saving lives. However, I don't remember anything, anything significant . . . If that call hadn't been interrupted, but as it is . . . Let's put our faith in Divine Providence. It could be that in the design . . . of the Almighty . . . whoever's in danger is to be left in it. It can be punishment, it can be mercy."

Was the Cardinal's behaviour equivocal? Heavens! What an idea! Here was a dotty old man, an eccentric old fellow, and yet he was known to half the world for his religious zeal and humanitarian fervour; here he was now running the risk of becoming a questionable character, the phantom head of a conspiracy no less phantasmal! And who was the target, anyway? And yet, what about that sore on the back of his left hand . . . ? A disease, the Cardinal had explained, Lyell's syndrome. Well, it would be easy enough to check, or ask someone who knew. How shameful, how absurd to suspect the Cardinal!

Then it suddenly occurred to him that the clue he was worried about finding maybe lay inside his wallet; the photograph that had come into poor Assunta's possession, by what means it was anybody's guess, and for reasons he couldn't understand, was very hot property. He withdrew to one side and, feigning a nonchalant air, began rummaging through his wallet, as if he were meaning to dig out a note or phone number. He fished the snapshot out between thumb and forefinger and then lost himself in contemplation of those faded features of a man and a boy. Yes, they were faces he knew. Then came the flash of revelation. A lot of time had elapsed, twenty years or more, but those two smiling faces, whose likeness transpired in their obvious consanguinity, but even more in an undercurrent of shared complicity, those faces belonged without a shadow of a doubt to the Minister of the Interior, Orazio La Calenda, and to Ciro De Fiore. Father and son. The Calabrian terrorist was the Minister's illegitimate son.

"Such a dear memory?" asked Lucilla Opitz in jest; she had silently crept up behind him.

"You've been spying on me!" Pantieri chided her, though he did not have the face to hide the photograph. It would have been a pointless precaution now that Lucilla had seen the photo and grasped its meaning.

"Rubbish. That photograph's dangerous . . . it's an accusation . . . It's the document that Conti's searching for, although I've no idea what he intends to do with it . . . Don't tell me you've only just realized what it is!"

"I hadn't thought about it. Intrigue's not in my nature, I don't think that way."

"Maybe, but with that photograph someone could destroy the Minister of the Interior, La Calenda, the father of a small-time delinquent, of a man charged with the bomb attack on the Discount and Savings Bank, a suspected terrorist . . . It'll be no use claiming that a father is not to blame for his son's misdeeds. Of course, the photo might have other possible uses. It could be sold, and it could be auctioned. There's a lot of money to be made from it. On the other hand a pretty family portrait like that could be consigned to the flames. A noble, disinterested gesture. The gesture of a person who doesn't want to dirty his hands. What will you do, Inspector?"

"I don't know," Pantieri replied, replacing the snapshot inside his wallet with meticulous care. "I need to think about it. I need to understand."

"Look," said Lucilla suddenly, and, taking advantage of their isolation, she raised her dress a little to show him the inside of her thigh, disfigured by a sore larger than a postage stamp. "This isn't Lyell's syndrome. It looks almost like a flower, one that's bloomed for the last time . . . It's not a real and proper pustule, more what you might call a pustilence. It was for Gruvi, but now . . . I'd like you to kiss it."

"Why?"

"That way you'd belong to me. Life's no longer a question of knowing, but of belonging. Salvation lies in belonging. To a party, a union, a club, a company, a society, an institution, the television, the radio, the press . . . The fact of belonging establishes the right pedigree and guarantees a future to your children and grandchildren."

"And what do you belong to?"

"Oh, I've told you!" she said with a sigh of irritation and crossly tugged her skirt down over her leg. "Not all that long ago we were a sect . . . then politics . . . politics has taken over everything in this country, it doesn't give anyone room. Even our pustules, not even they . . . Tell me the truth, they've shocked you, haven't they?"

"Not all that much."

"You're right," said Lucilla, her eyes brimming with tears. "Even the sores are a trick, a very common trick. One day I'll explain."

"You haven't answered my question. You haven't told me what you belong to."

"I don't belong to anything," Lucilla said, with a sniff, "and I'm frightened."

Dawn was breaking when Pantieri reached home. It was no longer raining. The darkness was ochre-coloured, the mutilated trees were splashed with grey. Hooded apparitions in black oilskins were using their brooms to heave rotten leaves out of the blocked drains: the road-sweepers were endeavouring to drain off the flood-waters. A layer of slime was deposited on the pock-marked asphalt. Bitumen and concrete were breaking up and pouring into the bottom of new craters, together with an inrush of mud. The sweepers' voices were commenting on the storm and reporting gloomier disasters further afield: basements had been flooded (perhaps) in the Magliana, five buildings collapsed in the Tufello, a high mortality of fish in the Aniene polluted by trieline from a laboratory.

The four a.m. news on the radio was broadcasting a commentary on the economic situation. Inflation was galloping, the price of potatoes had reached eight thousand lire a kilo. What was to be done? Freeze excess demand, apply fiscal and credit controls at the same time. Sacrifices, sacrifices and more sacrifices . . . The same arguments endlessly repeated, complex circumlocutions to say that poverty was knocking at the door.

He crept into the apartment like a thief, not wanting to wake Mirella, but the telephone rang. It was Conti: "Pantieri, De Fiore's escaped. Talk of swashbuckle – it's something out of *The Count of Monte Cristo* or some bloody Japanese film. Got to hand it to him . . . Started last night, shouting about the shits and an upset. 'Oh, Mother, I feel ill, do something. I'm dying, hurry up, give me a Sympatol, a Coramine, a Microren, give me Milk of Magnesia, a cordial, a herb tea, anything!' Warder calls the guard, they go into the cell and find him on the deck, foaming at the mouth. They hump him down to the infirmary, call the quack, but he can't be found. Chaplain comes running up with his crucifix: 'My son, this is your last breath you draw, repent your sins and kiss this Holy Cross!' The guard and warder are taken in, they're convinced De Fiore's got one foot in the grave, so off they go hoping to run into the quack. Chaplain prattles on his devotions and in a flash the prize son of a bitch snatches the crucifix out of his hands, crucifies him over the bonce with it and has him falling down stunned. He makes off with the Chaplain's cassock and things, disguises himself as a priest and steals off with a blessing here, a prayer there and an exorcism to someone else! Well, he gets to the main gate, hears the guard's confession, and cocky as the Cardinal-Vicar he slips clean away!"

"And now what?"

"That's up to you. We think he might go looking for that wife of his, so you've got your hands on the bait. But even if we don't nab De Fiore, it's all the same to me."

"Do we know the results of the autopsy on Gruvi?"

"And how! Did you have any doubt about it? Cause of death, a primitive stabbing weapon that pierced the ventricles of the cardiac muscle. Lot of alcohol in the blood and a gall bladder full of stones. Nothing serious. Poor sod though, stuck worse than a pig."

It was to be expected, Pantieri thought miserably. They were marking the cards, as they always did when it suited them. De Fiore's escape had been rigged, too. Sure, Lucilla might have come forward as a witness, but even if she told the truth no one would believe her.

Suddenly a vigorous banging appeared to break the door down. It was Ciro De Fiore. Whether it was out of anger or jealousy or an excess of energy, he began hitting Pantieri. He struck him calmly, methodically, working on his face, stomach and ribs. He had been taught that the blows should land soft and muffled, that they should leave no marks on the face and he applied the lesson with the zeal of the boy at the top of the class. Pantieri considered defending himself, but he read a sly intention in his aggressor's look: if he gave a hint of resistance, De Fiore would kill him and then report that he had been forced to do so. With the blessings of Conti and the Minister of the Interior, his father, to boot. The son of a bitch wanted nothing better than an excuse to do him in, camouflaging the murder with a semblance of legality.

"This is crazy!" panted the victim. "What are you trying to prove?"

"I love that woman," said De Fiore sullenly and pointed to his wife. "She's mine. You're not fit for her."

"Let's talk about the Crux instead, or better still about the warrant for your arrest issued in Genoa."

"Don't know a thing about that, I don't. Not a thing."

"That's not true. Just as it's not true you escaped. They let you out. There's a difference. But you've got connections, you've got relations that count."

"What the fuck are you on about?" said De Fiore, withering him with a look that said if he heard another word on the subject he'd kill him without a second thought. "Bribed a copper, had my mates outside waiting, had all I needed. Even a Honda 750, a gem."

"I don't give a damn about your motorbikes. I want to know why they let you flit."

A silence like the grave. It was useless trying to insist. De Fiore wouldn't talk. Anyway, maybe he was a small-time thug, but he was still the illegitimate son of the Minister of the Interior: it was superfluous to ask him where his protection came from. But who could tell? Perhaps De Fiore wasn't playing a secondary role in this mysterious game. For a moment, Pantieri was tempted to fling the truth in his face quite brazenly, but the instinct of self-preservation told him to keep quiet. The secret about a certain blood relationship was worth more than the neck of a police inspector, as he had clearly read in the Calabrian's eyes. The din of a bulldozer on the building site next door butted in, another block was about to rise and it was obvious that, during the site clearance, the past, or what was left of it, was flying into smithereens.

"She's coming with me," said De Fiore brusquely.

"Where are you off to?" asked Pantieri dully. "They're looking for you . . . or aren't they anymore? Strange. You go about on a motorbike without a care in the world . . . Where do you want to go? Or rather, where do you have to go?"

De Fiore didn't reply. He darted a last hate-filled look at Pantieri, grabbed Mirella by the arm and dragged her off. They vanished down the stairs like two phantoms and, a second later, came the accursed roar of a motorcycle. How would Peter Ilych Tchaikovsky have reacted to the din of engines? He'd managed to bury himself in the countryside all his life. But then he'd been a spirit open to novelty. The Moog? Ah, Tchaikovsky would have gone mad for one! And then there he was, by the association of ideas, thinking about Lucilla Opitz and the sore she had shown off to him a few hours before. A trick, Lucilla had warned him, without any further explanation. Then he remembered about Raymond of Touraine. Who was the mysterious character hiding behind that name?

Politics, everything was politics. The right to work, to a career, to respectability, to success, even good health and the salvation of one's soul depended on belonging, as Lucilla had said. Besides, even the opposition, which for ages could do nothing but whinge, was shouting for a bigger stake in belonging: it was no longer capable of creating ideas, ideas that had nothing to do with repletion.

He went out. He had little time at his disposal, not that he had much idea of how to employ it anyway. The autopsy report following Gruvi's murder had been altered and this could only mean one thing: Conti meant to incriminate and have him arrested. Maybe the warrant for his arrest had already been issued. He had to escape, to hide . . . But they'd catch him very quickly and then it would be all the worse.

Passing in front of the porter's lodge, he rapped his knuckles on the doorpost. He didn't know when he'd be coming back and thought it wise to leave his keys. He knocked repeatedly, but Byron didn't reply. He looked inside but there was no one about. Only the morning and Byron already drunk? Unlikely. He leaned his weight on the door and to open it had to overcome the resistance of an inert body lying on the floor. It was the porter. Wrapped up in blankets and shawls, he lay on the streaming wet tiles among potato peelings and cigarette ends; his hands were clasped between his thighs, he was curled up, his teeth chattering; he was racked by fever.

"High fever," he stammered. "Very high . . . Ate too many rigatoni with *pagliata** . . . Nasty indigestion, I think."

"I'll get you a doctor," Pantieri said, and was about to bend over and help him find a better position when he was gripped by a feeling of revulsion. Horror, probably. He remembered the *Mastomys* drowned in the footbath and shuddered. Nonsense! Byron was a brute; he could easily have eaten ten-day-old *pagliata*. Before disappearing, Pantieri repeated: "I'll get you a doctor."

He kept his word. At the nearest tobacconist's he telephoned for an ambulance and then, feeling at ease with his conscience, he had an inspiration: he needed to find a safe place for the snapshot that contained the Minister of the Interior's secret. He bought an envelope and a stamp, writing his name on the envelope. But what address? Certainly not Via Monte Pelmo, which was as good as sending it to the Prosecutor's office. He put Biraghi's address in Lavinio, slipped the picture inside, stepped outside and posted it. The treasure that had fallen into his hands by chance was safe, at least for the moment.

* A heavy sauce made with calf's intestines, typically Roman . . . (Trans.)

FOUR

Where to now? To the Protomoteca, to hear Opitz's speech? Well, why not? Not that he could expect much light from that quarter, but Savings Day was attracting a crowd of top people; all those who pulled the strings were there, along with their puppets and – who could tell? – a string might break and some fleeting revelation might emerge. And, perhaps, as one anonymous celebrity among so many, the company might include the jeopardized Raymond of Touraine.

It began to rain again with a vengeance. The 124 wouldn't start, the distributor cap was wet through. Damn nuisance, but he couldn't wait. Ignoring the rain, he set off towards Via Nomentana and was lucky to catch a bus. It stopped every so often to pick up more people: housewives with their shopping bags, pensioners with too much to do, two Dominicans, and a teenage girl wrapped up in a black mac. Very romantic. Pantieri generally had little sympathy for the young; he found them an impudent tribe of ne'er-do-wells, who made a big fuss about yesterday's problems. But that girl was quite romantic. My goodness, women in macs out in the rain . . . there was something about them, some throwback to Carné films perhaps.

Mirella, who knows if . . . He'd just abandoned her, but her husband had reappeared and Ciro was a violent man. Yes, he'd like to be in love with Mirella or at least with some woman, a formal love, signed and sealed. But it was such an unlikely, such an absurd situation. A narrative woven by the imagination. In the end, every great love story grew in the shadow of impotence and premature ejaculations; perfect, athletic technique in the act of love was a myth of the age, it was humbug. It didn't tally with his recollection of brothels that Peter Ilych Tchaikovsky would have deplored. To love Mirella not as she was and for what she was not . . . Pantieri's heart was teeming with photographs, not one of them truly like the original, rather they were all tarted up, every one of them. Had he been a writer he would never have been able to create an authentic female character: maybe he was to blame, maybe women simply were elusive.

The hall of the Protomoteca was crowded. He found standing room at the back. He scrutinized those present: plenty of people in the public eye, plenty of personalities, many illustrious. The illustrious from the better families were crowded behind the chairman's table, more cheek by jowl than the disciples depicted in *The Last Supper*, elbowing each other to gain more space and thus more attention from the television cameras. One couldn't put a finger on the essential quality of these V.I.P.s; it was a question of gold teeth, rings on fingers, handkerchiefs in top pockets. Next to Opitz sat the Rt Hon. Lauro Croce Sabbioneta, and at one end of the table, sitting apart as if the others wanted to ostracize him, was the Minister of the Interior, Orazio La Calenda, rubbing his glasses with a small piece of chamois leather. Cardinal Meschia, seated in the front row, was holding up a placard with the words:

SAVE FOR WORLD FAMINE AID.

In a fluty voice, Opitz began his speech: "I have just returned from the bloodied fox-holes of the Carso. A lonely pilgrimage of meditation, and with no false modesty I confess in my heart I still feel emotion for those places sacred to our native land, where memories of ancient deeds spring up in the mind that consecrate the virtue of heroism to eternity. Let us honour the dead of the Carso!"

An embarrassed silence descended, for a very long time. A shabby old crone, whose provenance was uncertain and whose presence inexplicable, pulled a lot of faces and appeared about to throw up, but removed her dentures instead, which she placed carefully in her lap, opening her mouth wide in a flabby smile, red with mucous membranes.

Opitz continued: "Nor can I fail to mention another pilgrimage of mine, through the fertile vales of the Ossola, fecundated with the blood of those who opposed the barbarities of the Fascists. They died thinking of a different Italy, and with their sacrifice they permitted the rising generations to create free and democratic institutions. Let us honour the dead of Ossola!"

An even more embarrassed silence followed. The shabby old crone took off her shoes, doubtless because her feet hurt, while Cardinal Meschia waved his placard around three or four times with its slogan for the starving.

Opitz cleared his throat, took a sip of mineral water and plunged on: "Savings are, technically speaking, that part of income which is set aside, to be translated later into consumption or investment. Time-honoured experience teaches us that savings fuel the investments of borrowers, never of savers. We have refined instruments at our disposal to deprive savers of a return on their savings: inflation, fluctuating exchange rates, stock-market crises, tax on interest, capital-gains tax . . . Thus there's an overriding question: who the f . . . ?"

He was not able to finish. There was a shot and a poppy sprouted on his breast; for a very brief moment Opitz looked incredulous, his mouth open in a wan smile, then he opened his arms wide, waved them about with ever decreasing force, and fell heavily among the chairs. He mumbled softly: "I was going to tell the truth . . . I swear it . . . I was going to tell the truth about sav . . ."

A spout of blood cut the word off. He kicked once, then a second time, hitting Sabbioneta in the shin as he was bending over him, more out of curiosity than pity, then spat more blood and died.

A great pandemonium followed. Pantieri saw Lucilla Opitz cleaving through the crowd, making for her father's body, with Conti following close behind. Sabbioneta drew to one side with La Calenda; they were engaged in a heated discussion, with angry gestures and little sympathy. Cardinal Meschia knelt down and withdrew into prayer. But the majority of the crowd had a mind to clear off with the greatest rapidity possible, forgetting any social proprieties and making no attempt (despite the occasion) to economize on the use of elbows. The Carabinieri tried in vain to restore order. An unknown voice shouted out that potatoes were now at nine thousand lire the kilo, which announcement only increased the agitation and the anxiety to get out. The slatternly crone nobody knew was complaining that she had lost her dentures and some willing souls crawled under the seats to look for them. In the end they came to light, but had so suffered from the trampling feet of the fleeing public that they were flattened and would not go back into the old woman's mouth; she began to cry.

Pantieri reflected. He'd be better off disappearing; he had nothing to gain from being found at the scene of another murder. But then what? No, all things considered, it would be much better to face up to Conti and try to make a deal: the Prosecutor wanted an old snapshot from him and he was in a position to satisfy him. But perhaps it wasn't that simple. Conti had been Assunta's lover and harboured an ancient rancour towards him . . . It was difficult to make a decision. Amid such reflections, Pantieri had walked with little conviction towards the exit, but there was still quite a mob, so every step was very slow. It was then that he felt a hand on his shoulder.

"Pantieri, now what you up to?" came the wry query from the Prosecutor. "Trying to hook off? Seems hard to believe, but there only has to be a murder or any kind of slaughter, and you're on the scene. But then I should be pleased: I was going to introduce you to the daughter of the late lamented, but I see you two already know each other . . . High society! I had the pleasure two years ago, when there was a bit of trouble over a building licence. Now get this, Pantieri: the time's come for handcuffs – I'm having you arrested. I don't know if you shot the girl's father, but you've still got to answer for the killing of Dr Gruvi. Your position's pretty critical."

Lucilla Opitz, a little to one side, was softly crying. Cardinal Meschia went up to her and held her in a long, paternal embrace; he mumbled incomprehensible words of consolation, and brought up some reference to Baget Bozzo; his ulcerated hand touched the girl's hair with a hesitant caress. The hall was now cleared and the Carabinieri were losing no time: they were tracing outlines in chalk, taking photographs and fingerprints. Conti followed their movements out of the corner of his eye and sometimes made a gesture with his hand for them to get a move on.

The Minister of the Interior came up with a quizzical air. On his way towards the Prosecutor he bumped into Lucilla; he flinched, as though put out by this encounter, but in a fraction of a second he regained his composure and even mumbled some expression of condolence. Then he moved on and as soon as he reached Conti fixed him with a wordless look that was a demand for an explanation, all the while tapping his foot and polishing his glasses with the piece of chamois-leather.

"A classic case of *aberratio*," said the Prosecutor by way of excuse. "Article 82, paragraph 1 of the Penal Code."

"I didn't ask for a dogmatic clarification," croaked La Calenda. "There'll be plenty of time to go into all that *sub specie juris*. A shot's been fired at the speakers' table, do you read me? I could have been killed myself."

This eventually must have struck him as such a portent, such an enormity, that he stood there for a moment with his mouth open, visibly shaken by his own words. A world in which the life of a Minister of the Interior could be placed in jeopardy was indeed the jungle.

"I'm afraid the murderer's got away," mumbled Conti, crestfallen. "I imagine he was hiding the weapon in a raincoat or overcoat and was brass enough not to take off straightaway. He was counting on the confusion, the chaos and mayhem, and went off mingling with the crowd. I don't think anyone would have seen him, it wasn't difficult to take up a strategic position. 'Course, the police surgeon'll be able to establish the bullet's trajectory and generally indicate the point where the shot came from, but . . ."

"Fiddlesticks!" said La Calenda, cutting him short. "They won't find out a damn thing, the inefficiency of the police is almost proverbial. But I don't want this to be a case of inefficiency on the part of the subversives . . . do I make myself clear? Gracious heavens, when the forces of order and the terrorists are as inept as each other, what kind of future does a country have?"

"So you agree with the hypothesis of *aberratio*," said the Prosecutor, a little relieved. "You'd claim it was a case of mistaken target, too . . . That's fine, that bucks me up."

"It is only a surmise," said the Minister of the Interior, trying to spell it out by emphasizing each syllable, but as he arrived at the "mi" his voice played him a cruel joke and broke into a squeak, so the last syllable died away in a trembling bleat. He inhaled deeply, swallowed, took hold of himself, and went on: "I'm not at all convinced that the murderer meant to kill Sig. Opitz. We could be dealing with an error, the grossest error . . . That's unacceptable! I mean, such unsteadiness, such confusion is unacceptable . . . I think that the new law on civil rights and institutional reform will be passed."

He turned on his heels and went off without greeting anyone, while the Carabinieri hurtled off in his wake, completely forgetting their duties with regard to the body of the construction boss, Gerardo Opitz.

"Let's get out ourselves," Conti hissed to Pantieri. "But as far as you're concerned, that's only in a manner of speaking, because you're going out, but you're also going inside. I'm committing you to the Regina Coeli, Pantieri. And strictly between you and me, that makes me very happy."

The sky looked about to clear and the waters were ebbing, gurgling towards the drainholes, but round about, the houses, the monuments, the paving stones were all damp and sad, a premonition of winter, a mist of tears, a *lachrymae rerum*. A ray of orange sunlight thrust out through the clouds. It was a diseased sun. It disappeared, reappeared, playing at reflections among the ruins of Imperial fora and the balcony of the Palazzo Venezia. An ambulance parked nearby, in case of any non-lethal bloodshed, set off with its sirens blaring, and no one understood why.

★

In prison, Pantieri had an ample cell. With bitter irony he went over his arms, hands and legs in the useless search for a sore; but those sores were a trick. Perhaps the whole of reality was mere artifice, the result of a sleight of hand that involved everything and was the cause of all the bedlam. The door bolts groaned . . . , or screeched? Linguistic conventions veiled thought; they tempted one to judgement on the basis of false archetypes. The rattle of rusty locks was not of necessity the portent of misfortune, and in fact a warder put his face to the grill and asked politely: "Would you like the Vidal perfumed bath foam, Inspector?"

He refused with a shake of the head, then threw himself down on the bunk to think. He had done nothing but that since he had been locked up behind these walls and, for a little while at least, would have been glad to stop the inexorable flow of suppositions, second thoughts, plans, hopes and dreams that his brain transmitted to him like a non-stop telethon. If that couldn't be done, it would have been enough to remain tuned in to those potentially gratifying VHF waves (memories of childhood, commemorations of non-existent loves), but the presenter's voice kept on insisting on the trials he had yet to overcome. Trials he had yet to overcome occupied almost the whole space of Pantieri's life.

Then . . . and then? A light came on. My God, how could he have failed to grasp Conti's allusion immediately, which La Calenda himself had spelt out? The *aberratio* was an error of identity, of the victim's identity. The bullet fired in the Protomoteca had not been aimed at Opitz but . . . who had been sitting next to him? There was no doubt that the intended target had been Lauro Croce Sabbioneta. A logical conclusion which allowed answers to other questions. The person whose life was in danger was Sabbioneta, the person whom Gruvi had wanted to warn, if only someone hadn't silenced him. And as a precautionary measure Gruvi's old mum had been silenced too. 'Cleon V.I. Cercato' was the coded message from which the doctor, a passionate crossword puzzler, had deduced the sentence of death. But how? A cryptogram, a rebus, a palindrome, an anagram? It was no good racking his brains: the sequence of events confirmed that Gruvi had seen things correctly. Certainly, one then had to admit that the mysterious Raymond of Touraine, the head of the Crux, a sect of obscure aims and, in recent times, perverted ones, might be the incorruptible Sabbioneta, but the conjecture was not far-fetched.

He spent two days fretting away and during that time they remembered him only to feed him; it looked as if they had abandoned him, as if his life was destined to waste away in self-contemplation. On the third day the warder tossed him a newspaper and a comment: "Times are bad, Inspector! Folk are dying of 'flu in the streets. And that other poor sod . . . what's his name? Senzameta . . . Stabbioreca, . . . whatever, abducted, kidnapped, vanished. Happened while he was having a peaceful slash in the Stazione Termini loos. They killed the bodyguards, five Carabinieri, but they don't count . . . poor folk are just cannon fodder – don't we know it!"

There it was. The irreparable had happened and he hadn't been able to stop it. The reports didn't add much to the warder's bare recital. It had happened around two in the morning at the Stazione Termini. Sabbioneta was about to leave for Hamburg in a sleeper. Before boarding the train he had expressed the desire to withdraw to the conveniences. The bodyguard had waited outside, as the station was deserted, the only people present being the usual railway men, busy tapping carriage wheels and changing accumulators. An atmosphere of weariness, listlessness, sleep. A dense fog floated lazily between the platforms. Feeble lighting. No witnesses, or at least no eye-witnesses. A burst of machine-gun fire, only one, and the man responsible for the points on Platform 5 thought an engine had gone off the rails. An effort to understand, to co-ordinate, and draw inferences. The bodies of five Carabinieri piled one on top of the other; the youngest a lad of nineteen, from Basilicata, from the South, naturally.

The MP's attaché case had been thrown to the ground, open and cleaned out, the documents stolen. A piece of blue cashmere overcoat spoke of what could have been a ferocious struggle. Blood. Blood which streamed over the pavement and wrote the headlines for the next days's papers. Lauro Croce Sabbioneta evaporated, like an equivocal genie torn away for ever from his lamp.

FIVE

It happened one afternoon, after two weeks of inertia and expectation: there was a huge blast, and the walls and gratings of the Regina Coeli prison disappeared in a swirl of dust; in less than a minute that venerable Roman institution was nothing more than a heap of smoking ruins.

The following day the papers spoke of the acrid smell of cordite and the horrible carnage. They listed the dead and injured, reported that the chaplain was found naked but otherwise unhurt, described the self-denial of the warders who had taken off, scattering through the fields in the direction of Monteporzio, and mentioned the visit of the Minister of Justice, who had raised the morale of twenty-four survivors and a hundred thousand cubic metres of rubble.

Miraculously unharmed, Pantieri leaped from one pile of débris to the next, slid down fragmented staircases, ignoring the cries for help that gave life to the ruins, and, in a word, fled.

Being on the run excited him, it was an experience that gave him feelings he had never known before. Life was a boys' game, a game of cops and robbers, and by chance, by the merest chance, he had, up to now, been on the side of the pursuers. Finding himself in the role of pursued, he relished the taste of transgression.

He walked along the Tiber towards Piazza del Popolo. Although the traffic was light, he thought he could be recognized at every step, as if everyone knew about him. A Carabinieri jeep went past, and Pantieri's heart leaped into his mouth, but Appointed Authority ignored him just as it did any other passer-by. His anxiety began to ease, he was beginning to understand. There was no need to find a hideaway, because he was already hidden; an anonymous face among millions of anonymous faces; if he had the prudence not to attract attention, then no one would notice him. The metropolis was safer than a den; all he needed was to avoid the grand hotels and their red tape. Anyway, not far from the Stazione Termini there were refuges of inexpert swindlers and expert prostitutes, where they didn't quibble about filling in a registration card. Conti would have a job getting his hands on him again.

He went towards a news-stand that was black with newspaper headlines and, out of curiosity, peeked in. There would be nothing about the attack on the Regina Coeli as it was too soon for them to have digested the news. He fished in his pockets, but hadn't a lira. In prison they'd taken away his watch and everything he possessed. Even his shoelaces. Here was a real nuisance, to which he'd given no thought. Life without money or shoelaces had its problems. But at the moment he was consumed with anxiety to learn what else had been happening. He satisfied himself with a glance at *Il Messaggero* hung up for publicity and for the benefit of penniless readers.

He was thunderstruck by the front page publication of the photograph showing the Minister of the Interior, Orazio La Calenda, together with his illegitimate offspring Ciro De Fiore. So, the secret had been revealed, it was being clamorously publicized and brought to the attention of the humblest citizens: a Minister of the Republic, a powerful and feared man, was the father of a questionable character who lived on the fringes of the law and who, in all probability, was a murderer, and maintained obscure links with the world of terrorism. But how had this compromising picture come into the possession of the press? He remembered addressing it to himself, even if it was care of Biraghi at Lavinio, and posting the envelope before going on to the Protomoteca. Either the Post Office had committed an unprecedented impropriety (when was correspondence ever opened and stolen?) or else Biraghi had abused and tampered with . . . This second hypothesis was too disturbing for him to be able to formulate completely. A bystander with a feverish look pointed a finger at the revealing photograph

126

and said: "So what's the big deal? Even a two-year-old knows that it's the sins of the fathers get their sons in the shit, not the other way round."

"D'you think so?" asked Pantieri, perplexed. "But a public figure, with heavy responsibilities in the government, he shouldn't land up in such a . . . singular position . . . it's not normal. Anyway, a father's morally responsible for his children's behaviour."

"Come off it!" cried the man, indignantly. "That was true back in the days when Rome was blitzed and Pacelli was Pope, but now the basis of family life's been stood on its head. Now it's the kids who teach their parents what's what. Kids today are more mature, better educated, they're clued in. What can their poor parents do?"

But at the height of this peroration, the unknown bystander's teeth began to chatter, and although he was well motivated to continue the debate about parents and children, all that came from his mouth was a clatter of castanets. He rolled up his eyes and keeled over, scattering the pavement with his keys, wallet, pen and Bank of Sicily pocket diary which had evidently been crammed any old how into his baggy jacket. Pantieri lost no time in appropriating the wallet: a bad deed, for sure, but it was justified by his parlous condition, and anyway, he looked upon it as a forced loan, not an outright theft.

"I wouldn't shift that bloke too much, if I was you," said the newsagent slyly, leaning out of his kiosk. "He's the second one to hit the deck after reading *Il Messaggero*. They say it's the 'flu, and they've got it all under control, no cause for alarm. Could be . . . seems to me it's catching and if you pick it up, that's your problem."

"I'll go and fetch an ambulance!" Pantieri lied and fled away at the double.

As soon as he was safely away, he shot a glance at his booty: faded photographs, identity card in the name of Semenza, Beniamino, age 52, from Matera, a holy picture of S. Francesco of Paola, a parking ticket and fifty-four thousand lire. A fortune! He clambered onto a bus and migrated towards the more accommodating world around the Stazione Termini. The

127

muddy yellow light of a pestilential sunset filtered in through the windows; faces equally muddy and yellow inside the vehicle were discussing the La Calenda/De Fiore case and the 'flu epidemic. Everyone was agreed on two points: the sins of a son should not be visited on the father and antibiotics meant immortality.

Inspector Pantieri found refuge in a pensione dedicated to vice: he didn't sleep a wink all night. He was assailed by a swarm of ideas, and even more by his incapacity to establish any order in them. Yes, he'd escaped from Regina Coeli, by God, but his situation was more precarious than ever. He was no Philip Marlowe, still less a Lemmy Caution. And then it bothered him that La Calenda's secret had been fed to the world at large (why? how? and by whom?) and also that sickness was settling over the city like a marshy exhalation. He remembered the *Mastomys* drowned in the porter's footbath: perhaps there was a connection? The destinies of mice and men intersected at crucial moments. He lit a cigarette and went to the windows to examine the dawn: streaks of saffron and indigo, five or six airships up there cruising, spying on the population's sleep. What should he do? Transgress, and what you needed was imagination, inventiveness, the ability to make choices and decisions; it was the harder part.

He left the hotel, bought a bundle of newspapers, and went to ground in the station waiting-room. It was a safe place, safer than any other, an inexorable coming and going of passengers, no one would disturb him, apart from the nuisance of the many exploding announcements. But it was only voices exploding. The newspapers teemed with news. First of all, Ciro De Fiore had escaped to South America, and nothing more would ever be heard of him. Whether or not he was a reformed character, or even a redeemed one, it was certain that he had gone as far away as possible to build a new life. That left the matter of the Minister of the Interior, Orazio La Calenda. Should he perhaps resign? Should he abandon his place at the helm? Not at all, quite the opposite. After Sabbioneta's kidnapping, everyone, or almost everyone, was pressing him to head a new ministry of national security. Hordes of Calabrians were marching on the capital to attest their love for a man who had been sorely tried by fate. Come now! Only a barbaric or semi-barbaric society could charge a poor father with the degenerate actions of his son. And then, after a very rapid but exhaustive investigation, it was found that, at the end of the day, there was not a minister, MP, or senator who didn't have at least one terrorist or delinquent in the family. Terrorism had become a vice like tobacco, cards or women, an inescapable social disease. There wasn't a man in power, or even an ordinary citizen, who didn't have at least a brother-in-law who was implicated. Orazio La Calenda deserved to rise to greater responsibilities.

Nor was that all. From the prison in which his kidnappers were holding him, Lauro Croce Sabbioneta was issuing messages. By post, special courier, telegram, poster and dustbin . . . Glance at any scrap of paper and there was a ninety per cent probability it was a letter from Sabbioneta. What was embarrassing was that the public's conscience was growing accustomed to considering the statesman a martyr to the cause, even if it wasn't clear what the cause was; and the fact that the interested party was reluctant to resign himself to the role, that he insisted on having his say, preaching on a discordant note, was quite off key, it defied logic.

Sabbioneta sent word of grisly things: he had been tried by a revolutionary tribunal, he had been condemned to death and he had no intention of dying. The pretension of the man! Why this bee in his bonnet about saving his own skin at any cost? Because his fellow party members were all scoundrels. Because the political game was a load of crap. Because he couldn't wait to get back to fooling around with his stamp collection. Absolutely scandalous! If Sabbioneta had written such lunacies, then he'd been drugged, or coerced or ill-treated; he was certainly not himself any more. Furthermore, the price being asked to reprieve the prisoner was out of the question: the release of a clutch of terrorists awaiting trial.

A day full of anguish. Pantieri wandered haphazardly through a somewhat harassed, worried crowd; the concern, though, was no longer over political developments, because in fact every news item was received with the same general indifference accorded to a change in the railway timetable.

The people on the street were harassed for other reasons that lay even closer to the surface. The 'flu epidemic was assuming more threatening features and, furthermore, there were doubts as to whether it was a question of straightforward 'flu. After their usual silence and reticence, the newspapers were now displaying alarming and funereal headlines. People were dying from this illness. An isolation hospital had been set up at Lavinio, not far from the Convent of the Blessed Oblate Sisters of S. Daniela Crisci; there will have been some notion of profiting from the naïve fervour of the nuns. Word was circulating that all means of communication with the capital were about to be cut off. And if it was the plague? My God, an outbreak of plague! That would provide the perfect finishing touch to the aesthetic of the society that flowed from the Altar of the Fatherland.

It was getting dark and Pantieri hadn't eaten a bite. How long had he gone without eating? It was important to take nourishment because without it . . . Of course! The very thought of food made him feel sick and his neck was bothering him. An old lady wearing a veil gave a start: she was a step or two ahead of him and gave such a violent jerk she must have had her handbag snatched or her withered beauty subjected to assault. But neither was the case. Leaning against the wall, she began to vomit, and struggled in a vain effort to swallow back what her stomach was regurgitating, but only for a fraction of a second: her gaping mouth poured out an orange-coloured cascade, until a long bright red dribble soiled her patent-leather shoes. That dribble was blood.

"Ugh!" said a priest, passing by in a hat hirsute with fur and priestly dignity. "That's what happens when you stuff yourself!"

Pantieri turned the corner into Via Arenula. He was walking very quickly, almost as if he wanted to hide the guilt of an unperpetrated crime or avoid an undeserved nemesis; but all of a sudden a familiar voice called him, just a shade mockingly. It was Biraghi.

"Oh, it's you," said Pantieri, uncertain whether to be pleased or not over the encounter. But curiosity was stronger and he plied his friend with questions: "What about that photo of La Calenda and De Fiore? How did the press get its hands on it? And those rats? Those damned rats of yours?"

"Hold on, hold on," Biraghi smiled, and thrust two fingers netherwards; he had his own burden of affliction, to be rationalized after a different fashion. "Too many questions all at once. Much better if we sit down in a café and talk about it in an orderly fashion. Yes, I understand . . . you're a wanted man, but I've got my own problems. I read the accounts of your arrest and escape: the headlines were barely visible, you're nothing but an extra. Anyway, no one will take any notice of you in a bar, barley syrups and tamarinds are a catalyst for anonymity."

They took a pavement seat in a café on Via della Conciliazione. The sky was turning grey and dark streaks were forming; the clouds were unravelling, but it would have been vain to hope for the twinkle of a star. The air was muggy, tainted with death. A bat fluttered around a street-lamp. Coaches were going up towards St Peter's Square; other vehicles were following them. Shouts, curses, invocations re-echoed. An undercurrent of barbaric sounds, bells and trumpets began to spread. A roar ascended from a crowd in a ferment.

"That will be the Calabrians," Biraghi sighed. "They've rushed to give La Calenda a hand . . . As if he needed it! There'll be a vote of confidence for him tonight in Parliament and we'll have the new government of national security with a NON-DETERMINING CONTRARY ABSTENTION from the opposition parties. It's an abstruse formula I don't follow, but it seems the best practicable. There'll be an immediate vote on the new law on civil rights and institutional reform."

"It's important?"

"No. Nothing's important."

Beneath Bernini's colonnade, voices were seething, trying to hit upon chantable slogans, but they could give voice to nothing but atavistic rage and irritation. Some had set up a rather half-hearted refrain: "The son's a sinner, the father's a winner!" In the dark, they were lighting oil-lamps, torches and candles; the shadows were pierced by thousands of gleams that washed over slanted faces, seething with age-old vendettas.

"Would you like to explain . . . ?" said Pantieri, slowly.

"Certainly," Biraghi assented and signalled the waiter to bring him another ice-cream. "It's rather difficult to find the right words. Maybe I could put it this way: there came a point where I decided to join in the game myself."

"Do you mean to say you're a terrorist, something like that?"

"Please. The terminology is not without significance. A combatant. Let's say I've been a combatant . . ."

"And now you're not fighting any more?"

"Not any more," breathed the magistrate, savouring his pistachio ice-cream as if it were a semtex bomb. "I'm not a reformed character, nor do I wish to dissociate myself, nor am I a deserter. But I knew that I was about to be sucked into the system . . . the system that appropriates everything. Even terrorism and revolution and death. And I'm tired. For the record: the attack on the Discount and Savings Bank was my doing . . . well, my group's doing. As was the recent attack on the Regina Coeli; I didn't care to see you in prison."

"And the photo? Don't tell me you opened my letter . . ."

"Of course I opened your letter! What d'you think? . . . I'd been hunting after that snap for ages, I'd come to stay with you specifically to turn it up and I wasn't going to back off in the face of a trifle like confidential correspondence. And anyway, it all backfired on me! Don't you see? I counted on annihilating our Minister of the Interior, I thought he'd be deluged under a flood of indignant censure when I publicized the family tie between him and De Fiore. And all I've done is attract the popular approval he was perhaps lacking! I've paved the way for him! I've provoked a scandal and made his fortune!"

"How were you to know!"

"I'm guilty of an error of judgement," said Biraghi, shaking his head bitterly, "or rather an error of logic. I thought I could take transgression and turn it against society, but it was a silly idea, because transgression is precisely what society feeds on. I created more opportunities, more justifications and more alibis for the system! Alberto Arbasino's made an illuminating observation. He wrote that nowadays it's enough to spring out on the local milkman and bash his brains in to make you a revolutionary leader. Those aren't his exact words, but that's his idea. There's no misdeed that doesn't have its touch of dignity. Think about it: you'll realize that everyone who passes for an unexceptionable person has a secret life. He has a clandestine side that parallels his official side. And I've been inoculating bacilli into an organism that simply feeds off them."

"Talking of which," said Pantieri, stiffening, "I'm deeply disturbed by those *Mastomys* of yours . . . It appears that an ugly epidemic's broken out. I hope you can reassure me . . ."

"I'm afraid I can't," the magistrate admitted. "The *Mastomys* provokes a terrible disease, worse than the plague. One out of two die; it's called Lassa fever."

"Oh my God!" cried the inspector, in a strangled voice. In the face of an outrageous admission he was at a loss for words to express his indignation, and croaked: "A plague-spreader . . . an unspeakable plague-spreader . . ."

"In a way," agreed Biraghi, dropping his eyes, though his contrition was not untinged with pride. "But you see the *Mastomys* only represented a back-up, they escaped before the appointed time, before I'd taken a decision. Things went awry, well, almost. That storm and the cellar flooding . . . However, I'm glad things have panned out this way: I'd have released the rats myself at this point."

"You'd have released them?"

"Unquestionably. Society's got to be changed, and punished in some degree. But I've toyed with every act of aggression, and it's useless . . . I've told you, this society appropriates everything to itself. So I became convinced that it was necessary to fall back on a biblical scourge. A lot of people will die, it'll be a catastrophe."

"You're mad, completely mad . . ."

"I'm afraid so," Biraghi murmured after a slight pause, "but I don't think I'm any madder than the rest. I'm weary, there's nothing I want any more. And then someone in my group must have spilt the beans, I suppose. Now I'm in an almighty pickle, I've got a house full of guests, while I'm a misanthropist myself. And then they're meddlesome, dangerous guests, and I can't chuck them out. I can feel Dr Conti breathing down my neck. Great heavens! What a witchcraft trial he could set up! And if that wasn't enough, I've been struck by a philosophical reflection: it's impossible to live in a world without ideas, but the ideas are all wrong-headed. Must we make do with wrong-headed ideas? I've retired to Lavinio in order to find out the truth. I'm studying gynaecology, comparative law and Egyptian history. But I grow only more weary and discouraged. If only they'd leave me in peace . . . The only real solution has to be collective annihilation: with humanity annihilated we'd do away with the need for ideas, we'd do away with wrong-headedness. Cosmic homicide, instead of the cosmic suicide predicted by Edward von Hartmann."

The Adagio movement of Tchaikovsky's Sixth Symphony surfaced in Pantieri's heart like the sigh from a death-bed. My God, was there really any need for ideas? If they led to the lunacies of Biraghi, it was almost preferable to pin one's faith in a government built on a NON-DETERMINING CONTRARY ABSTENTION . . . Perhaps a world of feeling was better, a world of instincts decked out in gladrags.

"You know something," said Biraghi all of a sudden. "I know who killed Gruvi. I've discovered all that's happened and what's still going to happen. But then I've acquired a bit of a nose for intrigues and plots."

"Well, I wish you'd explain, the problem's crucial for me . . ."

"Too bad! I can't tell you a thing. Besides, you presume too much, the world does not revolve around you, you see. And as for me, I told you, I'm weary. I've bought a fabulous blue overcoat, a cashmere one . . . but so what! In reality, things happen to me I can't define. I'd like to go about on all fours like a dog, or I'd like to subvert the language. I've learned to abhor words, they're so old, so conventional, so ambiguous. I remember an idiot boy (the son of an alcoholic); his whole language was limited to a few sounds for expressing the basic necessities. Just look around you, look at these wretched Calabrians and their lights. If you were a writer instead of a police inspector, think how you'd be cobbling rhymes together to make it leap from the page: gleaming vermilion, saffron perihelion . . . That idiot boy used to say PLOP! and it was simpler and more beautiful. This unruly mob charging into St Peter's Square – it's pathetic, utterly pathetic! I was speaking about transgression and I forgot the saddest, silliest one of all; that of the poor sod that just gives him peanuts, and never really pays off. Anyway, I think we're chattering on to no purpose, and I can't stick around any longer. I have to be on my way. I'm sorry about the epidemic, but it was indispensable."

He leapt up suddenly, seemed about to lose his balance but bent forward and, imitating a dog's gait, he sped off, still bent double, and vanished into the night. In that instant the Calabrians found words to cement their hatred, and sang out in unison in response to the invitation of their cheer-leader; he was piercing them to the heart of their most sacred heritage, religiously handed down from father to son, inviolate and unvanquished for centuries.

"Up their arse!" the cheer-leader cried. "Up whose? Up mine? Up yours?"

"Up the government's arse!" roared the angry chorus.

They shrieked all night among their lamps, and when next day the radio announced that Orazio La Calenda had formed a government and that he hadn't got it up the arse, but was up theirs, they didn't understand. They left satisfied, eating their bread and salami, dreaming of woods, feuds and knife-attacks.

135

SIX

Next day the papers published what was taken to be the last message from the Rt Hon. Lauro Croce Sabbioneta, but even this extraordinary news was relegated to the inside pages, because the headlines were full of the epidemic. They were starting a count of the victims. Illustrious clinicians held forth on the nature of the illness. The smoothest pens rose to the challenge of writing descriptions of people collapsing, agonizing, decomposing. *La Repubblica* opted for an unknown form of highly contagious tetanus and ran the headline in block capitals: OPISTHOTONOS. This threatening word, which in itself was enough to arouse horror and dismay, was, however, followed by a question mark.

What to do? thought Pantieri. His head was still hurting him and his arms and legs were trembling with a fever. He began to wander around the city again. People seemed to have disappeared. Through the streets of Rome, down Via Sistina, along Via Condotti, usually so full of sweet, languorous life, where enchanted apparitions indulged themselves before the splendours of the shop windows (that made extravagance look so reassuringly innocent), and scarlet lips and nails re-enacted the sorcery of Circe, there was not a soul about. Everything had a diaphanous transparency. Under the trees of the Borghese Gardens there was only silence, a pitying and meditative silence in which the leaves were fluttering and the last flowers fading. Pantieri sat down a little out of breath by the edge of the ornamental lake, where once festive boatloads pursued well-fed swans with their cries (they knew nothing of Hans Andersen). The grey, leaden waters merged with the sky in a desolate horizon that was generous with solitude.

He didn't know why, but Croce Sabbioneta's last message came to mind, his spiritual testament composed several days earlier, when the condemned man had no further doubts about the inevitability of his sentence. Absurd, totally absurd. His preceding letters had already destroyed the myth of the man and gone beyond the bounds of decency, but this time the eminent statesman had discarded all shame. He wished a thousand plagues on his party colleagues, reaffirmed his visceral love for his stamp collection, asserted that human life had no purpose but ingestion, digestion, defecation and, every once in a while, copulation, and ended by stating that the thought of imminent death left him annihilated and confessed that he was "shitting himself with fear". These were his precise terms, penned with a schoolboy's realism, free of any concern about the image he would be leaving for posterity.

Sabbioneta's swansong . . . Unbelievable. Certainly his horror of death was plausible, it was only human and yet . . . when dying lost its place in the scheme of things, living also lost its place. It was at this moment that Inspector Pantieri slipped or perhaps passed out and slipped: he plummeted right into the lake and was drawn away from the shore by an invisible current. He lost no time in coming to his senses, and realized that he had to swim, but the discovery didn't surprise him; the space between being and non-being was filled with amniotic fluid; staying afloat was *de rigueur* for any person required to make a choice between the two.

The water was murky. An unlucky or peeved flower-seller had thrown her withered bouquets into it and now decomposing chrysanthemums were surfacing like seaweed. Every few seconds Pantieri found a rotting flower-head glued to his lips and brushed it away with a weary gesture; but more lumps of putrefied petals came up and he was enveloped in a sweetish smell of ether and iodine. The stink of a hospital ward.

"You're a new boy," observed Signorina Candiani, very clearly. It was a statement of fact, and also a condemnation. Forty eyes from the children at the other desks feasted on him, and he knew they would laugh at him. A show of hatred towards an outsider was a way of stating their own partiality for the teacher; every creature not forming part of their microcosm was edged aside, humiliated by their indifference and derision.

"And what a strange idea," she went on, "bringing me chrysanthemums! They're flowers for the dead. Perhaps you wish that I were dead? Or did you bring them in the hope of worming your way into my good books? Well now, you see, I'm going to take your nice little bunch of flowers and throw them in the waste bin! You're a new boy, so don't go getting wrong ideas, it's not something you can wipe out with a bunch of flowers."

I want to cry, but it's not dignified, thought Pantieri, and then she'll think I'm tiresome.

"I hope you're not going to start crying," she said harshly. "You're new here, you don't know my way of doing things. I won't tolerate cry-babies. If you start crying, then I shall laugh and all the other children will laugh with me."

Bursts of laughter showered on him from the desks, a collective, automatic hilarity; a conditioned reflex, whose reward was a wicked smile that lit up the dusty dais for a brief instant.

Some mud came surging into his mouth; he coughed and spat, but didn't tarry over the matter, he was too busy trying to ward off the rotting heads of chrysanthemums. If only the petals would break off and float away . . . then he would swim in a stream of them, and if he wanted to cry, no one would stop him.

Now Signorina Candiani was musing. It was a long and involved cogitation, as her index finger was stuck up her nose, excavating snot, encrustations and thoughts. She amalgamated the treasure she had captured using the pressure and rolling movement of excavating index finger and thumb, forming a round green ball of mucus, and flicked it in his direction. A shudder of disgust. He'd have done better to have remained impassive, but he hadn't been able to stop himself.

"Does it revolt you?" she asked, tetchily. "What else do you think life is made of? Snot, vomit, spittle, sweat and urine: those are life's raw materials!"

"There's also 'poo'," the top of the class chimed in.

"Shut up, you," Signorina Candiani scolded him jovially. "There's no need to be vulgar."

Ingestion, digestion, defecation . . . Signorina Candiani and Lauro Croce Sabbioneta saw eye to eye. He went back in his mind, enumerating snot, vomit, spittle, sweat, the top of the class's 'poo', dead chrysanthemums . . . then the great Adagio of Tchaikovsky's Sixth Symphony invaded his thoughts; the wing of a requiem that was spreading out and by some alchemy plucked from the filthy crucible the suspicion of a different way of being mortal.

"Hey, there's someone drowning!" a distant voice shouted.

"Oh, yeah?" replied another voice, sceptical. "Drowning in whisky."

"Yeah, fathead!" the first voice bawled, "the poor twat's really drowning, can't you see?"

But Inspector Pantieri couldn't hear any more.

Very little was known about Lassa fever. In the first place, it was difficult to recognize. In fact, for some people it was a recrudescence in an insidious form of Asian 'flu from Hong Kong, but with ugly pulmonary complications; while for others it was the return of the notorious Spanish 'flu (nearest relative to the so-called swine fever virus, HswN1), which claimed twenty million victims at the end of the First World War and remained embedded in the memory of the late construction boss, Gerardo Opitz.

As soon as the true nature of the disease was discovered, a tropical fever unknown in the Western world, the sense of doom increased. The calamities of Africa were the prerogative of its coloured populations; if one of those calamities had now shifted to a Western country, then something in the mechanism of natural law or divine justice had jammed. Lassa fever was highly contagious and, according to the statistics, the mortality rate was fifty per cent. It had been diagnosed for the first time in 1969 in three missionary nuns, who were taken ill with it in Lassa, Nigeria. One of the three died, followed by Dr Jordi Carols, who was treating her, and then by the virologist who had undertaken the laboratory tests. Here at last was a virus which preferred medical personnel! The aetiological agent came from the Arena-virus family and was transmitted by an innocent little rat, the *Mastomys natalensis*. Antibiotics were of no use, neither were other pharmaceuticals (only cortisone allayed some of the more serious symptoms); the search for a vaccine had its attendant problems associated with the high risk-factor of the cultures; in London, in fact, another virologist had died, after being over-lavish or too incautious. In 1974, the transportation of a sick clergyman, the Rev. Bernard Mandrella, had required severer precautions than those taken in the handling of radioactive material.

The fever's course was rapid and spectacular. In delirium the patient was shaken by tremors and convulsions, not unlike a person suffering an epileptic fit. If the patient was not intubated at once, suffocation would occur. The neck glands swelled and tumescence was such that the neck itself became a hard, misshapen mass of inflammation, marked by nodules and hematomas. It buried the lower half of the head and the mouth, which was already dry with fever, looked similar to a distorted fissure which contracted in a series of grimaces and, in between the lymph glands that were enlarged and hard as wood, fished about in search of air.

After searching for relief on the outside, the dilated and thickened tissues then started to exert pressure on the trachea, which became blocked full of catarrh. From that moment, suffocation began, and the only hope, as we have said, was intubation. If this didn't happen, the patient stopped kicking, instinct warning him to conserve his energies for a greater ordeal: that of extracting a breath of air, despite having an occluded trachea. Suffering the last throes, the patient started to sink; his viscera were by now in a state of advanced putrefaction and, rolling up the eyes, he would emit a rattle, until breath, mucus and agony were fused into a single raucous cry of stupor. It was then that death occurred.

During the first few days, the spread of the epidemic was alarming: many cases, many deaths, few recoveries. The health services, logically enough, failed to rise to the occasion, even though instances of corruption multiplied and a small bribe was needed even to gain access to the communal grave. The isolation hospital and the general ones were overflowing, the burial of the dead was held up, often without the necessary precautions being taken, and quarantines were not respected. Nevertheless, the Blessed Oblate Sisters of S. Daniela Crisci, who had assumed the task of aiding the nurses, worked with heroic devotion. By the end of the eleventh day, 26,000 deaths had been counted, of which 6,800 in the previous twenty-four hours. Things were growing steadily worse.

What happened, then? Someone spoke of a miracle, but it is more correct to seek an answer from science. On the twelfth day, the graph-curve of fatalities dropped away sharply, and the daily death-toll gradually declined to a couple of dozen, then just about tailed off altogether. In a few months, the cycle was over; nevertheless, every autumn, Lassa fever returned, but in a limited number of cases and for the most part in a benign form. An atrocious epidemic disease had turned into an everyday endemic one, as had already happened with cholera in the south. Engulfed by phagocytes, absorbed by the environment and hence disarmed.

It's difficult to make sense of this change, even more so in that it happened so suddenly. The isolation of a vaccine, and the programme of mass immunization played their part, although there were gaps. The immunity gained by those who had recovered had a little significance as well. But apart from these obvious considerations, science was forced to admit that, by some mysterious genetic factor, the Italian people were able to produce antibodies capable of neutralizing the Lassa fever virus. This conclusion raised many questions, and the medical journals pullulated with learned articles. The question, in fact, remains open.

At the end of the year, it was established that deaths from Lassa fever barely outstripped those from a virulent Hong Kong 'flu strain. The statistic induced the health services to take credit beyond their entitlement.

The transition from the disease's acute phase to its benign one was marked clearly by a very violent storm which descended on

Rome after the showers and cloudbursts of preceding days. For a whole night the sky was furrowed by flashes of lightning, while thunderclaps exploded above the rooftops like bombs or else rumbled in the distance with the pretence that they were moving away. Hail machine-gunned down on rooftiles, then the rain rattled down in bursts, its rage inexhaustible. Wind and water swept up a Carabiniere patrol and rolled it into the Tiber, where the current swallowed it up. A few night-birds met the same fate. The sewers were overflowing and the river was bursting its banks, flooding the streets. It was like the end of the world and the sick were forgotten. But the following morning, the sun shone luxuriantly down on the capital; on its gardens, on the Ghetto, on the Talenti district, on the warrens of Via Serpentara and, naturally, on Piazza Navona. Half the city was flooded. The houses seemed to be floating in a swamp; the yellow, muddy waters gave no sign of receding, but sat there and with a gurgle returned what they had swept up. More epidemics were feared.

Instead, Rome was able to breathe in that fecal miasma and, for no obvious reason, found it to be quite a tonic. The floods lasted two or three days, no corpses came to light and people spoke of bodies assumed into heaven. But the more sceptical thought it was the sea's greedy suction.

A Fiumicino fisherman recounted having seen a column of rats several kilometres long, endless so far as he could see, throw itself squealing into the sea and make off southwards, swimming with a desperate energy, to regions that were less tough on them and more hospitable. But no one believed him.

Rome recovered its normal aspect of languid indifference, and nobody noticed. People avoided talking about the epidemic, and if anyone persisted with the topic, it was devalued with little falsehoods, the most brazen being that there had been a spot of measles at the Magliana and a few children had died. People said "children" because, given their natural spontaneity, any lapse of taste could be forgiven in them.

The last victim of the malignant fever was the Health Minister; as soon as he had been warned about the gravity of the danger he had barricaded himself in his house, communicating only via the telephone and even that way with reluctance. What proved fatal to him was a chink in the window he had opened the better to look over the drowned city; it was rightly given out that he had been taken ill while helping the sick. A tablet was dedicated to him with pretty citations including Aesculapius.

Lastly, the isolation hospital restored high society to Lavinio. This unhappy and neglected town had enjoyed fame immediately after the war; cellulitic mothers burdened with babies went there on holiday for a therapy of baths in the sun, the sand and the sea; in other words, ablutions that didn't rise above the knee. Their vacation found its necessary finishing touches in rigatoni, roast lamb, strawberry ices, sessions of canasta, swarms of snake-haired and spastic aunts, and devotion to De Gasperi. Lymphatic kids passed the threshold of seventy kilos; they caracolled on flat feet, entrusting their wobble of jelly to the rays of the sun. Everything was health. Then the mothers were driven out by the building speculators and the dust, especially the latter; a cloud of it had sprinkled Lavinio and the holiday villas that had sprung up, which were already disintegrating and falling down. For ever. In the dust ladies of the tawdry Suburra, half-witted kids, pimps on a hiding to nothing, thieves and kidnappers had made a permanent settlement. Oily waves washed ashore seaweed and general decomposition. The seaweed was seen to diminish daily: it was the last of a botanical species condemned to extinction.

The isolation hospital, later transformed into an orphanage, brought a breath of fresh air to the languishing area. The people who mattered (and also those who, even if they didn't matter, tried to act with style; the commonest genus of Roman fauna) transferred the rite of the aperitif to the shadow of that place of suffering. The rich, real and feigned, soon disappeared, but after them came the crowds. Then an amusement park was opened (it outdid the nearest rival for noise) and cafés, trattorias, and gimcrack shops mushroomed. The inauguration was graced by the presence of five professors of semiotics and the sociologist Alberoni. A clandestine casino also opened its doors, about as hush-hush as contraband cigarettes in Naples. Lavinio sparkled with fairy-lights which were just as soon dimmed by the implacable minuet of the age-old dust.

ACT III

ONE

A rubber snake, very long and thin, was hanging from the wall, sliding down towards him; it bit him on the inside of his arm, but Pantieri felt no pain. It was clinging on to him, but he had no power to react, let alone decipher the meaning of the scene centred around him. A hospital ward, probably. Subdued lighting and muffled sounds. Now a needle was being inserted in an arm and someone was cursing at the drip that was running too fast. Other voices were cursing the ESR and others the leucocytes. Nothing was good for anything, certainly not for the histrionic needs of medicine. You'd better pray, my love. It had been a woman's jesting whisper. Better get out, drop down into depths in which an end might be discovered. He descended by a weightless lift in a magenta trail of invocations.

When he woke up, he was well. Weak and groggy, but well. Now convalescence awaited him. For how long? The doctors weren't sure, it depended how the epidemic developed, on the experiments they were now conducting, on preventative measures, the phases of the moon, the will of God. But never mind: he was alive and, as a fugitive, he'd find the isolation hospital just what was needed. In the middle of the crowd, that was still the secret.

Semolina, veal escalopes and tablets. The hospital organization occasionally left something to be desired: they'd serve up a double ration of escalopes in place of the pills, or a double ration of pills in place of the escalopes (the really irritating error, this), but little by little life picked up again. True, one patient had died of starvation, another had died of poison, but in all the hurly-burly the odd human error could be forgiven.

Anyway, life had become cheap; death was less to be deplored, more to be stoically accepted, especially when it was others who were doing the dying.

He was cured, technically and also bureaucratically. Without any burdensome formalities he was discharged from the isolation hospital, giving false particulars and no one bothered to check his identification or pursue enquiries; these were not times for splitting hairs. He thought he'd go back home to Rome, an act carrying a minimal risk as it wasn't very likely that it was still under surveillance. They'd surely given him up for dead or assumed he was hiding in the underworld, and wouldn't waste men to stake out a house which they supposed he'd stay clear of. Sort out ideas: reflect, decide and then move swiftly. Go to the heart of the problem, without getting sidetracked.

A cold morning. You couldn't catch a sound, only the whispering caress of tyres over the asphalt. But the traffic was sparse; a few cars passing and one or two trucks with their freight of frozen meat, exhaustion and risqué window-stickers. Then there was an immense juggernaut, slipping by red as flame against the saffron sky, vaunting a trademark along its length. A shadow prevented Pantieri from reading it, but suddenly the speeding sign rose into view, tossed up on high, and it was stated that PEZZUTTI'S THE GORGONZOLA EVERYONE LIKES! A revelation which lasted but a flash. The cheesy epigraph, the sky's ochre and the crimson lorry became fused together in one single glow, then the road and even the landscape with them. After a stormless thunderclap a vague zone of smoke was left behind, a backwash of cosmic nothingness among the fallow fields and tumbledown farmhouses.

"Another bomb!" cried a pensioner angrily. "Made mincemeat of that place . . . Because it's as I say, you know, they plant that explosive, they don't do it by any old chance. When someone's made the target, it's never a surprise. And if they know, why don't they stay at home? It's the last thing you do, driving a lorry around, putting folk at risk!"

"It'll be for the scandal about that poisoned gorgonzola,"

a housewife commented. "A little boy died last month in Maccarese, after he'd been taken ill eating that rubbish."

"They've no social conscience," pursued the pensioner. "Stone me, now the road's up and I bet the bus for Rome won't get away before this evening."

Too right! The bus wouldn't get off before the evening anyway because of a lightning protest-strike. People were rushing up, a disorderly start was made to clear up the debris, curses and entreaties were flying; but of all the terrorists, the gorgonzola was the guiltiest. What's more, the price of potatoes had reached fourteen thousand lire a kilo and this would seem to justify gestures of protest, however excessive, however short on logic. In any case, getting back to Rome was now a problem.

And how! Inspector Pantieri wandered about Lavinio among the crowds and, as dusk was falling, ventured into the amusement park; he felt safer than ever among the noise and bustle, the light-hearted frolicking and the excitement of everything a-twinkle. He was sucked in among the aimless throng and let himself be carried hither and thither; he wavered between little shops that sold everything, roguish, questionable cafés and minute cinemas that were more than a little saucy. He was dazed, and thus ran slap into a tall, gnarled and somewhat masculine nun who was casting a critical eye over a display envelope packed with stamps. A chance flush of philately at a cut price. There was a fair number of nuns about, not surprisingly: the Oblate Sisters of S. Daniela Crisci had rushed into the breach – nuns sprang up spontaneously wherever there was infirmity, with its attendant bedpans, syringes and enemas. Like mushrooms in the woods after rain. Most of them were robust, arrogant and tyrannical.

"I'm sorry, Sister," Pantieri excused himself, "I didn't mean to bang into you."

"Huh!" snorted the nun, angrily, and vanished into the crowd.

How rude, thought Pantieri, abashed. But his attention was immediately distracted by the tight-fitting rotundity of a pair of faded jeans. Those curves were not unfamiliar to him. She was bent over the same window which had tempted the gnarled sister to her swift and tetchy contemplation. But this girl was in no hurry as with sinuous wriggles she'd stand on one foot and caress the air with the other, dallying thoughtfully among turquoise rings and coiling bracelets. Her hand would reach up to brush the hair out of her eyes; the neon's golden pallor glowed around her like a halo. Signorina Candiani had warned him about the soul's immortality, but the body's rotundity was more apparent.

"Mirella," said Pantieri, and she turned round with a jump of recognition, pleased to see him.

"I never thought I'd bump into you here," she said. "I knew they'd put you inside, then they blew up the Regina Coeli and the epidemic . . . Did you catch Lassa fever, too? They let me out this morning and I was just strolling about. There was some problem about getting back to Rome."

"To De Fiore's house? There's been a certain amount of commotion about that husband of yours."

"I didn't know a thing about it. I underestimated Ciro. All that's happened must have led you to harbour some nasty suspicions about me, but I've never deceived you."

"Do you mean to say you never knew you'd married a terrorist? Nor that he was the son of a Minister?"

"I didn't know, far from it, I swear."

Oh my God! But if she swore to it, there wasn't any problem, that must be the truth, and nothing but. The occasion deserved solemnizing with a dry martini. The bar-trattoria was some distance away, facing the sea: it was no different from the joints that adorned the streets of Rome, with the same rhetoric intent on celebrating the authenticity of the cuisine, even if it relied on supermarket mayonnaise. A cartwheel, glowing with lights, hung from the ceiling; the walls dripped with salami, provolone cheeses, red peppers and garlic, while the ramshackle tables offered a tart's smile in red and white check. It was remarkable, but in a few days Lavinio had assumed all the appearance of Rome, though its stigmata were harsher, its winks more wanton. The sea and the night washed against the shore, which curved back on itself in a horseshoe. From one extremity an exhalation of lighter shadow rose, a milky cloud of dust that wasted away with the height. The incinerator.

"It's difficult to believe you," Pantieri sighed, passing a hand through his hair. "But, you see, I remember Papasidero . . . And then I had an intuition: innocence is forbidden, it attracts punishment. If you were implicated as well . . ."

"I'm not," said Mirella, lighting a cigarette. "Of course, I'm not stupid. After my husband dragged me off from your place, I did hear things. Snatches of conversation. Not much, but as I say, I'm not stupid. For example, the poignard was stolen by your porter: the door was always open and he came and went as he pleased. Then Conti let me go, as long as I could keep out of sight. There was some understanding between him and Ciro, a project. Then they said Ciro had escaped to South America. Conti kicked up a hell of a row, wanted to know the people I knew . . . who I mixed with. You follow, I suppose?"

"And you?"

"I kept quiet. I couldn't tell him that Sabbioneta . . . Oh, damn! Well, now I've gone and said it."

"You knew Sabbioneta?" said Pantieri, emphasizing every word to make sure he had understood. "But he's known for being a saint . . . or almost a saint, a kind of national monument to public and private virtues."

"I don't know anything about the public virtues," Mirella quipped, "but as for the private . . . Oh, I don't know how to put it! He was depraved. I saw him once a month, more or less. There was a devil gnawing away inside him."

"How revolting," moralized Pantieri, but he felt a secret excitement that surprised him and flung him into a small chasm of uncertainty.

Well, not all that small a chasm. To start panting for a woman like this one, a woman who'd really lived her kind of life, well, it was obvious Signorina Candiani wouldn't have approved, but neither would the people who were equally critical of gorgonzola hauliers and of those who did them in. And that was wrong. Mirella's observation about Sabbioneta, that there was a devil gnawing away inside him, was true for everyone, and nowhere was it laid down in sacred fashion that you had to spend your life exorcizing evil. Quite the opposite, it was welcome. The great love affairs had absolutely no connection with Paradise; if anything, with Hell . . . they always ended among sulphureous vapours, unless a weary, desperate piety took over.

"I met that girl with a limp," said Mirella, out of the blue.

"Girl with a limp? You mean Gerardo Opitz's daughter? How come you know her?"

"Oh, come off it! She was Gruvi's lover, everybody knows that. I met her two or three times, at his house. But we weren't on the same wavelength. She was mad about telepathy and spiritualism. Not my scene. We can find her at the casino."

"Rien ne va plus!" a distant voice shouted. A wall of disembodied heads intruded among the tide of smoke, whisky, bejewelled cleavages and nothingness. Something circled in the depths of the firmament, a minor star, a clove of garlic or an ivory bead; it journeyed with the speed of light, fell into the dish of the roulette wheel, jolted, pirouetted, rolled, then got itself into the heart of number 32. Thirty-two, roared the disembodied heads. That's the seventh time this evening. If that isn't sorcery . . . If only I'd covered the pair! The other comments were drowned in the throng.

It was a matter of getting used to the filter that was bathing the casino in a green light, and the heads recovered their bodies. A school of batrachians, its monotone hedge punctuated at intervals by rounded buttocks, glittering and enticing. Pantieri reproached himself irritably for the attention he was dedicating to those punctuation marks, but the more tenacious passions were the less avowable. With an effort of the will, he set aside his forbidden cogitations and began investigating the faces in the crowd. Green faces of Pythagoreans, scored by numbers or rounder than a zero.

That was odd: just to the right of the croupier sat the gnarled and faintly masculine nun whom he'd just bumped into; she was erect and stiff, with a rosary in her hands. Her eyes were circling with the ball.

"What's a nun doing in a place like this?" Pantieri asked Mirella.

"Praying for our souls!" Mirella joked. "It'll be one of Cardinal Meschia's brainstorms, he's scandalized by what's happening to Lavinio. She's a chilling presence, that valkyrie."

An aristocratic lady materialized out of the crowd; she was short, fat and bloated, and was taking no notice whatever of the game. Her penetrating eyes searched about and eventually fastened on Pantieri; he felt she'd snapped his picture, and quailed. Alright, so he was on the run, but the inquisitive look of the aristocratic lady, whom Pantieri mentally baptized "Marchesa Palla", had served to satisfy her curiosity and nothing more . . . He'd better not start over-reacting.

"You here as well, Inspector?" The dumb question belonged to a melodious voice. Not Lucilla Opitz's style, but it was her nevertheless. Pity she was lame. Pantieri's attention came to rest on her neck: smooth, white and slender. The comparison with Modigliani's necks was perhaps banal, but then what did Modigliani see in necks? It was useless trying to guess at an artist's motivations; better to content oneself with a periodical glimpse of a beautiful top storey and avoid the degrading lure of the nether regions.

"I'm worried," Lucilla went on, without giving him time to reply. "It's lucky I met you, I need some advice, or help."

"Is it a private matter?" Mirella butted in without a greeting. Her tone was sarcastic.

"Maybe," said Lucilla, uncomfortably. "But I'll not take up more than a quarter of an hour of the Inspector's time."

"Take your time," enunciated Mirella dryly, and vanished into the crowd.

"I hope she's sore," Lucilla said. "She's detestable, like all women who aren't crippled. Do we have to talk here? Wouldn't it be better to go to one side?"

"Better to go to one side," agreed Pantieri. "There's too much of a shindig here. Okay, so what's the gist? You start: I've got a pile of questions afterwards for you."

"Alright," Lucilla smiled, and made a move towards the exit. "First of all, I've identified the stuff that was used to poison Gruvi. Amanitine. I'm sure of it now. All you have to do is make an infusion of some pernicious toadstool for a few days and you'll derive a fatal decoction. Easy, anyone could do it. But there's worse. Incredible, you're not going to believe it! I've just met . . ."

She wasn't able to go on. The hand of the masculine nun had seized her dress and pulled her back. Pantieri thought it was an attack, but was reassured seeing the two confabulating. An indecipherable whispering, but it was clear that the nun was asking her a favour. Lucilla sat down in her place, while the nun went away giving thanks with exaggerated nods of the head.

"She's asked me to keep her seat for a minute," Lucilla explained to Pantieri who had drawn close. "She had some bursting business, had to run off to relieve it. Frailty of the flesh."

The ball darted round another turn and was already vacillating in search of a number, then suddenly, clack! the sound of the mains switch and night tumbled in from the window, blackening everything under an equal wash of ink. "Oh!" exclaimed the gamblers. The lights had failed. "Could be a power failure," someone observed, and many people said what a bind it was when technology went on the blink. The inky blackness began to fade, then quiver with a green phosphorescence coming down from outer space; distant gleams slid by dragging a swarm of sparks in their wake, shaking out golden comets' tresses. "Night's not so bad, you know," a voice remarked. "It's enough to take your breath away," replied Lucilla. It was in that moment the woodcutter let his axe fly; thwack! everyone heard it, but where? It had been very close and Lucilla had taken fright, letting out a gasp. "What on earth's going on here?" the earlier voice bawled. "Clack!" went the mains switch a second time and back came the lights. "Ah!" sighed the gamblers with relief, but the Marchesa Palla pointed to Lucilla and cried hysterically: "That girl hasn't got a head any more!"

It was true. Lucilla was sitting primly, hands in her lap, feet together, but she was rigid and without expression, necessarily.

Her snow-white neck had been neatly struck through and where the head used to be a circular wound had appeared; a steaming, pulsating beefsteak of cartilage, glands and arteries, not even bleeding all that profusely. All eyes focused upon the petrified body which, after allowing itself to be admired, tottered and fell to the ground in a spatter of cinnabar red. "She's ruined my dress!" protested an elderly lady. "The dry cleaner's can sort that out, now let's see where the head's got to!" exhorted the "power-failure" man authoritatively. But there was no need to look. Lucilla's severed head was resting on the roulette table like a sculpture of extraordinary, though bloodcurdling, naturalism; her eyes were popping out of their sockets and the tongue hanging out. A symbolic detail: its tip held the ball on the zero.

"Merciful Heaven!" invoked a character in red overalls appearing suddenly at the door. It was Cardinal Meschia who, with his hands clasped together, was murmuring a prayer. Perhaps he murmured more than one, because he seemed to take a very long time about it. He had come from a pastoral visit to the Convent of the Blessed Oblate Sisters of S. Daniela Crisci and was making a tour of Lavinio, bringing his blessing to those who wanted it and still more to those who didn't. He thrust out his arms and inveighed: "Headhunters! Cannibals! Have we come to this?"

Each time there was a crime, Pantieri couldn't help but notice that Cardinal Meschia was present. He opted for retreat, not wanting to be recognized, placing a barrier of stunned people between the prelate and himself. A hand touched him on the arm and Mirella whispered: "Hadn't we better beat it?"

"Sure, but let's wait a minute and see what happens."

Nothing happened, at least not there and then. There was consternation, indignation and desperation; while the Cardinal was waiting for a reply to his invective, the air was dark with suspicion, because everyone was thinking that, when it came down to it, the executioner could have been the person right next to them. Anyway, switching the lights off had not been by chance nor had the blow been struck fortuitously; Lucilla Opitz had been a chosen, not an accidental, victim, even if the crime's motive remained a mystery. Mystery? Well, perhaps not. Perhaps it was as clear as the sum of a simple addition, only he didn't know what figures were involved. Giving a face to them, then adding them up, that's where the enigma lay.

"I am waiting for an explanation," Cardinal Meschia spelled out. "You decapitate a girl and feel no need to justify yourselves? Divine goodness is infinite, that's true, but let's not overdo it!"

"We didn't do it," the Marchesa Palla blurted out, making herself spokeswoman. "The lights went out and we heard a great blow in the dark; when the current came back, we found the poor thing had lost her head."

"Is that so? And who could have committed this bloody deed, if not one of you?"

"It could have been anyone passing through," she mumbled, with little conviction. "A sadist . . . a madman . . . a drop-out . . . someone who wormed his way in, then slipped off in the dark, if you follow me."

"In other words, it could have been me?"

"Not possibly, Your Eminence," the Marchesa muttered dutifully. "I think it would be suitable to call the police, they're people used to these matters, they do it all the time. What I mean is, they know how to pick up the pieces . . ."

"The police! That's just the way we shirk our office of piety, and our duty as Christians. Before anything else, take that poor head off the roulette table; it's already been sullied enough. Every year there are millions of children dying of starvation and you play at roulette! Abysmal! How were the numbers falling tonight? Any not showing up?"

"The 4," replied 'power-failure' promptly. "Haven't seen it for two weeks. While this evening the 32's come up seven times."

"System player?"

"Rough and ready."

"Well, at all events," said the prelate, cutting him off, "get that head off the baize. It is not an acceptable sight. Get a basket, do things according to the rules."

"To tell the truth," 'power-failure' dared to object, "we

shouldn't touch anything before the police arrive. That's what it says in all the whodunnit novels. I don't want to be accused afterwards of tampering with the evidence. You know how it is, Your Eminence. They come along, look at everything under the microscope, find a hair, a cigarette-end with lipstick on it and a nutshell. They go by induction and deduction, they investigate, interrogate and auscultate and bang! they nail the culprit."

"Bang my foot!" responded the Cardinal. "I don't give a hoot for all that nonsense! You don't unmask the culprits with cigarette-ends, but by letting them have it in the teeth! Now I don't want to see that head on the baize another moment. Enough! It's absolutely disgusting."

The Marchesa Palla looked circumspectly about her, hesitated, then approached the severed head with little mincing steps; she bent over to scrutinize it and couldn't suppress a look of disgust. She stretched her hands out to pick it up, but stopped dead a few centimetres from her goal, not knowing where and how to place her grip (an exhausting mental effort, causing her to moisten her lips with the tip of her tongue). In the end, she had an inspiration and grasped the head by the ears, lifted it a little with an imperceptible air of triumph and showed it off to the crowd; but immediately, resuming an air of melancholy, she dropped the pitiable remains into her dress, after quickly gathering up the hem.

"That's better," commented Cardinal Meschia. "Now, if you like, you may call the police, but first I must put you on your guard. It's not only a matter of a decapitated girl, which is already deplorable enough, but something that touches you all and the lives you lead. God is not dead. That is a cliché and like all clichés, it seems like the discovery of America, while it is only a f . . . f . . . a foolish catchphrase. God is more than ever present; and if one day He really should die, we will all die with Him. The death of God means the return to chaos. It is up to you to decide, while you still have time."

This said, the Cardinal shuffled away as was his wont, leaving his listeners deep in thought; most of all the Marchesa Palla, who was forced to hold the severed head in her dress. An obliging person dashed off to phone the police. Then someone dared to make a comment, which in a certain way served to break the ice binding them all together, because another immediately followed and still another, until, in short, a furious criss-cross of remarks began to shatter the prevailing air of calm. Nevertheless, and it was quite an achievement, a cry pierced through the market-place hubbub. "I know who the murderer is!"

With Mirella in tow, Pantieri went up to the man who had spoken and caught him while he was brandishing the lethal axe he had discovered on the floor between the gleaming shoes of the croupier – who uttered a moan and fainted away. On the wooden haft the riddle which had tormented Pantieri for so long, and had cost the life of the Gruvi family, had been carved with a penknife. Those not in the know read the semblance of a Christian name, two initials and a surname: CLEON V.I. CERCATO was scratched on the handle.

"But what does it mean?" a gambler objected. "Is it conceivable a murderer would put his signature on the murder weapon?"

"And anyway," observed another player, "do you call that a surname? Have you ever known a Mr Cercato?"

"Seems more likely it's a secret message," said a third, attempting to clarify things. "Something in code. And *cercato* is a past participle, means that something is being 'looked for' or 'wanted'."

"It's suggestive, but arbitrary. Although we do have to find someone or a meaning."

"The fact remains that leaving your signature after a murder makes little sense . . . I would have thought it was a secret message myself and I wouldn't be drawn in too much by the word *cercato*, it's a studied trap to divert attention. After all, we know we have a murderer to find."

"Of course, but how do you interpret a secret message? It's not easy. Words are surprising hiding places. Sometimes it's enough to change the order of the letters and, for example, 'Cleon' becomes *oncle* in French."

"Blimey, what on earth have 'French uncles' got to do with it?"

"Anagrams and transliterations! Take the letters of each word separately and toss them in the air like dice . . . try every possible combination . . . it's possible that the real message will spring out."

Police sirens were wailing in the distance, a distance that was diminishing, from which in a few minutes would appear the minions of the law and start interrogating. Christian name, surname, address, previous convictions, profession, alibis, guardian angels. Very embarrassing. And then more questions: why had the decapitated girl's head been removed? Why had Cardinal Meschia insisted so much on it? Had the grand old man the force needed to deal such a blow?

"Let's hop it!" said Mirella peremptorily. "There'll be trouble if the police catch us here."

Night. Always night. It seemed to Pantieri that the sky's dark cavity was sucking them in, dragging them upwards while below them sand dunes were enveloping the rest of humanity lost in the desert of sleep. The sky was a box shaken by an invisible hand; new stars, new planets, new destinies appeared and disappeared in darting trails. The letters of the alphabet were in flight, scattering silver dust, flying with the velocity of comets across an unknown astrological house. They were writing the latest constellation: CERCO NECAVIT L.O. Lucilla Opitz! Cerco, I'm looking for her murderer . . . Cerco had killed Lucilla . . . then CERCO became CROCE, and CROCE became CRUX! The Crux had killed her! The solution to the anagram was there, glowing with a deathly pallor among the pallor of the other stars.

TWO

They arrived in Rome very late. During the journey they had barely exhanged a word, lulled by the swaying of the bus, their thoughts and the ambush of sleep. Soon after Ardea, threatening ink-blots had furrowed the dark well that imprisoned the world with black velvet dreams. Airships? Pantieri and Mirella had exchanged mute glances. It was difficult to distinguish between the signs released by the imagination and those spread about by a mysterious other, whose fancy was more potent and derisive. The airships had disappeared towards the sea, driven by the instinct for adventure and perdition.

But, good God, what did it matter? Lopping the head off Lucilla Opitz had been an outrage that remained inexplicable despite the presumed message in the anagram. Besides, one of the gamblers had observed that words were surprising hiding places. All you had to do was invert the message's last two letters and you had a different victim. CROCE NECAVIT O.L.: The Crux had killed Orazio La Calenda. But why go in search of him in a clandestine gaming room in Lavinio? It didn't make sense. Pantieri had to think about anagrams and transliterations until he reached the truth! But he was tired.

A taxi took them to Via Monte Pelmo. There wasn't a living soul about. Unless a couple of plainclothes men were hiding away somewhere . . . No, it wasn't the way with the police, they insisted on relying on the intimidating power of a uniform. The apartment was as Pantieri had left it: the G-Plan furniture, the display cabinet with its sets of glasses, the cretonne-covered sofa, the panoply of arms, with its hint of heroism. He was afraid that strangers might have entered to turn the place over and rummage through things, but on the contrary, no one had taken it upon themselves to pry into the pitiful secrets harboured between those walls. So much the better.

He threw a window open and the moon appeared in a patch of sky swept clean by the wind. It was a white and mild-looking moon, murmuring depraved words in the firmament, and problematic stars were spinning a web of obscene confidences. What a cheap spell! Mirella was bent over to straighten the quilted bed and, all of a sudden, an adverb penetrated Inspector Pantieri's heart. A homely adverb. Roundly. Perfumed temptations of grammar and vocabulary, the worst of all temptations. Was it possible? To repeat an adverb in a low voice and shiver with forbidden pleasure. Signorina Candiani had initiated him in the sublime beauties of the immortal soul and every small renunciation had cost him an irksome, latent remorse; but now he was girding himself up for apostasy. He trembled with fear as he sensed the disdainful, threatening grimace of his schoolmistress in the jagged edges of a cloud.

Roundly, Pantieri thought once more and then he remembered Horace's lines: "Nox erat et coelo fulgebat Luna serena/ inter minora sidera,/ cum tu, magnorum numen laesura deorum,/ in verba iurabas mea . . ." He felt the sour taste of betrayal in his mouth and knew he didn't find it unpleasant; unchastity was a woman's most beautiful ornament. And then he thought he was sinking into a whirlpool of bad literature; Horace and Liala had little in common but, on the other hand, the most realistic and unspeakable sins were denied to Liala's female readers. At most they could aspire to Purgatory; Hell was a privilege reserved for poets and those who loved poets.

The quilted bed was a railway station where there was a train about to depart, waiting for them. There wasn't a minute to lose. The way dogs did it, why not? Pantieri looked towards the window in front of him, finally untrammelled by a damp pillow plastered with hair, and night assailed him – crossed by the gusting passage of witches. He found it intoxicating to think he was committing a shameful act and that he had found an accomplice more sordid than he was; those hips were quivering too much, even in so much filthiness there had to be a limit!

They were animals, weren't they? Chaos was complete. Making love meant an act of commingling whose memory would bring a blush; a tacit obligation to master oneself in wickedness.

Was that love, then? To desecrate and be desecrated? There was something wrong, thinking of it like that, an infantile hangover from which he couldn't liberate himself. The height of voluptuousness coincided with the height of solitude? Useless thoughts. Who knows, one day or another piety would overtake him, and with piety a different love; he would learn affection, tenderness; he would accept Mirella's thoughts, troubles and hopes as his own.

The morning after, Pantieri was forced to admit it was time to do something: set about finding Conti, for example, and reveal himself before being discovered. But it was dangerous to go near him. He'd be returned to prison at the drop of a hat, or end up drilled full of lead by a twitchy Carabiniere. The twitchiness of the police (traffic cops included) was one solution to the impracticability of the death sentence.

He fretted away for a week, the more so because Mirella made such fretfulness not displeasing, until one evening the radio broadcast the news that everyone had been waiting for, and which they had been sure would happen. On the beach at Ardea, a few steps from the lapping waves, a Volkswagen Golf had been found, completely burnt out. Only the blackened and twisted metal parts were left, already turning to rust in the briny air. In the boot the unrecognizable remains of a man had been found, but science (and what had science not mastered?) had undertaken to bring some order to those pitiable exhibits: a gold chain, cufflinks, watch, a fragment of identity card, dentures, a lock of hair and a toenail, which had all escaped the flames . . . Infra-red rays and chemical reagents had been employed, a goldsmith from the centre had supplied information, and the Records Office had offered the missing pieces to the puzzle's solution: with mathematical certainty, beyond any possibility of error, the man was Lauro Croce Sabbioneta. After a captivity of inexplicable length, the death sentence had been carried out. The Prime Minister, Orazio La Calenda, had made a brief homily; Sabbioneta would have hit upon more touching and convincing words, but he was dead and could not speak his own commemoration. A pity.

Pantieri fretted away for another three days and in the end . . . Yes, that was it! A confrontation with Conti was called for, at whatever cost. The Prosecutor had to revoke the warrant for arrest, restore his juridical status as a free man and, as for the rest, well, he was ready to tender his resignation, they could all go to hell, he'd never cared for the job of police inspector anyway. As if he'd ever got promotion! However, this was not a question of establishing humble truths, but of guaranteeing clamorous lies; it wasn't his scene.

"Watch it," said Mirella, solicitously. "Conti's not to be trusted."

"Don't worry. By the way, I don't know if you've read the papers, but word's going round that Ciro De Fiore hasn't taken off to South America and, well, he's still around these parts . . ."

"Let's hope not. It would be dangerous meeting up with him."

Pantieri went back to where he had left his Fiat 124 and, after several unsuccessful attempts, he managed to start her up: Fiats thrived on strikes, water and neglect, especially models of that year. Not far from the Pincio, he stopped and continued on foot. Heavens, he would have to sort out a plan or something. The city had its usual appearance, and was thronging with workers, teachers, students, loafers and working-class women on the make, with their shopping bags . . . He heard a voice cursing that potatoes were now sixteen thousand lire a kilo and another voice expressing faith in a prompt increase in salaries. Yes, that was the inflation spiral and, in order to break it, either prices or wage-packets had to be reined in. As to the intentions of Prime Minister La Calenda, the second solution was the more likely.

The Pincio with its milling crowd on Sunday mornings! . . . Whoever hasn't experienced this spectacle hasn't known angst and death's mischievous invitation. The dusty air polluted by flying kites, multi-coloured footballs, and celluloid model aeroplanes; the aimless wandering of fathers, mothers and overdressed children, with vacant eyes lost in the contemplation of even more unfathomable vacuity; the never-ending scrape of new shoes in the gravel; the consuming reek of petrol and vanilla; the flight of screaming children and the flaccid wobble of breasts as mothers pursued them; the assault of pirates on board their bicycles and pedal cars in a squall of idiotic laughter; the frown of marble heroes behind the backs of soldiers in mufti on weekend leave; the rush of mangy or be-ribboned dogs in identical quest among the mortified and vanquished trees; it was into this scene that Pantieri plunged, regretting that the world had to have children. He looked up to examine the sky. It was compact, like chalk; there was no room for gleams of turquoise now.

"Well, if it isn't Pantieri!" boomed a familiar voice in apparent affability. "Come on now, stay happy! There's nowt can't be mended, except death!"

It was Dr Conti, who had suddenly appeared behind him, his lips wide in a conciliatory smile and his whole mien an open invitation simply to knock and the iron gates of his magistrate's heart would be unlocked.

"No accident, this meeting of ours," he added sweetly. "It's not fortuitous. We've always kept an eye on your house, you old lag, and now we meet . . . Inevitable, this meeting, predestined . . . the fateful hour that strikes on history's dial! I could have you arrested forthwith, but you're an intelligent man, and I want to have a word with you before I do. Like to propose a deal, give you a break, as they say. Mind, I'm playing this out to someone else's script and putting my own feelings behind me, because you know I can't stand you, and you know why, too. You killed my woman and I can't forgive you for a monstrous deed like that."

"Your woman! Who ever gave you the right to appropriate my wife and now her memory as well?"

"Ah, shut up, you nincompoop! She didn't love you and you didn't love her . . . What Italian law and its true, holy, indissoluble marriage means is the cuckold's horns! It's orgasms that get folk wedded, not stuffy old priests! That's philosophy, that is. But I won't bore you with private matters. I'll let you into a secret: I've got an inkling it wasn't you who put away our Dr Gruvi."

"Oh, so it's no longer me?"

"It wasn't you if you'll listen to me and if you'll go along with what I say; if not, I can't help you. And I can give you some advice: you can't be a freelance nowadays, no one'll come touching you up. That's politics, the art of the possible, which means the art of living in the world. Now, the story began during De Fiore's interrogation, the husband of your little friend. Talk about a coincidence!"

They were walking along the edge of Piazza del Popolo; the presence of an escort was betrayed in the crooked smiles, blue suits and pomaded hair-dos gleaming round them. Conti was walking slowly to help the labour of his stomach, which was busy digesting his breakfast of two *cappuccini* and four croissants. Every so often he put a hand to his mouth to repress or disguise a belch, but if his wind was giving him a spot of bother, he scarcely troubled to hide it.

"It begins with De Fiore's interrogation," the magistrate resumed. "You tried to mix it with the Crux . . . Yes, I don't know how to put it now. In the beginning it was like a freemasonry, just nonsense, pissing about . . . nothing more than a game. I was well aware that they were doing revolting things . . . well, nothing really, a bit of cunt came my way . . . and it was even a leg up, a little string to pull . . . for getting on, having some lolly in the bank (credit guaranteed to your old dead dad), getting well in, knowing the bigwigs. Besides, the head of it was Lauro Croce Sabbioneta, alias Raymond of Touraine. The greatest prank was that of the pustules. Pretty effective, if you didn't know the trick! Even you were fooled. Holy cow! Two drops of turpentine injected under the skin . . . method used for provoking experimental abscesses in laboratory animals. A matter of dosage, you follow? But then word got round and, well, the time of the good old pustules had to stop. We even had a stream of folk parading pimples, boils, impetigo, baldness, genital warts and corns! Hell of a to-do. Wanted to take advantage, they did, too much advantage! Anyway, a little at a time, the Crux began to change:

the odd kneecapping, the odd murder, an occasional bomb outrage . . . Terrorism was a way: it strengthened democracy, because everyone was shitting themselves with worry that it was under threat. The best way to keep the invalid on its feet, see, was to kick him in the balls. I didn't do badly out of it, to be honest: but it was peanuts, small potatoes. Perhaps I wasn't liked by the bosses. So, De Fiore's arrest was my big chance. Found myself with a treasure in my hands and never had to lift a finger. De Fiore had nothing to do with the attack on the bank, but he was compromised with another clan and they were playing a risky game. A very risky game. And then De Fiore wasn't just anybody, he had a father, hadn't he? A detail that came out straightaway. Assunta and I suspected that His Excellency La Calenda had a compromising secret, something to hide, and just when the blessed lady had found out . . . before she could tell me . . . you had her kill herself, you rotten son of a bitch. And then you were such a dunderhead, they whipped the photo from under your nose . . . or maybe you sent it to the press yourself . . . I don't know and in the end it's your hard shit. His Excellency La Calenda couldn't have hoped for better propaganda. But that's by the by. Fact is that De Fiore was working on a project they were ready to touch the match to, something they'd had in the pan for months. He'd bumped off Gruvi and his mother, poor old thing, because they couldn't keep it under their hats: poisoned the Doc and strangled the old bag. Nice work."

"So you've found out who *is* guilty?" Pantieri observed, "and you know I had nothing to do with the crime you're accusing me of!"

"Fancy that!" smiled Conti, baring his teeth so that it looked as if he were about to take a bite out of him. "Try and understand, Pantieri, I thought I'd made myself clear. In a world where the crime, the offence, is commissioned work, a gang giving orders, I'm sorry, Pantieri, but even justice has to fall in with the rules. De Fiore did for Gruvi and the old dear, but we have to nail the culprit, we've got to choose . . . it's a question of expediency."

"I see," said Pantieri bitterly, passing a hand through his

hair, "so all that theatrical set-up with the poignard, and the trap at the Bela Motel . . . were used to set *me* up."

"Yes, that's about right. You were about to meddle, stick your nose in, ask questions, in short, you were dangerous and I couldn't leave you to your own account. We had to be careful. That pantomime at the Bela Motel was funny: four tarts and seven girls from the Convent school of the Blessed Oblate Sisters of S.Daniela Crisci. The tarts went off the rails, they seemed to make a lousy show beside the schoolgirls. Then we wondered whether you'd get to the right place at the right time, the message was a bit sibylline: but everything went off perfectly. Besides, a climate of doubt and suspicion was vital; otherwise the business would have been no fun . . . you need to bear in mind posterity telling the story, and even reading about it. The transfer of Gruvi's body went off like clockwork, too. Very smooth job. Mind you, I knew nothing about the plan to do away with Sabbioneta, in fact I was taking my orders directly from him. De Fiore let me in on the real situation and won me over. Eventually it was my turn to distinguish myself and reap the fruits. A change of colours was enough or, if you prefer, in stuffy language, a feint, a betrayal."

"I'm not surprised."

"Oh, come on! Traitors are more necessary than heroes, how often do I have to repeat myself? Betrayal's the indispensable antithesis for creating a synthesis: the dialectical process is stuffed with betrayals."

"I think I follow," whispered Pantieri huskily. "So De Fiore killed Lauro Croce Sabbioneta."

"Not a bit of it," scowled Conti. "It's someone else snuffed out Sabbioneta: that's the rub. Between you and me, as an assassin De Fiore's a dead loss. I've got to put up with him because he's got pull, he's the PM's son, and you know how these things go. The terrorist who makes a balls-up is a social pest. Well, De Fiore starts at the Protomoteca, misses his aim and kills Opitz, who's got nothing to do with it. He should have got Sabbioneta in the shoulder. There was an ambulance waiting outside and it would have been child's play in all that mayhem to whip him off on the pretext of taking him to hospital . . . Never mind. In the end De Fiore finds his target at the station, grabs him and hides him . . . guess where? Well, where doesn't matter, it's by the by. Sabbioneta starts writing his messages . . . All his own work . . . no need to dictate anything to him, nudge him, drug him or slap and kick him. All his own work, signed and sealed. Besides, Ciro's almost illiterate and Sabbioneta was spreading shit on himself very well on his own. So then what? De Fiore lets him escape, doesn't he? But he doesn't give up, he goes off in search, hunts all over, thinks he recognizes his man dressed as a nun, but hits the wrong target once again and lops the head off Opitz's daughter. Real bad luck for that family, they were doomed from the moment they crossed Ciro's path. He should weep for shame. But that's not the point. You know that Sabbioneta's corpse was found and they gave him a wonderful funeral and fitting send-off, laying him to rest for all eternity in a tomb with cherubs all over it, better than a museum. What the hell more could a man want? But it wasn't De Fiore who killed him, and I'm asking myself who did."

Pantieri lit a cigarette and inhaled two or three lungfuls in silence. Then he spoke severely: "You've listed God knows how many crimes, actual or attempted, though I'm not clear whether you set them up, took part in them or at any rate connived in them; but it's never crossed your mind to start proceedings against anyone, unless it's against an innocent person like myself!"

"Pantieri, it's clear you haven't understood a bleeding thing. Sometimes I'm almost ready to give up on you. Look, even if you come to me now and tell me I'm the instigator, executioner or accessory to these crimes, and even if you're right, where does that get you? Am I expected to incriminate myself on my own? And, excuse me, was I doing all these crimes just to get myself flung in the slammer? I was saying that Sabbioneta's been killed and no one else knows who did it. De Fiore, who of course never left for South America, is on the loose, prowling and scratching about . . . But I have my doubts. You, though, you're a policeman, a professional."

"I'm supposed to find out who the killer was? What for?

You only have to invent one. You could even prove it was me."

"That would be a good idea, but that's not the point. This gang of cut-throats who steal our ideas and nick our clients . . . I don't care for them. Could be dangerous for us. Perhaps they want to start your actual revolution or, after that last bit of dirty work, they're hatching some fresh mischief. Pantieri, I'm not ready to pop my clogs. I want you to investigate . . . Then we'll see . . . I don't think you'll retire a simple inspector."

"Then I'm free? You'd revoke the arrest warrant?"

"Now take it easy. You're sort of free, we're all sort of free. I can help you, I can watch your back, give you a few tips, but just don't keep asking questions and above all, don't hassle me. So, I'm telling you, do your job discreetly, keep your head down and don't try any funny business."

"I was there when Lucilla was killed," Pantieri mumbled pensively. "I would never have believed that that tetchy, gnarled old nun was Sabbioneta. Now it's clear what lay behind that grisly act. I suppose that Sabbioneta had given De Fiore the slip only a short time before."

"Half an hour at the most."

"Right, otherwise he'd have had time to think of some less precarious and farcical disguise. Then what? I mean, after the girl had been killed?"

"Evaporated. When he was found, he was a charred corpse, as dead as could be, with five bullets in his belly. That's what's driving me mad: who could it have been?"

"After Lucilla's murder Cardinal Meschia showed up. Not that I'd like to formulate a suspicion or, worse, an accusation . . . But society's in such a mess!"

"Sacred words, Pantieri, or rather, the right words. Even sanctity makes me a bit wary . . . it almost gives me the creeps. I really don't believe in sanctity, I think it's hypocrisy, rather. Come on, what's it to you that some poor sods are dying of starvation? Who are you kidding! When I've eaten, the whole world's eaten. Oh yes, even the Cardinal could be a first-class son of a bitch."

"That's not what I meant."

"Who cares? I wanted to put a doubt to you, you can think what you like. Anyway, we've talked enough, more than enough for my taste. I was forgetting . . . Pantieri, don't get ideas about double-crossing me. *In primis*, double-crossing the double-crossers is bad manners, it's not done in good society. *In secundis*, I'll say it's a pack of lies and put you away for killing Gruvi. *In tertiis*, with your hangdog look, you'll have to resign yourself to being the thesis in the dialectic. That's your cross. Forget all I've said, if it bothers you. Do your job, Inspector, find me Lauro Croce Sabbioneta's killer."

He turned on his heels and, as was his habit, went strutting off, this time trailing a protective wake of pomaded locks and *camperos* boots.

THREE

Cardinal Meschia was without doubt a singular character. It was a strange thing, but every time blood was spilt, he was there. A saint or a devil disguised as a saint? My God, what a ridiculous suspicion! The whole world retained memories of Meschia's charitable works. But what about that sore that disfigured his hand? It was the object of veiled allusions. Could it be that this extraordinary man of the Faith had injected a drop or two of turpentine under the skin to produce the revealing pustule? The Cardinal was obsessed by the apocalypse and sometimes prophets tried to bring about what they prophesied. Perhaps this man of the Faith had a truth of his own to confess . . .

The eminent prelate lived in the Prati district, in a secluded side street. It was a humble abode, which tried to hide its cracks and the ravages of time behind a mass of creeper that was climbing towards the roof. The Cardinal wasn't at home, and wouldn't be back until the evening; he was tied up with a funeral Mass and a polemic with some journalists. Pantieri promised he would be back later, but decided not to leave the vicinity. The Prati was a cheerful family quarter; forgotten smells were percolating: the sharp scent of geraniums, the softness of jasmine, the freshness of washing, the pride of *melanzane alla parmigiana*.

He telephoned Mirella from a bar. Briefly, he brought her up to date, without worrying if the phone was bugged, which was more than likely. Her distant voice sent an almost forgotten shiver of tenderness through him; the desire to escape sometimes became irresistible.

"Here's the latest," Mirella said with feigned indifference, "my husband phoned this morning."

"Ciro? Where is he?"

"He was evasive on this point, but I gathered he was in Turin, at Caselle Airport. I distinctly heard the loudspeaker calling passengers for the Turin-Amsterdam flight . . ."

"What does he want?"

"I don't know. He'll be waiting for us in Biraghi's villa in Lavinio; the pair of us, at midnight. His tone was threatening; we'd better do as he says."

"He's not to be trusted."

"If we take no notice, he'll kill Biraghi first, then the two of us. And that was a promise."

The sun went down. The chalk sky seemed to break up, boulders of night weighed down heavily on people's hearts. From an open window, a gramophone was playing music for a little blonde girl who was pale and unhappy . . . Who knows why she was unhappy? That was a twist of Pantieri's imagination. People lived, and that was that. He remembered Sabbioneta's last message: ingestion, digestion and defecation . . . A crude synthesis of the human parabola, but perhaps . . . Society was the evil, in whatever form: an evil born from the organization needed for living together. Lewis Carroll would have persuaded the pale, blonde little girl to allow herself to be photographed with almost nothing on: capturing an image with a photograph, or more probably a dream evoked by an image. Up to a certain point, Lewis Carroll had enclosed his personal universe in a photograph collection. There was an insight there: you had to freeze-dry the world and store it away. To be used according to the imagination.

He went back to knock at the Cardinal's door. In his domestic intimacy, he was touching; the red overalls were off and he was wearing a tattered dressing-gown, while a yellow scarf protected his throat. His study was a collection of ruins. Two wooden beams had come loose from the ceiling, a collapse which had occurred some time in the past and, fortunately, at a sufficient distance from the writing-desk. Dust and cobwebs had accumulated on them. Even the bookcases were falling to pieces; every now and then, under the combined assault of rats, bookworms, and the water dripping from the walls, a volume with no further chance to maintain its balance would topple to the ground with a thud. To approach the writing-desk that stood beyond the steeply inclined beams was dangerous. No less so was the occupation of the seat in front of it: half caved in, soiled by ancient abuses, as it received the visitor, it unsheathed a broken and rusty spring from under the greasy upholstery of indefinable colour. In the middle of this disaster area, an Art-Nouveau lamp spread an austere magenta warmth through its quiver of beads, tassels, sequins and little bows, enveloping the ruins disseminated about the room with equal consideration. A tray was placed on the desk with his supper: two onions and a glass of *zabaglione*.

"You'll be thinking I don't practise what I preach," the Cardinal smiled, taking his place and pointing at the glass. He was thin and very pale. An ugly sore disfigured his face and a bandage imprisoned his left hand. He stretched his right hand out to the *zabaglione* and tested it with his index finger, sucking the tip and closing his eyes under the impulse of a chaste rapture. He opened them again and sighed: "I have a public image to defend, but I'm only human too. My health is precarious and the doctor has ordered me to take a nourishing diet."

The echo of one of the songs the pale, blonde girl was broadcasting to the neighbourhood drifted in; a rather indecent one, this. The singer was burbling on about the cobra, with its prurient innuendo.

"The snake's always been a phallic symbol," observed the Cardinal. "In Christian iconography it's identified with the devil. True, that song's not a good example of modesty, even if the tune is rather pleasant. However, it's pure exaggeration attributing a diabolical power to the . . . you follow me. The cobra always manages to get its head up, despite age and infirmity, while . . . Won't you have a little?"

"No, thank you. I don't want to deprive you and anyway I'm not hungry."

"Have you read Baget Bozzo's article on events in the Middle East? It's so futile it's mind-boggling. The truth is we're already at war. The suspicion of war is a portent of its outbreak; and we're already at that stage. I'm speaking of a universal conflict, a deflagration that will mean deaths counted in hundreds of millions. The skirmishes in the Middle East are only the aperitif. I'm certain that before the end of the millennium the whole world will be in flames for the third time . . . it'll probably be the apocalypse."

"The purifying war of nations?"

"That's a nonsense. I'd say the inability, perhaps the impossibility, to live in a way that is universal, eternal; the two categories are not strangers to the human spirit, but it is only in tragedy that one knows how to achieve them. This is the punishment for Original Sin."

"No need to afflict yourself about sins that remote in time. I wanted to ask you about the Rt Hon. Sabbioneta's death. Your opinion would be of interest."

"Merciful heaven," invoked the Cardinal, and he wiped his mouth with his bandaged hand. "It's a subject I would prefer to avoid. Not that I have any revelations to offer, nor even a tessera of truth to slot into the general mosaic. I know nothing about his kidnapping and death, except what the newspapers have published. I was a great friend of his, thought a lot of him . . . certain things I would like to pass over in silence."

"Don't be afraid," encouraged Pantieri. "I know now that he wasn't what people thought, that they still think even now . . . I know he was an unscrupulous, cynical, corrupt man, an untrustworthy man, maybe even a pervert. I know that he was ready to stoop to anything in the political struggle and that there was nothing he'd stop short of."

"Exactly," the grand old man confirmed. "Politics served to satisfy his worst vices . . . I suspect that he became enormously wealthy through it, even if I have no proof of what I say. And, at risk of shocking you, yes, his death has inflicted an incurable wound in my heart, but in a certain sense, I also saw the hand of God in it. The wisdom of Manzoni often comes to mind: 'It can be punishment, it can be mercy.' Forgive me. Then in the mystery of his death there lies another."

"What do you mean?"

"The messages . . . take no notice of the lies about their not being true. In reality Croce Sabbioneta never wrote with greater sincerity. It was his soul undergoing purification, it was the truth slowly coming to the surface. A man who identified his own particular situation with the universal and who was desperately asking to live in the only way he knew how: for himself and not for others. Above all, a man who admitted his own carnal nature, and his feebleness at ridding himself of it."

The pale, blonde girl, unwittingly at odds with Sabbioneta's testimony, was currently held in the spell of less fleeting emotions; the gramophone was now playing the powerful attack of Tchaikovsky's Piano Concerto. The light encircled the music in its magenta universe and for a little, and only for a little, the Cardinal's study was bathed in the happy beauty of unhappy loves and unhappy dreams.

"In the face of death . . ." hazarded the Inspector and then dried up.

"Yes, of course," the Cardinal went on. "Fear is a good cleansing agent. Nevertheless, Sabbioneta had already been showing signs of a rethink, of second thoughts, in private at least. A few months ago I was worried about his health; I thought he was working too hard and wrote to ask him why, with a view to urging him to take a vacation. This is how he replied to me. Do read it, please."

He fished in his dressing-gown and extracted a crumpled note from it which he proffered like a holy relic. Pantieri reluctantly took hold of it. He smoothed it out as best he could and, with the hesitancy of a first-year primary-school pupil, he carefully pronounced:

"Because urgent grounds give extenuating reasons, for abnegation means invariably nicety, exemplarity and infinite dutifulness.

Lauro"

"What do you think?"

"Well, it's a highly distilled language, improbable, rhetorical, learned . . . A text that harmonizes with Sabbioneta's public image."

"It's an acrostic," whispered the distinguished prelate conspiratorially. "I mean that the initials of each word form a complete sentence. BUGGER FAMINE AID, that's what it says. It's an affront, an insult."

"It could be a mere coincidence," Pantieri began, but instantly bit his tongue. That fifteen letters of the alphabet should just happen to form that combination from among so many was absurd!

"Rubbish," said the Cardinal with a smile. "It couldn't be a mere coincidence. And anyway, why insult me? Why wound me in what has been my life's mission? Perhaps his soul was already beginning to purify itself, was already beginning to feel disgust for the hypocrisy on which a certain way of life is based. At first blush, I took offence, I was angry, I felt wounded, but I wasn't long in understanding. And his letters from prison, if I can call them that, made things even clearer."

"How do you mean?"

"I mean in the only way possible. He had thrown off the mask and, not without ostentation and braggadocio, was confessing to not cherishing, and never having cherished, any faith in the public, whom he had always exploited in order to accumulate wealth, honours and power. At the expense of the weakest, needless to say. He refuted any kind of social regeneration, he judged it impossible. And he strenuously claimed his right to his privacy and to the meanness, mediocrity and stupidity that go to make it up. That's to say, his right to the only space accorded to human beings. A dreary conclusion. Which anyway I wouldn't like to repudiate . . . if only faith had taken a look in! You can see to what his 'preoccupation for the life that has to end' brought him. If Sabbioneta hadn't been massacred, in such a stupid and barbarous way, would he have stayed on in politics? Or would he have chosen a different path, a less ostentatious one perhaps, but in the end more sincere, more honest and more genuine?"

"That I don't know," said Pantieri. "Certainly he would

have been a different man . . . But these discussions won't bring us to any conclusion. Too many ifs."

"That's true," the Cardinal murmured. "But perhaps they will give us a key to interpretation. A man like that, who was so attached to this earth, would have done anything to avoid being killed. Anything. In the Revelation of St John, it is said 'and death and hell delivered up the dead which were in them.' In the end, is it really certain that the charred corpse discovered on the beach at Ardea was Sabbioneta's?"

"No doubt at all. Science has made giant steps . . . It was possible to determine the blood group by analyzing a toenail."

"From a toenail . . . ? Then I won't say another word. Nevertheless, if I were you, I'd go and take a look not far from the scene of the tragedy. I believe that everything occurred roundabout there. I feel it in my bones."

The gramophone was silent, the pale, blonde child had gone to bed. In the evening quiet, the Art-Nouveau lamp made a denser rain of shooting-stars: the eminent prelate's face was damp with it, and it was perhaps this unreal light that was distorting the serene composure of his austere yet benign expression. A tear seemed to bathe his cheek. He immediately rubbed his eyes with his hands, smearing *zabaglione*. He didn't notice and went back to his usual stolid contemplation, without the yellow splodge above one eyebrow impairing his dignity or diminishing the reverence he inspired. He smiled with impalpable bitterness and when he spoke, there was no flaw in his voice.

"You suspected me, Inspector. My sores have no relation whatsoever to any others . . . I'm ill, very ill. My skin wastes away every day and my poor flesh becomes naked. A disease of burnt skin, Lyell's syndrome, that's how the doctors diagnose it. I will die of it in a few months, perhaps in a few weeks. In some ways my situation is similar to that in which Sabbioneta was living before his execution. My God, it may seem scandalous for an old priest to pose a question like this: can one hope that death won't always come like a capital punishment?"

"Oh, dear Father!" exclaimed Pantieri. He felt he was saying words he had read once before. "We'll see each other again, won't we?"

"In heaven, I hope," whispered the Cardinal, repeating a famous reply.

He stopped the car a kilometre before Lavinio. The sea was alien and hostile, but there was no fury of crests and spume rearing up; it rippled with the softness of a swamp and streaked the sand with corrugated caresses, spreading a desolate fixity, extinguishing every sign of life in an identical image. The newly whitewashed house, geometric and not very large, stood out in that phosphorescent universe and was imbued with it. Not far off was the Convent of the Blessed Oblate Sisters of S. Daniela Crisci.

"I think you'd better wait for me in the car," Pantieri said quietly to Mirella. He gazed at her for a long time and imagined, or thought he imagined in the darkness that the girl's face was marked with wrinkles; he felt a twinge of conscience, almost as if it were he who had put them there, followed by a pang of tenderness.

Biraghi opened the door and, without a word, led him into a drawing-room no different from any respectable person's. A green-silk-shaded lamp shed a dismal, ominous light. Knick-knacks, silver ornaments, G-Plan furniture, a sofa, an upright piano, and two solemn armchairs under wraps; a whiff of mildew and cooking. Yes, he was familiar enough with that household smell, containing garlic, onion and bleach; it re-minded him of furtive, penny-pinching arrangements from his prehistory. His late wife gliding about on pieces of felt with a skater's grace, disappearing into an inner sanctum of detergents. Good God, that green light with its cargo of ectoplasm . . .

A Val d'Aosta-style wardrobe in the hall seemed destined for visitors' outdoor clothes. Pantieri went up to it to free himself of his raincoat, but was stopped by the magistrate, who put his fingers to his lips with a peremptory gesture.

Biraghi was behaving most bizarrely, as though tipsy, were it not for his pallor, and the feverish spark in his eyes, which were straining to replace his mouth as the organ of speech.

Pantieri threw the raincoat on the sofa and attempted to sink into one of the armchairs and cross his legs, but was forced by the protective shroud to sit on the edge. He lit a cigarette and caught sight of a bottle of grappa on the table.

"Why don't you offer me a drink?" he asked, with a forced smile.

"Impossible," mumbled the magistrate. "That's a bottle of trieline."

"You shouldn't keep the bottle labelled as spirits, then. Oh, I was forgetting . . . you like playing dangerous games. You pulled the same trick on me a little while ago. I remember it well, you were about to poison me. Only, if the worst came to the worst, with that trieline you could kill someone who's distracted. The *Mastomys* are another matter."

"Pah! I don't like talking about my failures. Let's drop the subject."

"That Lassa fever nearly cost me my life! I agree with you, better to change the subject. Do you know the reason for my visit?"

"More or less, more or less," Biraghi whispered, inserting a hand down his trousers, whether in search of relief or refuge, it was difficult to say.

"Did De Fiore warn you?" Pantieri asked. "I had to be here with his wife at midnight, on the dot."

"I think so. At least he telephoned me and told me . . . anyway, I don't think there'll be long to wait."

"Why a meeting like this? What's it all about? And what's your role?"

"None at all. I told you. I'm tired and I want to live in peace. I've no idea what De Fiore has in mind."

A very long silence fell. A woodworm in the Val d'Aosta cupboard creaked and Biraghi gave a start, but then, as if ashamed of his over-reaction, he recovered his composure and straightened his trousers over the knees; he offered his guest a foolish smile. The bleating of a goat could be heard from behind the house. A goat? It wasn't possible. The rush of the surf captured the waves of the imagination as well, which returned them with unbelievable vividness; all the emotions running through his soul were being churned in the panting of the sea. But another bleat broke in, this time quite unabashed.

"D'you keep goats?" asked Pantieri, circumspectly.

"Well, only one . . . the milk's light and delicate. Good for the skin. It prevents acne."

"You drink goat's milk?"

"Now and again."

Good God, there was something unnatural about the conversation they were having. Sparing of words, and those few wrenched out with tongs and, above all, devoid of any sense or logic. As if they were not alone and someone, hidden behind a curtain, were spying on them. For a few moments Biraghi devoted himself to a disjointed mimicry, as if he wanted to signal some obstacle or danger; but his expressive capabilities were modest and all his gesticulating turned out to be indecipherable, if not a little crazy. What the devil did he want? Perhaps a magazine left beside the bottle of trieline? Pantieri politely got up to go and get it. An insignificant little rag, *The Philatelic Courier*, a fortnightly magazine, available at your local newsagent's.

"Are you interested in stamps?"

"Not me. You know, I don't know if you're already aware, but Sabbioneta was hidden at my house during the kidnapping. Against my wishes, needless to say. I've got nothing to do with the gentlemen of the establishment. A nightmare, believe me. But I was susceptible to blackmail for my transgressions – I still am – as you very well know. They had me by the short hairs, and I could only suffer in silence. De Fiore and a bunch of hoodlums, calling the tune; they soiled my armchairs, spat on the floor, belched . . . And then the chap himself in a complete panic. Not that Sabbioneta gave me much trouble: he kept writing letters, notes, wills, doing his accounts. He also wrote a couple of epigrams. For him, writing and living had become one and the same. Reality sprang from his ballpoint. It was a mania with him. And then his insistence on never taking off his overcoat."

"He was a man who felt the cold, everyone knew that."

"Very well, but such an attachment to an overcoat . . . morbid. An unnatural relationship. And the joke of it is that, when he escaped, he fled in his underpants. Opened the bathroom window and vanished."

"And afterwards?"

"Afterwards . . . Afterwards . . . ? How on earth should I know? You've heard the radio, read the papers . . . It's assumed somebody killed him. An ugly end for the poor sod, burnt to a cinder in the boot of a car."

"And De Fiore? And the others?"

"How on earth should I know?" the magistrate repeated with a groan, shooting anxious glances at the Val d'Aosta-style wardrobe. "Disappeared. After all, they'd really got themselves in a mess, letting the prisoner escape, and in such a stupid way."

"Why didn't you tell me?" Pantieri quizzed. "We were in that café in Via della Conciliazione for nearly an hour! You could have told me, or asked for my advice, or help. Instead you behaved like an accomplice!"

"What an idiotic thing to say! You were in a mess, yourself. Anyway, I did try to put you in the picture. I explained I had intrusive and dangerous guests . . . There was no room for acts of heroism; they would have killed me, they'd still kill me now! It's all a regrettable business. You know very well that De Fiore's turned up, and fixed a meeting with you. In my house. A respectable house turned into a den of thieves!"

The Val d'Aosta wardrobe creaked again; under the woodworms' attack, it was collapsing and the destruction was being accomplished with a racket out of all proportion to the cause. Its joints were groaning and, for a moment, a fantastic shuffle of feet scraped the insides of the huge cabinet.

"There's someone inside the wardrobe," Pantieri observed.

"I don't think so," replied Biraghi, evasively. "They all took off, and I live alone."

"Wouldn't it be better to take a look?"

"Oh, no. Absolutely not. Better not to open it. There's the stink of mothballs and camphor . . . I've just put my autumn clothes away. There's my new overcoat as well, the cashmere.

I told you I'd bought one, didn't I? The same as Sabbioneta's, but more elegant."

Pantieri paced about the room in long strides, with an increasingly uneasy feeling. However, to suppose that an unknown person was holed up in the wardrobe or in some other corner – that was the stuff of fiction. Odd! The apartment had been finished less than two months ago, and already it felt old; but it was an impression created by the knick-knacks piled on furniture that was too old and too over-crowded. There was even a fustiness about the books. Textbooks on gynaecology and obstetrics, complete runs of *Foro Italiano* and *Massimario*, Manzini's manual, and a paperback whose dog-eared condition betrayed frequent consultations. He delicately flipped it out and read the title: *Techniques of Extermination*.

"What's this?"

"Oh, philosophy. New techniques which connect with von Hartmann's theories. An attempt at synthesis between the moment of aggregation and the moment of destruction."

"I don't follow," said Pantieri tersely, and he rapidly flicked through the volume. A page came loose and floated on to the tiles. It was framed by bold markings in red pencil. Pantieri gathered the page up and read aloud: "In 1977 scientists were concerned with the Rift Valley Disease. Known up till then as an epidemic disease from Kenya, characteristic in sheep and goats, it unexpectedly attacked the Egyptian population and over 200,000 people contracted it. There were 600 deaths; a restricted number, explicable by the imperfect maturation of the virus (belonging to the Arbor virus family) and thus by its limited capacity to attack human beings in a lethal way. Nonetheless there is reason to suppose the mutant strain is in an advanced phase, so much so that the United States has prohibited imports of the virus for study purposes. Contagion occurs via the bite of the mosquito and other bloodsucking insects, but, in the developed disease, it occurs via the breath and even through touch. The developed disease causes a very high fever, terrible pains along the spinal column, encephalitis, diffuse and very severe jaundice, and blindness. It is always fatal . . ."

"Quite a serious disease," Biraghi commented, without being able to disguise a shade of pride and smugness in his voice.

"The goat . . ."

"Is pregnant, of course. I'm not absolutely sure it's got the disease; I was unfortunately forced to make my preparations in a bit of a hurry, but I hope so."

"Why this fixation with exterminating humanity? Why do you want to assume such powers on other people's behalf? Couldn't you make do with your own suicide? You could do away with yourself in an atrocious way, I mean without denying yourself the opportunity to expire in the most horrendous agony."

"You're simply superficial and antisocial, you can't push your own individualism to those extremes! The solution has to be adopted by the collectivity and regeneration presupposes destruction. It's no longer possible to live alone, and therefore it's no longer possible to die alone. It's a theorem. Anyway, I'm all in . . . I can't take any more . . . I'll tell you everything, yes, the lot. Beginning with Sabbioneta's overcoat, or rather beginning with that wardrobe . . ."

The magistrate's voice which, until that moment, had been subdued, rose and rose until it became a shriek: his last words, which in truth made very little sense, turned into a crash that drowned the bleating of the goat and the soughing of the sea. The wardrobe doors were thrown wide open, perhaps thrust off their hinges, so instant was the apparition, among a thicket of clothes and umbrellas, of a character who preferred to turn up to appointments with minimum notice and a great deal of noise. That character was Ciro De Fiore.

183

FOUR

"You won't tell a damn thing," pronounced De Fiore, and to show he allowed no interval between the word and the deed, a shot rang out, a rifle-shot. Only one. The magistrate thrust out his arms and, for interminable fractions of a second, fluttered as if he were trying to lift off in an impossible flight, then came crashing down, cracking the back of his head on the pedals of the piano, whose wires, thus rudely pressed into action, emitted a requiem that vibrated for a long time on the enervated air. The bullet had entered at the neck and, after performing acrobatics which it would be the police surgeon's job to describe, it had come to a halt just above a cheekbone. An eyeball had impacted itself on the ceiling and, viewing this vale of woe from on high with detachment, it wept its last tears.

"Real hornets, these bullets!" explained De Fiore, with pride. "5.56 calibre, and they go where you tell 'em. Got a displaced centre of gravity, set off straight, then rotate."

"Why were you hiding in the wardrobe?"

"Don't be daft. What should I have done, wait there or find you'd laid a trap? Perhaps you'd have shot me in the back of the head, without me having any time for last words. Where's my wife?"

"Here I am, Ciro," said Mirella, who had appeared all of a sudden at the door to the drawing-room, drawn first by Biraghi's cries and then by the noise of the shot. She was pale and the delicate line in the middle of her forehead was more than a hint. "I've done what you said, but I don't want any more bloodshed. You understand?"

"I don't know," De Fiore replied, "The Inspector's

dangerous . . . He knows too much, too much poking around."

He spotted the bottle of trieline and lifted it up to look at it against the light. He shook it, then glanced round to grab a glass, finding one on the drinks trolley. Six or seven bottles were on alluring display: Glen Grant, Chivas Regal, Fundador, Marie Brizard, Amaro Lucano, Mistrà Pallini . . . The brightly coloured labels and their contents shone against the rays from the green silk lamp, sending out amber reflexes that had the soft inconsistency of the world during a hangover. De Fiore weighed the bottles up one by one, showing perhaps more affection for the Mistrà. He went back to the trieline. Delicately with his fingertip, he cleaned the rim of the crystal goblet he had appropriated. He wasn't satisfied. Taking the shirt-tail out of his trousers for an improvised duster, he ran it vigorously round the inside of the glass.

"I'm all for hygiene, me," he exclaimed conceitedly. "That's how they learned me."

He started to pour, then suddenly stopped and hesitated; he shrugged and went on pouring. A few drops of trieline slopped onto the table and ate into the varnish, frothing and spluttering, emitting deadly vapours.

"Nothing better than grappa," De Fiore observed, lifting the glass up. "Cleans your guts out, disinfects them. A drop of this here liqueur and you forget everything, it's like leaving for another world."

"Don't drink it," said Pantieri. "It's not grappa, it's poison."

"It's grappa!" De Fiore roared back. "Very old, fine, distilled in the home. The best."

He took a generous gulp. His eyes came out on stalks and his mouth sagged open. He inhaled and exhaled with the fury of a bellows and with one hand massaged his belly. He coughed, cleared his throat, swore and spat blood. Then he said: "Pretty damn strong. Seventy proof, at least."

With another gulp he drained the glass. He walked up and down in the grip of a mysterious agitation, began to massage his stomach again and breathe with his mouth open. Then he let out a cry that was halfway between a cold shudder and a growl of animal delight: he trumpeted like an elephant, and after three or four trumpetings flopped down on the sofa with his head in his hands. But he didn't forget his rifle, which he slipped behind his back.

"You've just drunk trieline," Pantieri allowed himself to say. "And if you weren't so stubborn you'd go to the bathroom and vomit. Not that it would do you much good, by now I think you've had it . . ."

"Sod it," trumpeted De Fiore crossly. "I'm afraid you're right. It's possible that wasn't grappa I drunk."

He grasped the rifle and pointed it at Pantieri, but a fit of coughing persuaded him to desist and, leaning on the weapon like a stick, he began to fire off protests, curses and gobs of blood. Every so often he raised his head and looked at Mirella and Pantieri, who were crouched in front of him and wanted to try and help, though with little idea of where to start; they suffered only mild anguish over their ineptitude. De Fiore's eyes were like those of a wounded beast, but one nevertheless resolved to fight to its last breath. Droplets of thick yellow sweat were welling up on his forehead, face, moustache and hands; his body was racked by ever more violent and frequent tremors.

"*Madonna mia*, save me!" said Ciro. "I knew I wasn't well . . . right when I'd finished too . . . but I've warned the Prosecutor, and how! When he learned the news, he was stunned. His blood froze. Petrified, wiped out. Could really have done without the dying! Holy cow, what rotten luck!"

"Tell me the truth," Pantieri asked with a slight edge to his voice. "Was it your father who sent you to kill Gruvi and his mother?"

"He sent me alright," De Fiore replied with a last flash of lucidity. "It helped my old man, he needed it, so it was a good thing. What rotten luck, Mirella! After seven or eight years of you out whoring, we could have got a nice little house, with a little garden: I'd have put prickly pears in it, apricots, carnations, sweet-smelling flowers and basil, too, and parsley, and pellitory of the wall . . . I was born of a laundress who got herself into trouble, but the La Calendas couldn't be compromised by a little bastard, could they? . . . My mother died and I grew up an orphan, with no money and no one to guide me: that's how I came to learn the trades of robbing and killing. I thought my father was noble, a gentleman, because he was a Minister: except it turned out he robbed and killed too, but on a bigger scale. He was the Fiat corporation when it came to murder, theft and fraud. He ran it up in Rome on an assembly-line in the corridors of power! It was there the money was made, there they had the mill and the granary . . . a mill that turned on treachery . . . My father taught me things, whoever kills one poor sod's a murderer, and whoever knocks off a hundred's a statesman . . . Mirella, don't you hear me? The scents of lavender and spikenard . . . the scent of life that's fleeting . . ."

The green table lamp flickered with varying intensity, went trailing off into alternating dapples of forest and night; in Lavinio it often happened that the electric current was a little unsteady on its legs. It gave off gaudy effects of intermittence and the overworked eyes blinked away to more soothing horizons. Then the light nearly failed altogether, a trace of phosphorescent mould remained from the lampshade: like a fixed star, it regulated the movement of the shadows in the room, which was sinking step by step into the gloom. The green star focused its single fragile ray on De Fiore's exhausted face. It plumbed his depths. It was a face stiffening in the rigidity of death, it mingled hate and fury in a mask of exhaustion, in the realization of hopelessness. His mouth quivered, he whispered secret words, confiding a message. All that came through, however, was a regret, or a pointer: "At Papasidero . . ."

Was it another leg, maybe the last? Was it the epilogue, the end of the adventure? Or was it a sanctuary to which the dying man, in the act of discharging his punishment, had looked, hoping to undertake a journey that would have led him up there among the ancient oaks and wild cyclamen? My God, wouldn't it be beautiful if a paradise of flowers existed, Pantieri thought, biting his lip and ruffling his hair more anxiously than usual.

The electric light exploded again into life; with the obscene

187

unsubtlety that is in its nature, it lit up the lifeless corpse of Ciro De Fiore, illegitimate son of the Prime Minister, Orazio La Calenda. Other mills, those of which Longfellow speaks, had ground for him – rather different from those within the precincts of Government; but this was no more than a moralist's supposition.

"Poor Ciro," murmured Mirella and modestly made the sign of the cross. "I didn't quite catch his meaning. Why was he talking about Papasidero?"

"Perhaps it was a romantic idea," said Pantieri, attempting an explanation, "a dying man's thought. He was thinking back to the scenes of his childhood, to the places where he'd been happy."

"No, that's not it. Ciro came from S. Nicola Arcella, he grew up by the sea. He used to scoff at mountains and mountain folk . . ."

"Who's to say what passes through a dying man's head?"

"He wanted to give a clue. Papasidero was a clue . . . Don't forget that Ciro was after Sabbioneta's killer like us."

"It's ridiculous. Who on earth knows about the existence of Papasidero? And why should the murderer be hiding up in those ruins?"

"I don't know. Anyway, that wasn't all he said. He said he'd told Conti, but what about?"

"Biraghi mentioned Sabbioneta's overcoat," Pantieri observed and, after exchanging a long glance with Mirella, he made for the Val d'Aosta-style wardrobe. It reeked of airlessness, mothballs, the odour of reabsorbed dampness from when the iron thumped its caresses. Old and not-so-old clothes, umbrellas, three raincoats greyer than a rainy day, a herringbone overcoat, and a blue cashmere one . . .

"A blue cashmere overcoat!" Pantieri exclaimed. "It looks like Sabbioneta's, but Biraghi also had one like it."

"Take it out!" cried Mirella, electrified. "What's the point of yakking?"

It was a very beautiful overcoat, but it didn't look like a recent purchase. Indeed, the collar and cuffs betrayed many years' stubborn and affectionate wear. The labels revealed little:

an elegant shop in Rome and the usual guarantees in English about the product's excellence. The cloth was torn next to a button. A tear, not a rent seam. The pockets were empty, absolutely empty. Well, perhaps it had been Lauro Croce Sabbioneta's overcoat, but there was nothing sensational in the discovery. It was known by now: immediately after the kidnapping, the statesman had been brought to this house, and in this house had remained a prisoner for many days. He had escaped in his underpants via the bathroom window. Of course he'd had no time to slip into his overcoat, and yet . . . The cashmere was a soft fabric, but one hem of it was hard and matted, as if it had been sewn with steel wire. In the lining, something clinked: an unexpected harmony of crystals lightly touching.

"Let's see, let's take a look!" Mirella cried, and she tore at the lining with feverish fingers. A pizzicato of violins found new notes, the harmony of crystals rolled to the floor and the green glimmer of the lampshade was outshone by the rainbow-hued flash. They were diamonds.

"How many are there?" Mirella asked, counting and recounting: she kept having to start again, because her fingers wouldn't obey her. "Fifty-two, no, fifty-six, oh, I don't know . . . we'll have to check better . . . They're shuttle-cut, blue-white. I think the smallest must weigh five carats, it's a treasure from the Arabian Nights . . . Don't you see? Sabbioneta carried around with him precious stones worth millions!"

"Pick the diamonds up," said Pantieri. "Put them in your handbag. Take care, it's a mindboggling sum. I still remember Uncle Giacchino's hospitality, and his eggs cooked under the ashes . . . Do you think he'd put us up for a few days?"

"You want to go to Papasidero?" Mirella shrieked, exultantly. She was about to go on when a triumphant bleat led her to look towards the back of the house. She ran to the window and peered out into the night's conniving murk. Festive bleats faded away in the direction of Lavinio.

"The goat!" cried Mirella. "It's escaped, it'll spread an epidemic . . . Wouldn't it be better to destroy her?"

"Let her go," Pantieri sighed. "Let's leave it to fate. I shan't be surprised if some day a shepherd tells me he's seen a herd of goats dashing into the sea to escape to another country."

"There are two dead men here. Are we going to go . . . just like that? Without any formalities?"

"They'll think they killed each other, or else one killed the other and then committed suicide. Or perhaps they'll think it was a double homicide and invent a culprit."

Pantieri bent down over De Fiore and, hesitation giving way to impatience, rummaged through his pockets. He took out some coins, a holy picture of S. Francesco di Paola, a box of matches and a bus ticket, which caught his attention. It was a flimsy piece of paper with a date-stamp on it. It carried the usual printed information: the name of the company who ran the service, a warning about the ticket's non-transferability, and a sequence of towns. The last place, printed in capitals, was Scalea. The conductor's clippers had perforated the second p of one of the names on the list: Pa . . . asidero, he read. There was no room for doubt. It was then that Pantieri rushed into the kitchen and, without paying any attention to Mirella, who had followed him, he lifted off the lid to the waste-bin: on top of the potato peelings and leftovers of pasta, there was a wig and a false moustache.

"Good God," Pantieri murmured, "I think I've got it. I know who wiped out the existence of Lauro Croce Sabbioneta."

"Who?" asked Mirella, with an anxiety which even she could not have explained.

"All will be revealed in the epilogue," said Pantieri with a sad smile. "We're nearing the end of the story. Let's be off, there's nothing more we can do here."

FIVE

They got into the 124 and Pantieri thought they were in for a
rather long journey. The truth had finally come out, the character of the late Rt Hon. Lauro Croce Sabbioneta had been laid
bare and explored as if it had been on a dissecting table. There
wasn't much more to know, and when all was said and done,
it was fairly futile disclosing the statesman's murderer. Why
should they? Hadn't he accomplished an act of reparation and
justice? Or more cynically . . . who could say? It was always
difficult reading into a man's mind. "It can be punishment, it
can be mercy," as the Cardinal had quoted.

He looked up and thought he saw airships sailing towards
the east; an apparition that no longer had anything sensational
about it. Perhaps the meaning of the whole story was hidden
in the night's worn velvet, in the white warp revealed by
transparent patches and shades of meaning; there was a design
in the not very dense weft of the darkness, but it was an
exhausting business establishing its shape. Night absorbed
everything, even the sea, which was now a thin streak. An
orange moon rose above it, a paper circle that gave off no light
and was ringed by no haloes; a huge orange thrown into the
rubbish tip of the dark.

He looked tenderly at Mirella. He had never loved a woman,
other than in an occasional and fragmentary way. Little had
been required to decree the end of his immersion in passion:
the nose blown trumpet-like, a moronic remark, an impudent
wart that caught the eye. The conviction of another dimension,
more lasting and more worthy, had stayed with him and
he had wandered there in pauses that led him as far as the
bougainvillea: real women were those whose foreheads were

creased by a little frown . . . They were reality and not a
fevered imagination. The pas de deux from Tchaikovsky's
Nutcracker Suite slid from the moon to the black line of the
sea . . .

"Liar," said Pantieri in a low voice, and smiled.

"Who?" asked Mirella, nonplussed.

"Tchaikovsky, but he was a good one."

Snow had fallen at Papasidero, which was normal, given the
season and the altitude. However, now that he had arrived
(Mirella had fallen asleep with her head against his shoulder),
he found it difficult to recognize the grey bastions of the
houses which several years before had suggested emotions and
auguries. The drifts of snow had altered the profile of that
ancient lump of stone, oaks and goats. Noises faded into a
dense silence, like the sky which was white and swollen with
more imminent snow.

Uncle Giacchino was warmly welcoming. His house was
still very beautiful and ramshackle: made of dry-stone walls, it
crept up the mountainside one floor after another and, from a
small balcony under the roof, a dangerous one because there
were no railings, it looked out over the valley and the mountains, which was as if to say, over the whole world. There was
a smell of scalded milk; the stones, the harsh and massive
furniture, even the soft piles of snow filling the flowerpots in
the windowsills were imbued with it. It was a good reassuring
smell, and it conveyed a sense of peace to Pantieri; but everything belonging to the old man, copper pans, kettles, figures
of saints and trophies of faded photographs, the nightlights
burning on the chests of drawers, the wash-stand, a 1936
Marelli radio, an oil-lamp, a wind-up gramophone complete
with horn, all fossilized the dimension of time, as if the calendar
hanging on the kitchen wall, and three-years-old to boot, was
only a useless ornament.

"Come and warm yourselves up," Uncle Giacchino
suggested, extending his blackened and martyred hands
towards the open fire. "Would you like an egg roasted in the
ashes, or with some pork crackling? It's a cold winter, this one.
Have you heard how that wolf's scratching in the snow?"

The old man's conversation was basic: the alternation of the seasons, the weather and food came down to forming the only plausible reality and all the rest was only contingent and possible.

"Another war might break out," Pantieri said, trying to engage his interlocutor in a less sparse conversation. "A lot of people are saying so."

"Yes, looks so," replied Uncle Giacchino, indifferently. "I've seen so many wars, the first was in Libya. Do you like wine?"

He never ceased from filling their glasses and with that slightly tart wine, pressed from *uva fragola*, and the gentlest of smiles, he urged toast after toast on Pantieri and his niece. They drank a lot and the old kitchen became imbued with images that were misty, smoky and full of bright red reflexes.

"Open the window," said Uncle Giacchino, "and let a bit of fresh air in."

The fresh air entered, and with it the night. It was a night white with snow, a swirl of flakes that fluttered between the shuttered houses (closed and inaccessible worlds), in a never-ending vertical flight. The old ruined castle, the one in which the feudal baron had spent his days waiting for his wayward wife to return, rose and rose as well . . . The whole world was drunk, filled as it was with phantoms.

"I can see spirits wandering in the ruins," Mirella giggled and raised her full glass of wine.

"I don't know about spirits," Uncle Giacchino replied, "but when the north wind blows . . . Ah, how it howls! It's like a werewolf."

But for that night the north wind kept its distance in the secret world of the tempests. Pantieri and Mirella slept holding hands and perhaps they dreamed; for a moment Pantieri thought he heard a furtive movement below at the front door, but he was sleepy and had no wish to investigate. It must have been a stray dog wanting to take shelter from the snow, he deduced, as soon as the noise ceased. He dropped back into his well of cobalt.

The next morning Uncle Giacchino suggested that Pantieri

go with him along the river. They walked down a path from which the snow had been more or less cleared. Pantieri remembered there was a legend attached to the river, too: the Lao's waters glittered with gold. Many centuries ago, someone, a king or a knight, had sunk some treasure there. But the unfortunate gentleman had died without resuming possession of his fortune, so that the spot where so much wealth lay remained a secret. It was known only that it was in the river-bed.

"I heard some outlandish noises last night," Uncle Giacchino said. "And the night before, as well. Folk coming and going together, in a group."

"Are you sure?" asked Pantieri anxiously.

"And then," Uncle Giacchino continued, ignoring the interruption, "there's the fact of that damn great bird. It's three nights now I've noticed it. The first time was a week ago. I heard a beating in the sky, like the ticking a reel makes winding wool. I set myself to have a look, but it was nearly dark and there were clouds, so you couldn't see much. But when the bird appeared, there was no doubt: black it was, great big thing, and it stopped there, hung in the sky. It looked like it was pecking under the wings with its beak. Not long. It shot down like a thunderbolt and landed behind the castle of the last Marquis."

"Perhaps it was an aeroplane."

"No, it couldn't have been, an aeroplane can't stop in the air. It was a bird alright. A great big bird of prey. An eagle. I even saw its eyes, round and sparkling like ice."

"Uncle Giacchino," smiled Pantieri, though with everincreasing alarm, "perhaps it was a cloud. There aren't any birds with eyes of ice."

A gust of wind sailed by, bearing a memory of juniper, rosemary and myrtle; another gust further away expanded like the soughing of a shell; it settled in without let up, wrapping the snow-covered sheep tracks and broken trees in a single background noise. At the bottom of a slope, tangled with leaves, a line of spurtings, frothings and spray cascaded downwards. It was the Lao. The air was now saturated with a haze of water that bore the sulphurous smell of mould and rotting vegetation; beyond the veil of microscopic droplets a meander scar, where a manna ash experimented with a precarious existence, sent out a golden glimmer. Below the limpidity of the water, it looked as if the stones were gleaming, that they were precious gems set among the waterlilies.

"The treasure!" cried Uncle Giacchino, and he dashed towards the scar, heedless of getting his whole body soaked. He came back with disappointment in his face. He was holding a waterproof bag with the bottom half-falling out, from which issued tins of every description: tuna, jam, beans, pressed meat, almost a whole larder.

"Grub," he said with bitterness, and passed several items under review to console himself. "But it's good grub," he added.

"I think you're right," Pantieri assented, bending over to observe a tin.

"But what son of a bitch goes scattering God's plenty about?" Uncle Giacchino asked indignantly.

"I don't know," Pantieri replied, deep in thought. "That sack was dropped from an aeroplane and went off target; not too long ago. There's someone hiding around here."

Two days later, *La Gazzetta del Sud* carried the news of the discovery of the bodies of Biraghi and De Fiore. A lot of conjectures, nothing concrete. It was thought to be a double suicide come to a head in the sphere of terrorism (some rather compromising documents had been found; it appeared that the magistrate had also been plotting against the institutions of democracy). A partial rehabilitation of De Fiore followed; his participation in the crimes he was accused of was now in doubt; not so much a miscreant, more a man who had been led astray. La Calenda had pronounced a few moving words and the country, which understood what the Prime Minister was going through, had gathered round him in affectionate respect.

Another piece of news was less prominent: unknown thieves had forced their way into the apartment of the late Rt Hon.

Sabbioneta and stolen his precious collection of stamps, including the blue Eleanora of Zimbabwe without perforations.

Another three or four days passed and the sky turned white and swollen again. Sinuous exhalations of mist covered the mountains and stone houses and reality, or what was left of it, went to ground between the wall and a barrier into the unknown. Uncle Giacchino predicted more snow and pointed out that for at least two nights he hadn't heard the great big bird flying any more. Pantieri listened closely to Uncle Giacchino's tales, but he knew that in that archaic world fables took it upon themselves to expand dimensions that seemed too narrow. The windows facing the valley and the wood looked out onto unexplored solitudes, which had perhaps remained deliberately half-discovered; it was there that the spirits of the dead, the werewolf and the fairies unwound the thread of destiny, and prepared philtres and sorcery.

So that when, that morning, there came three knocks on the door, not one more nor one less, three peremptory and unusual knocks, which transmitted an order, not a request to open up, Pantieri, Mirella and Uncle Giacchino darted silent, questioning looks at each other, and only when the triple command was repeated with an even more threatening cadence did the old man decide to unlock the door. A shaggy fur hat complicated the identification of the visitor, but the protruding and penetrating eyes, like a person suffering from Grave's disease, the arrogance of the face, the haughtiness with which he crossed the threshold, stamping his heels on the stone floor, well, they were enough to eliminate any shadow of doubt. It was Dr Conti.

"Oh, come on, Pantieri," said the Prosecutor with hollow joviality. "No word of hello? Fancy running into you again! And Signor De Fiore's lady . . . sorry, his widow. What a lovely surprise! And this silly old bugger? Ah, a close relative. Not a bad little set-up, open fire as well! Get moving, Pantieri, and this floozie, too. Got to take a little walk, we have."

"In this weather?" asked Uncle Giacchino, hazarding a protest.

"Who asked you? Stay out of it!" Conti growled, pushing

him away with a slap on the back of the neck. "Let's go. Can't hang about."

They set off warily in the mist. Pantieri thought he knew the aim of the expedition, because they weren't going towards the valley, but climbing up a badly flagged path that grew increasingly narrow and soon dwindled to less than a mule track. It was difficult walking; every so often it was necessary to venture a leap or try a stone with the tip of the foot to make sure of its hold. The mist was rising in swirls and, during the pauses, allowed glimpses of the shadows of the snowdrifts all about, the deposits of ice between the rocks or a wild myrtle, but then it swallowed everything up in a milky sea.

"Where are we going?" asked Pantieri, taking advantage of a halt called by the magistrate, who was out of breath. "What's this all about?"

"Pantieri, get stuffed!" Conti rasped. "Always asking questions. Still that bad habit of yours. Can't you see I'm nearly winded. Serious and urgent business. Business of state. Came up by car from Rome, but the Carabinieri stayed down below. But they'll be joining me right now. Pantieri, we've been dogging your footsteps discreetly since the last time I saw you. Now the time's come to settle accounts . . ."

"Where are we going?" Pantieri persisted. "There's only the mountain in this direction, and higher up an old ruin, an abandoned castle. The local people are frightened of it, give it a wide berth."

"Frightened? Why?"

"Tales of one kind or another. There's one about noblemen, goes back to the last century. A baron was deserted by his wife and spent the rest of his life waiting for her."

"Waited for the trollop? That's very interesting. Well, my boy, that's exactly where we are going. The castle."

"To wait for the trollop?"

"Better than that. We're not folk to be kept waiting. We're going to pay a visit. Could be they'll even give us tea and cakes. Very nice cakes."

"A visit to whom?"

"You and your lousy questions! The answer is I can't say.

197

This is a surprise and, if I tell you, you'll catch me on the hop. Just look at you! Always wanting to skip to the last page! Can't you ever enjoy the flavour of a surprise? Anyway, tell me what else they say about this castle. Sort of thing that interests me."

"I don't know, they say all kinds of things. They're superstitious folk here, they believe in spirits and people rising from the dead."

"I believe in them myself!" said Conti, with an evil grin. "But what do they say about the castle?"

"That it's better to give it a wide berth."

They continued to climb, however. The path was becoming ever rougher, but fortunately the mist was thinning and accumulating lower down, so that it looked as if a layer of cotton wool had come down to hide the world. To protect it, and stop it from seeing. Then, after a last turn, the baron's castle appeared: it was less tumbledown than the local people made out; quite the reverse, apart from two walls crumbled away in a landslide, the place was not in all that bad a state of repair.

The path died out, giving onto a vast esplanade in front of the buildings and here it seemed as if the snow that had fallen the previous weeks had somehow been removed; it was a sheet of ice, marked by grooves that were not the effect of the wind. The main door, half torn off its hinges, sagged towards one of the statues which flanked the entrance and gave notice to the visitor of the mansion's nobility. They were two commonplace statues, now covered with lichen, and there was something perversely fascinating in their allegorical intent. They were representations of Love and Death, the one in the semblance of a young naked woman, the other a skeleton armed with a scythe, but the explanatory inscriptions cut into the plinths had been inverted, whether by mistake or caprice it wasn't clear. Wretched grass climbed right up the battlements, which were restrained, ornamental, timeless. Besides, the entire castle gave no suggestion of period; constructed perhaps one hundred and fifty years ago, it mingled every style and the monstrous result emitted an obscure harmony, an obscene beauty, as if someone had poured into it all the vices of the heart.

The ashen sky weighed down and minute, premonitory snow crystals, sifted by the wind, were already beginning to sprinkle down. In that grey air, coils of smoke were rising from the battlements, sewing arcs of tack-stitching in the clouds' fleecy cloth; this was a fact, not an illusion. Someone had lit a fire inside the building and wasn't worried about signalling his presence (or was doing so deliberately?); those black puffs sent from a hidden chimney were a confession, or worse, an invitation.

"There's someone in there," observed Pantieri, lowering his voice.

"Oh, Jesus!" exploded Conti, losing patience. "And what have I just been telling you, sweetheart? Didn't I say there was a treat in store?"

They went in. It was almost completely ruined inside; everything had been stolen, even the terracotta floor tiles, as the last martyred traces bore witness. Only the stones remained. Uncle Giacchino had been right, the castle was only a dump, imbued with an aura of graveyards and ill-omen, as spiders' webs and bats' nests suggested. From the half caved-in roof, a hesitant blade of grey light fell, diluting the shadows, but only a little; so that, as soon as they passed into the next room and were assailed by the gleam that blazed up from the fireplace, Pantieri gave a start. But it wasn't for the sudden vividness of the flames in that lifeless atmosphere, nor even for such details sitting oddly in that waste of architecture as a trunk against a less sorely tried wall, a suitcase thrown open on the ground, a radio transmitter/receiver, a stack of tinned food, and, for the hunger of the spirit, a battery-operated record-player. The fact was that, not far from the fire, towards which it was holding out its sensitive and feminine hands, there stood a phantom. But phantoms don't exist. It was a man: tall, elegant, polite and smiling. That man was Lauro Croce Sabbioneta.

EPILOGUE

"Amazed?" asked the eminent statesman *redivivus* with a sad, wry smile; he was piling clothes into the suitcase open in front of him. "The Prosecutor wouldn't be, I think. He knew he'd find me here. So, no surprise. I was waiting for you . . . I was warned of your coming. Even a man playing dead is forced to keep a minimum of social relationships. My eternal rest is furnished with every necessary protection. Some friends in Customs and Excise watch over me. They're experienced in passing one thing off as another, they can create reality on the basis of the consignment note and from mine it appears that I'm dead."

He paused a while over a bright red pullover, turning it this way and that in ironic contemplation. Turning to Mirella, he said: "A bit on the youthful side, don't you think?"

"Far from it," put in Conti, sycophantically. "I wouldn't like to flatter, but it's a Burberry, a classic line. Besides, you're a tall man, stand up like a lord."

"You think so?" observed Sabbioneta coldly and wedged the pullover in the case, without waiting for a reply. Then he sighed: "I imagine that this is the moment for some sort of explanation and therefore I shall try and throw light on events; not that I feel obliged to, or even think it necessary, but it will amuse me. It's more or less as if we'd arrived at the end of a detective story with myself in the role of novelist, following the well-tried technique of rehearsing the entire story in a nutshell, but from the opposite angle. A mundane tailoring job, turning a garment."

"This is nothing but a detective story?" asked Pantieri bitterly, thinking of all the deaths, the upset to his life and the solid certainties of which he had been cheated.

"That's for you to judge," Sabbioneta pronounced sarcastically. "But do avoid overrating and universalizing. Remember my pensée about ingestion and digestion, that's the only marketable truth."

"Blimey, what a footslog that was!" Conti observed, incoherently. "Got a hole in my socks, my tongue's hanging out, can't get my breath . . ."

"Then all the more reason to belt up," commented Sabbioneta icily. Then he turned sweetly to Pantieri: "Exceptional things come to pass, and leave you only one way out: have people think you're dead and make your exit. But it's better I start at the beginning. The Crux was my creation. The enigma that's cropped up so much is nothing more than my middle name in Latin. An elementary idea, crude even; I needed a monster that was ill-defined, but with disagreeable connotations, to which everyone would attribute the enormous evil that was occurring in the normal course and in the little more that I was trying to create. It was for aesthetic fullness, or rather, to fix attention on some crumb of horror, to detach it from the uniform background of outrages. So I made use of a pre-existing organization of much more limited objectives: under the name of Raymond of Touraine I had procured myself a charge of emotional stimulus, and was much gratified by Gruvi's support. Then . . . After all, between stubbing out a cigarette on a prostitute's thigh and planting a bomb, it's a mere question of degree. Well, what's a handful of deaths? After each miniature attack and each murder, people ended up feeling reassured; we were teaching humanity to be satisfied just to be alive."

"So that's the Crux . . ." Pantieri observed. "Nothing more than a power game. A bit cruel, not quite above board."

"No more," stressed Sabbioneta with a frown. "A pity. Everything had been studied with intelligence and imagination. I should tell you something about the folklore: the pustules, the airships, the priestesses . . . The turpentine trick is, I think, known even to children by now. As for the airships, nothing could be more banal. We'd learned from Goodyear that every so often, for publicity or some other obscure reason, they sent people on a tour over Rome and round about. Airships have an unknown hypnotic power; silent and cumbersome, suspended between the past and the future, they load the heart with questions. We took advantage of special atmospheric conditions, mostly at dusk with low cloud, and projected a film from a hidden angle, using the sky as a screen. A spectacle similar to those given on summer evenings in certain gardens and courtyards, *son et lumière*. A sure-fire effect, it couldn't fail. Besides, we'd studied Ian Fleming; we'd consulted poor Agatha, a few months before she died."

"Let's get to where I come into the picture," suggested Pantieri.

"Pantieri," broke in Conti severely, "just lay off, eh? Stop being so self-centred. Perhaps His Excellency is in a hurry and you're being a pain."

"By no means!" exclaimed the statesman politely. "Well, things were getting out of hand. It was a poker game in which we had reserved the right to cheat, but in no time everyone was cheating and God knows what was going on. A few hints were dropped. The bomb attack on the Discount and Savings Bank wasn't our work, nor even the attack on Regina Coeli prison, the one which allowed you, Inspector, to escape. Maybe the late Dr Biraghi knew a thing or two about those episodes, if the papers are telling the truth. And then there were too many airships taking flight, too many priestesses being wheeled out. Dr Conti, you went too far the night Dr Gruvi's body was discovered at the Bela Motel, hiring half the whores on the Tor di Quinto and an entire girls' boarding school! It's incredible what prurient appetites girls have today! Anyway, after needling the devil so much, he really began to stir. Something like the tale of the Sorcerer's Apprentice."

"The world's all changing," said Conti philosophically. "Men's hearts, too. The feelings of those of us who are no longer young are more refined."

"The Prosecutor's generalizing," smiled Pantieri. "And he's allowed himself to be tempted by rather grand notions."

"There's been a re-think in the private sphere, I'd say," observed Sabbioneta, "but I wouldn't like to say more than

205

that. We know the sequence of events which led to the murder of Dr Gruvi and his elderly mother. Equally we know the motive for the double homicide. Someone was out to ensure that the plots being hatched against me were not brought to my attention."

A very long silence fell. The fire in the hearth was dying and Conti approached with a piece of wood, but was stopped by the statesman's brusque gesture. Now the shadows in the dilapidated room were heavier; from one minute to the next it looked as if it might vibrate with the flight of bats or palpitate with some other graveyard apparitions. Conti kept rocking on his feet, as if a hidden thought were preventing him from being at ease. And yet he was not a person who was easily worried.

"Dr Conti knew all about that," said Sabbioneta ironically, "especially after he'd listened to De Fiore. The Prosecutor had a problem of choosing sides and didn't take long to opt for the one he judged was the winner. Isn't that so?"

"What's this? Doubting my word?" Conti rasped. "I nearly had a heart attack knowing that those villains wanted Your Excellency to do yourself in. Now even you . . . just because we're magistrates, you suspect us rightaway!"

"When Opitz happened to be killed in the Protomoteca, I was worried," Sabbioneta continued. "The bullet almost grazed me. I had reason to be worried: during my subsequent imprisonment, I learned that De Fiore, instead of wiping out the unfortunate new Chairman of the Discount and Savings Bank, should have wounded me in the shoulder. Lying in wait with a group of companions, his job was to steal me on board an ambulance. I decided to take some counter-measures. I had good friends and protection abroad, so I made up my mind to flee to Hamburg. I went to the station with my usual escort . . . Alas, too late! How things then developed has been reported in the press, with substantial accuracy for once. To conclude, instead of finding myself among my faithful allies in Hamburg, I was captured and taken to Biraghi's villa in Lavinio."

The fire in the hearth had now gone out; a pile of incandescent cinders remained, giving off an insubstantial, somewhat imaginary heat. And then the air shrank under the thrust of membranous wings that struck it; a maddened wave pounced with blind fury, but at the last moment, warned by the ultra-sound, it leaped upwards, trying without luck for the opening towards the murky sky. Mirella gripped her head between her hands and screamed that she was frightened it would get caught in her hair, while Dr Conti jumped here and there to avoid the danger. It lasted less than a minute: the bat, torn from its lethargy by the miserly heat of the flames, took its last flight. It looked for the gap in the ceiling, spread its enormous wings, rapacious as the night, then suddenly plummeted to the ground, exhausted and perhaps dead. It was simply a lump of black cartilage, from which a small face with human features appeared. Conti was quick to crush it beneath his heels, trumpeting his revulsion and triumph as he did so.

"Who knows where the hoopoe's nest lies," Sabbioneta observed in a literary vein. "I have a painful memory of my detention. I was scared stiff, and Biraghi even more so. But all in all, my captors didn't treat me badly. Of course, they were free with their foul language and abusive epithets, while I was used to language of a different kind. I was afraid they would kill me on the spot or very soon, but instead, to my painful relief, I realized that my imprisonment was to be a prolonged one. Perhaps my death sentence wasn't absolute, or perhaps inscrutable aesthetic considerations had suggested a deferment; I don't know, I couldn't begin to say, except that the delay was to save my life. I was allowed to read and write, so I could unbosom myself . . . I could confess . . . I could finally express what I had thought all my life. Unfortunately, no one took my messages seriously. By the by, the greater part of them were censored and destroyed; they were judged to be too corrosive and explosive, too dangerous for the survival of any kind of society. The little you know filtered through, and even then they created such a scandal."

Believing in those letters was no joke, thought Pantieri. My God, an ascetic, or semi-ascetic, on the threshold of the world to come, who sent word as a spiritual testament that the only aim of the human parabola was, word for word, ingestion, digestion and defecation: well, it had to be a joke, it was unthinkable that the eminent statesman could be so despicable, so colourless, so carnal; in a word, so human. Now Pantieri realized, established for himself that it was true, and still he didn't understand what prompted that urge to self-destruction, or rather, he looked at Mirella and was afraid he did understand. He remembered certain confidences picked up when he ran into the girl at Lavinio, but it was hard to ascribe a certain kind of self-indulgence to someone as hieratic as Sabbioneta. Bah! Sanctity and depravity were placed on the same circumference, and at some point, they met.

"As the days passed," Sabbioneta continued, "my captors' attention lapsed, which was logical enough. Besides, the police investigations were rather inept and desultory . . . Force of habit – a bad thing, that! They dragged the depths of Apennine tarns, the icier the better; or they lay in wait on rooftops with their machine-guns levelled, it wasn't quite clear why . . . The Carabinieri knocked at our door three or four times: they wanted a drink of water or to pass some, or to catch up on the football scores. Nothing ever happened. So I profited from that climate of general relaxation, and slipped out of the bathroom window one evening – it had been left open – and made off. I was in my vest and underpants and it was freezing cold. The Convent of the Blessed Oblate Sisters of S. Daniela Crisci was only a step up the road; I took shelter in a store-room, bumped into the Mother Superior and struck a sinful bargain which left me with clothes to protect me from the cold and change me almost beyond recognition. All right, so it wasn't a perfect disguise, but still, I did escape to Lavinio . . . I have to admit that we had a merry dance that evening, worthy of the finale of a James Bond film; there we all were, lying in wait, in ambush. I was that very tall, and, of necessity, rather masculine nun whom you, Inspector, collided with, politely excusing yourself. I was impolite and I do beg your pardon; but if I had spoken I would have betrayed my secret. Worse was to happen. I spotted De Fiore on my tracks and knew that he had spotted me, too. My only hope was to take refuge among the crowd, so I hid myself in the casino, but at a certain point I saw my persecutor making a beeline for me . . . I got away by a hair's breadth, but unfortunately Lucilla Opitz was decapitated in my place. If I may anticipate an objection: it would indeed have been simpler to reveal my identity and ask for help, but by then I had decided to disappear, and let people think I was dead. It was the only way to free myself from the obsession of more traps and to be able to live, to be born again, in my own way."

Sabbioneta enfolded Mirella in a long indefinable gaze, expressing gratitude and rancour. Pantieri thought he glimpsed a spark of that depraved sensuality that enslaved this man, who had once been so powerful and respected. It was a strange adventure Sabbioneta had planned, a fifty per cent suicide, perhaps more, perhaps less, it was hard to measure. It was a totally subjective calculation, linked to the marginal utility each person gives to physical survival. What is certain is that with the single stroke of the pen that had expunged him from the municipal and parish records, the illustrious statesman had abdicated from his own past, a past both more tortuous and less inspired than was generally thought, but one that identified him no less precisely than did other outward connotations. The colour of his hair, for instance, and shape of his nails.

"Here, I regret to say, I'm compelled to slip into the macabre," Sabbioneta continued with his story. "Benefiting from my nun's habit, I was able to gain access to the mortuary in the isolation hospital. The Lassa fever didn't worry me, I was taken ill with a mild strain during my imprisonment, just enough to guarantee my natural immunity. I foraged among the corpses lined up on the marble slab and, with a little luck, I found one that suited my purposes. My build, wearing dentures, and with my blood group (which was indicated on the medical card attached to the big toe, as with all the corpses). I stole a car and escaped to my house to take what I needed to leave the identification beyond doubt. In my hurry I forgot the stamp collection, which I had a reliable thief steal for me later on. I got back to Lavinio in little more than an hour. I exchanged dentures; very uncomfortable, quite disgusting. I couldn't speak for several days, but then I was helped by an orthodontist, who worked for the Customs and Excise. I switched my watch,

chain and ring to the corpse . . . I fixed up every detail of the
scene. Dressing up and transporting the corpse were very
tiring. Shooting that inert corpse in the stomach seemed to me
a deplorable waste. All this could seem far-fetched and indeed
would be were I an ordinary man, but don't forget I had been
an athlete. I drove as far as the beach at Ardea. There was a
rubber tube in the boot which I used for dowsing everything
with petrol; when the flames died out there were only fragments
of carbonized humanity left. I was dead. The result was so
realistic I suspected that I was truly dead and felt sorry for
myself. I wept over myself, and this did me good."

"I'd like you to confirm . . ." said Pantieri. "The instigator,
I mean the organizer of the plot intended to eliminate you was,
of course . . ."

"Pantieri!" interrupted the Prosecutor, breathing heavily,
"just what are you after? Mind your own fucking business! I've
got nothing to hide, but you always have to put your big
foot . . . I came to fetch you . . . you and this bit of cunt, this
trollop . . . I beg your pardon, Your Excellency . . ."

"Your language is scurrilous, Conti," Sabbioneta protested
disdainfully. "You're vulgar through and through. What you
meant to say was: this angel. Am I right?"

Pantieri thought he detected a shiver of pain and pleasure in
the statesman's words. He looked at Mirella, but the girl had
moved several paces away and either hadn't heard, or was
pretending she hadn't. A reticent smile was playing on her lips,
an admission that didn't steel itself up to total effrontery. She
had raised a knee and the leg, sheathed in reindeer, was showing
between the edges of her unbuttoned fur. The boot was resting
on a stone larger and squarer than the rest, a relic from time's
crumbling decrepitude.

"You're looking at the lady, Inspector," murmured Sabbioneta, nodding imperceptibly towards Mirella. "An adorable
crossroads where a thousand paths have met, including our
very own. Including De Fiore's. The intersection of private
spheres . . . because that's what left. But we'll talk about that
later. My story's coming to a close. The rest was easy. I had
money, dependable friends at home and abroad. This lady had

spoken to me of her native village and I had been touched by her words. A village cut off from the world, dominated by a ruined castle which no one would go near for fear of spirits. A romantic temptation. It was difficult to wish for anything more. So I had an emergency hide-out prepared here, given that a public man's life should never be without a secret alternative. It only remained for me to reach it and join in with the unanimous lamentation as soon as my death was discovered."

"I thought . . ." the Prosecutor stammered, but couldn't explain. He was so worked up, he could not speak. He was rigid, paralyzed with terror, bent forward almost as if he were making a tragicomic bow, his hands clenched in his pockets and his staring eyes fixed on a distant point.

"No one will be coming, Dr Conti," Sabbioneta muttered. "My men have kept a good guard up. Theoretically, I'm dead, that's true, but I'm not without money and that's almost a guarantee of immortality."

"What's this?" panted the Prosecutor, regaining his voice. "Men? A good guard up? Your Excellency can't be doubting my devotion . . . We've worked together for so long, we've wrecked Italy, and now we were going to deal with the Italians . . . You turd! What are you doing?"

An explosion prevented Conti from adding anything more. He staggered with both hands clutching his abdomen and with his great ox eyes gradually becoming emptier, he followed the last chink of light across a mist that was growing thicker and thicker . . . The fur hat flew off and away, and the magistrate fell heavily face down on a century of history in stone fragments. His thin, sparse hair ruffled and faded like venomous petals. Mirella approached him and, after a brief hesitation, crossed herself. Sabbioneta was contemplating the revolver still gripped in his hand with an absorbed look, bereft of emotion.

"You've killed him," Pantieri observed idiotically, turning to the statesman, who had gone back to cramming clothes into his suitcase.

"I think you're absolutely right," Sabbioneta confirmed.

"He was a traitor. As soon as he got his hands on De Fiore he immediately went over to the other side. It was De Fiore himself who telephoned him from Lavinio, informing him about my hide-out . . . How De Fiore had come to know I was still alive and that I was hiding out here, well, that's another story. But Conti wanted to kill me, and he wanted to kill you, too, Inspector, as well as the lady. He'd climbed up here to perform a mass slaughter. Better him than us. And then treachery is not always tolerable, a little punishment was necessary."

"Why kill me? And Mirella? Why?"

"You were too compromising as a pair of witnesses," smiled Sabbioneta, shaking his head. "Too dangerous. And then Conti had always loathed you. He couldn't stand your good faith, your lack of protection, your not being one of the boys. In short, because you were different. Above all he nursed a longstanding grievance, a jealousy on a matter of marriage. Now, having said this, I must make an impertinent, indeed vulgar request of this lady: I should like what's in your handbag, it belongs to me."

Mirella looked at Pantieri for a second and then, with a gesture of regret, she tipped the bag out onto the red Burberry pullover. A shower of diamonds poured onto the wool and Sabbioneta's eyes lit up with greed. He began counting them and then, with growing perplexity, counted them a second time. With an accountant's scrupulousness, he objected: "There are two missing."

"I don't think so," Mirella replied disingenuously. "Perhaps you miscounted. I've no more stones left on me."

"Except two," objected Sabbioneta. His austere look melted into a smile of sardonic understanding.

"Except two," said Mirella, blushing.

"The rightful reward due to someone who returns missing property," pronounced Sabbioneta after a pause. "Besides, how could we leave the two protagonists of so many adventures without a little treasure? Otherwise how could they live happily ever after?"

"You knew we had the diamonds . . . ?" Pantieri muttered, hesitantly.

"Absolutely not," the statesman smiled. "Mere intuition. I never believed in the suicide of De Fiore and Biraghi . . . These are fairy tales for the public. The fact is, during the commotion of that night in the villa at Lavinio, you, Inspector, also made your appearance; and you discovered a clue that led you straight to me. You hadn't a single reason for coming to Papasidero, except for a doubt, a suspicion . . . You're with me, aren't you?"

"I think so."

"The story of the diamonds is soon told. When I took refuge here in the castle, there was something that troubled me, something that stopped me from completing my preparations to leave the country with equanimity. My overcoat. I had accumulated a fortune in that cashmere and I would never be parted from it, not on any account. To be sure, there are numbered accounts, and even numbered deposit boxes, but the world is so uncertain nowadays. Switzerland doesn't merit the trust it once had. Unfortunately, as I fled from Biraghi's villa, I hadn't been able to take my treasure, and I couldn't stand the thought that so much wealth should finish up in the hands of some lout or simply be forgotten. So, once again I disguised myself. With a wig and a false moustache I was unrecognizable. I took a bus to Scalea, then a train to Rome and a bus on to Lavinio. Public transport guarantees an absolute anonymity. I wasn't polite with Biraghi, I showed him my revolver. But through one of those coincidences which happen in novels, and in real life are much more frequent, I bumped into Ciro De Fiore. He had also turned up, cool as a cucumber, to get rid of the magistrate – his other plans were not exactly good-natured either. We fought. I fired two shots, lost the wig and the false moustache, but managed to grab the overcoat and escape. But, oh dear, in the haste and excitement I'd snatched up Biraghi's coat instead of mine. De Fiore had managed to tear one of my pockets and my bus ticket dropped out. This was regrettable, because my hide-out would be discovered, as indeed it was. I hid in the usual store-room of the Blessed Oblate Sisters of S. Daniela Crisci and ran into the Mother

Superior once again: my safety cost me the customary sacrilegious and nauseating embrace. Is there anything I've missed?"

"What about the other characters in the drama?"

"Almost nothing to add. By the way, Inspector, about your wife, let's leave her to rest in peace. However, talking about her when she was alive, she helped us a lot in the choreography, she was a formidable organizer of rituals that encouraged the right atmosphere. It's rather sad that you lived with a person for so many years and formed such a false and conventional view of her; but I don't think it's an unusual experience. Marriage erases any impulses that lie outside the code, and besides, we have to admit that the most exaltingly wicked deeds stem from the perpetrator's being above suspicion. Biraghi wanted to have his personal revolution and Divine Providence sent him a sign, rewarding him with a bullet. We shouldn't be too surprised: in these times half the population of Italy messes around with mercury fulminate. The undertaker's business ties up a good proportion of the nation's wealth, apart from politics, of course. We know all about old Opitz; the construction boss was quite senile and therefore a man predestined for the highest responsibilities. A shame he was eliminated, even if, thank Heaven, there'll never be any shortage of fools. As for Cardinal Meschia, he has nothing to do with this business, but I think that was evident from the start. He's got a terrible disease and will not live long. He'll still suffer for world famine and for the ills which trouble his priestly conscience, and he'll still cross swords with Baget Bozzo. By the way, that acrostic was mine. For ages I'd been wanting to express what I really thought about the problem of malnutrition. Is there anything else?"

They went out onto the esplanade. The sky was low and swollen; it was eddying and drifting with uncertain undulations, shedding flakes of mist that wrapped around the white, subdued rocks. In a distant place a reel began to wind off skeins of snow and the earth seemed to meet the bed of clouds, but it was a meeting doomed to failure, despite the upward attraction of the eddying flakes. It was only an optical illusion, thought Pantieri. Before long Conti's body would vanish beneath the white cover being laid over it; it would not suffer from the silence that would descend to freeze the scene before the rigours of night. That silence had a sound. Could it be that the reel was broken? It was a clacking of wood against wood, and it was coming closer, growing in intensity and widening out. Now there was a roar as if of an aeroplane; sudden blasts disturbed the snow, scattering it in swarming clouds of blizzard. The black vulture was falling, falling; stretching out its claws, it landed in front of them. It was a helicopter. The propeller blades were beating the wind and it was impossible to talk, but the din was suddenly extinguished. Someone leaped from the helicopter and began to see to the luggage.

"It remains for me to talk about my, about our private sphere," said Sabbioneta with a bitter sigh. "I must confess: I'm not indifferent to the De Fiore widow. In my own particular, rather tormented way; the intimacy between a man and a woman is dirty, bestial, degrading . . . but here we're getting too personal. I'm about to leave and go far away and I'd like Mirella to come with me, but then I'm old . . . I'm beginning to grow fond of modest enterprises, a book, a plant to prune, a glass of wine. I'll entrust her to you, Inspector. Make good use of her. You could prostitute her, but that wouldn't be a new solution, even though a profitable one. You could send her to a nunnery, but neither would that be a new solution: I think there's a precedent in the theatre. Would you entertain a suggestion? Marry her! I'm sure that you would both be exquisitely unhappy, but you'll only find that out later on, and anyway that will be another story. For the present, the wedding march will ring out, the wedding veil a translucent white, albeit a little shop-soiled: and there'll be the orange blossom, the start of a new family and, at the end of the day, the private sphere will have its due. The flavour of a happy ending will remain."

The propeller blades moved and a roar of snow enveloped the confines of the rural scene in which the vulture shuddered. Sabbioneta dashed to the helicopter and then appeared at a window; he had to form his hands into a megaphone and shout to make himself heard, his words were crushed in a vortex of wind.

"You haven't told me the name of the instigator," yelled Pantieri, although he already knew the name and had done for some time.

"The instigator? The Prime Minister, La Calenda, of course. But he won't give me any trouble, nor you. Too busy watching his own back! The poker game continues. Besides, I've become a national monument, something between Giuseppe Mazzini and Cesare Battisti. It's not worth while making any more fuss and, above all, there's a need for martyrs."

"And Sig. Cleon V.I. Cercato? What was the solution to the anagram?"

"I'm not into crosswords, but the solution was a cinch. A silly little game, quite without importance, nothing more than a joke. O.L. NECAVIT CROCE, Orazio La Calenda killed Croce."

"Where are you going? I'll never betray your confidence."

"I don't know," Sabbioneta grinned. "To Afghanistan, I suppose. I'd like to teach those people what politics are about. What else d'you want to know? Do you want to know how it'll end? Frivolously, and the best of luck!"

The window rattled shut. White clouds were raised and it looked as if sky and earth would be swallowed in a cosmic avalanche, but the snow immediately reverted to falling in its quiet descent with flakes that seemed to rise upwards. Much farther up, ready now to vanish in the soft belly of the clouds, the black vulture beat its wings; the distant reel ticked on for a little and then the mighty breath of silence took charge of the world.

When Pantieri and Mirella went back down, it was no longer snowing. It was getting dark, but in an uneven and incoherent way; streaks of night were running across the sky, framing a slow-moving cumulus cloud over the tips of the trees, like a shroud hugging the face of the earth. A kite screeched and hurled itself from a peak into the clouds. It was then that the airships appeared; thirty, forty, even more. They were sailing slowly in a constant quiver of shadows, shading into transparencies; they headed off to follow a secret route, where the brushstrokes of the dark concealed any last conjecture. Perhaps it had been an optical illusion or perhaps the airships really were flying there; in either case reality was not definable, it only made free with presentiments.

"Who knows if they were real," said Mirella quietly, pointing a finger towards the sky. "But it's not a serious problem. I wonder if we should have hidden Dr Conti's body."

Nothing more than one more corpse, thought Pantieri. Killing was so easy. He was nauseated by all that had happened; a bazaar of murders, poisonings, deceptions, plots, disguises and resurrections from the dead; in short, all that abounds in the cinema, the television, and the worst kind of novel. However, it was also true that these ingredients belonged ever more to life and ever less to the imagination, because once it was the latter which had tried to imitate the former, while now the reverse was true. How much blood would have been saved if the taste for a *coup de théâtre* hadn't won the day? A difficult question to answer, but didn't all the chaos that was spreading through the world betoken a revolt of the imagination?

"Hide the corpse?" said Pantieri slowly. "There was no point. Not many people go up there. The odd shepherd, during the summer. There's no need to go poking around inside the castle. When they find Dr Conti, if they find him, he'll be just a skeleton; the sun and the fauna will see to picking his bones clean . . . People don't waste their time on skeletons; either they're catalogued or they stay in the cupboard."

"How did you come to realize that Sabbioneta wasn't dead?"

"Goodness, a deduction . . . That ticket from Papasidero, which carried that day's date, couldn't have belonged to Biraghi, who'd been barricaded at home for some time, and nor to De Fiore . . . who was in Turin that morning – you remember his phone call? Therefore, there was a third man, who'd been forced to disguise himself, as the wig and false moustache in the waste-bin revealed. Biraghi had no need of a disguise, he was totally anonymous, like me. De Fiore, maybe. But why a false moustache when he had a thick black one of his own? It had to be someone in the public eye who was coming from Papasidero and who had a serious motive for getting to the villa in Lavinio. The motive was supplied by the diamonds and only Sabbioneta knew of their existence; what with all the people who had come in and out, if anyone had suspected, the cashmere overcoat would have disappeared. However, the most important role was played by chance . . . Yes, almost everything happens by chance: like when you're writing and, without your expecting it, there emerges a hendecasyllable."

"You're really complicated at times, you are. But it doesn't matter, I love you for what you are. You know . . . I was thinking about Sabbioneta. Deep down, don't you feel a little sorry for him?"

"Sorry? He was cynical, corrupt, ironical, and a know-all, it seemed as if he owned the universe."

"Yes, that's true, but he had an intelligence riddled with anxiety . . . He suffered from everything, there was a sense of the tragic in him . . . perhaps it was for the sweetheart who died in the bombing, who knows?"

"Anyway, was it true, that story?"

"I suppose so. I caught one or two references to it. With me he had no need to maintain his public image. He was a very lonely man, and lived with his phantoms."

"And now what will you do?" asked Pantieri.

But he immediately regretted his words. After all, they could seek out a choice for the future together. This didn't mean dashing off to marry, as Sabbioneta had suggested; nonetheless, they could try setting out together, at least for a stretch of the way. It was a good idea, certainly the only idea that was worth a shadow of consideration. You had to resign yourself to the material conditions of the world and dedicate a greater attention to . . . how had Sabbioneta put it in his testament? Certainly an improper use of phantoms was all wrong, but perhaps it came to the same thing in the end; years and experience took it upon themselves to imprison you in an ever narrower space, to squeeze you into a narrow cell that allowed you to peer out on a ghetto of memories, dreams and nothing else. But at least less fleeting, less decadent paths might be tried . . . Allow the shadows to lengthen in their own good time and place, without rushing on ahead, in the end, who knows . . . and then nobody wanted a world of serious thoughts anymore, at each step in life you had to prohibit diagnostics; things went their own way and there were important decisions to be taken, like giving up smoking, dressing salad with lighter oil, going over to short-sleeved vests, taking long walks to prevent constipation, taking the odd bribe to live a less colourless life . . . These too were existential problems. Sabbioneta's message wasn't so meaningless, after all, who knows . . . Pantieri looked at Mirella and added with a smile: "If you like, you can stay with me . . . for a while . . . for as long as you like. Uncle Giacchino could put us up a little longer, couldn't he? I've not much to offer, but give me a few years . . . it could be even I'll learn."

"Uncle Giacchino will be happy," said Mirella in a low voice . . . "I'd like to taste his eggs cooked under the ashes and drink the wine made from *uva fragola*. After all, who knows . . ."

Uncle Giacchino welcomed them effusively. He laid the table with pork cracklings, dried figs and the flask of wine. He stoked up the fire in the hearth, and seeing that the occasion seemed to him a special one, he switched on the venerable radio, but with little conviction. He hated to waste electricity and thought that nothing of what happened in the world made any sense. From the news bulletin they learned that unknown terrorists had razed the town hall at Novara, with one hundred and thirty victims; that American and Russian warships were on manoeuvres between Malta and Sicily; that five missiles had fallen into the sea off Pantelleria; that the currency market had been closed; that an earthquake had destroyed Campobasso; that Parliament had approved a law reforming the new law on civil rights and institutional reform; that the Prime Minister, Orazio La Calenda, had been kidnapped at Roma Termini station, while waiting to leave for Hamburg. The death count was keeping pace with the rate of inflation. Potatoes had disappeared off the market.

"Ugh!" exclaimed Uncle Giacchino in exasperation and irritably snapped off the radio. "Always the same junk, nothing new ever happens! Now sir, you tell me a good story, tell me your story."

Pantieri passed a hand through his hair and smiled. He looked at Mirella snuggled up by the fire and tried to remember, because already it all seemed so far away, consigned already to the past. With a soft and pleasant voice, he began to relate: "Once upon a time there was a police inspector. He was looking out through the windows across the street one afternoon, when an elderly lady came to pay him a visit and, while he listened reluctantly, he gazed across at the familiar climber, and never ceased to take delight in the flame-like bracts of a bougainvillea . . ."